THE
Loyal Heart

Center Point
Large Print

Also by Shelley Shepard Gray and available from Center Point Large Print:

Thankful
Joyful
The Promise of Palm Grove
The Proposal at Siesta Key
A Wedding at the Orange Blossom Inn
A Christmas Bride in Pinecraft
A Son's Vow
A Daughter's Dream

This Large Print Book carries the
Seal of Approval of N.A.V.H.

THE
Loyal Heart

A LONE STAR HERO'S
LOVE STORY

Shelley
Shepard Gray

CENTER POINT LARGE PRINT
THORNDIKE, MAINE

This Center Point Large Print edition is published
in the year 2016 by arrangement with Zondervan.

Scripture quotations are from the *Holy Bible*, New Living
Translation. © 1996, 2004, 2007, 2013 by Tyndale House
Foundation. Used by permission of Tyndale House
Publishers, Inc., Carol Stream, Illinois.

This novel is a work of fiction. Names,
characters, places, and incidents are either products
of the author's imagination or used fictitiously. All
characters are fictional, and any similarity to
people living or dead is purely coincidental.

The text of this Large Print edition is unabridged.
In other aspects, this book may vary from the original edition.
Printed in the United States of America on permanent paper.
Set in 16-point Times New Roman type.

ISBN: 978-1-68324-099-0

Library of Congress Cataloging-in-Publication Data

Names: Gray, Shelley Shepard, author.
Title: The loyal heart : a lone star hero's love story / Shelley Shepard
Gray.
Description: Center Point Large Print edition. | Thorndike, Maine :
Center Point Large Print, 2016.
Identifiers: LCCN 2016022960 | ISBN 9781683240990
     (hardcover : alk. paper)
Subjects: LCSH: Large type books. | GSAFD: Love stories. | Christian
fiction.
Classification: LCC PS3607.R3966 L69 2016b | DDC 813/.6—dc23
LC record available at https://lccn.loc.gov/2016022960

To my husband Tom

Create in me a clean heart, O God.
Renew a loyal spirit within me.

—PSALM 51:10

Let us go home and cultivate our virtues.

—ROBERT E. LEE,
ADDRESSING HIS SOLDIERS
AT APPOMATTOX

PROLOGUE

❧❦❧

Johnson's Island, Ohio
Confederate States of America
Officers' POW Camp
January 1865

They were digging another grave. The third that week, which Devin Arthur Monroe, captain in the C.S.A., reckoned was hard enough without knowing it was for Rory Macdonald. Rory had been all of nineteen, the youngest member of his unit by far. Because he had been a private, he shouldn't have even been imprisoned with them in the first place. He wouldn't have been, except for some clerk's error.

The clerk's mistake had been Rory's good fortune, however. Conditions had been better for him here than they would have been in the enlisted prisoner-of-war camp in Columbus. Devin had been grateful for that. Rory had been a good man. He'd been a good soldier too. If they hadn't been captured down in Tennessee, he would have made sergeant before too long. The Confederacy had needed more young men like him.

Devin had been certain Rory was going to walk

out of their prison in the middle of Lake Erie, go home to his family's loving arms, find a pretty girl to marry, and accomplish something great. In short, Devin had been sure Rory Macdonald was going to do them all proud.

Instead, the best of them was going to spend an eternity in an unmarked grave surrounded by Yankee soil.

Just thinking about it stung.

"I still can't believe he won't be heading back to Texas. Ever," Lt. Robert Truax said as he tossed another patch of dirt over his shoulder. "Why did God have to go and decide the kid should die of pneumonia?"

Devin said nothing. Merely looked toward the dead zone—a line of fencing surrounded by a three-foot gap and another higher wooden fence. Their worthless Yankee guards were instructed to kill on sight any man who went beyond their restricted boundary.

Devin had seen them do it.

Lord knew, none of the structures that confined them were all that well put together. But that was the charm of their prison—at least for the Yankees. Even if a Rebel was able to escape the barricades without being shot and killed, the broad expanse of Lake Erie surrounded them. If the swim in the frigid waters didn't kill them, the frozen Canadian wilderness on the other side surely would. They were good and trapped.

And for the most part, bored out of their minds.

"It should've been me," Robert muttered as he propped a boot on the edge of his shovel, using his weight to help him dig into the frozen ground.

Robert had taken the boy's death especially hard. Devin figured that was to be expected. For all his rough-and-tumble ways, his second lieutenant had a soft heart. But the man's tone was dark enough to pull Devin out of his reverie.

Turning to him, he glared, his expression vivid in the moonlight. "Nothing we can do about the dead. Rory is in a better place. I thought you would have come to terms with that by now."

Impatience flashed in Robert's eyes. "The kid was only nineteen. Too young to die."

"You know the answer to that," Devin chided. "A great many men have died in this war who were too young. What you need to remember is that Private Macdonald definitely did not consider himself too young. And he'd likely try to box your ears if he could hear you saying that."

"He would box your ears for even thinking it," Sgt. Thomas Baker pointed out as he thrust his shovel into the hole they were digging. "Mac had no patience for anyone discussing his age."

"Well, now he's dead," Robert said. "He should have had his whole life ahead of him."

"I reckon the good Lord didn't see it that way. A great many men should have been looking forward to a bright and sunny future." Thinking of

9

Gettysburg, Devin felt his throat clog. He cleared it, at the same time pushing away the gruesome memories that never completely went away. "But they're gone too."

"It doesn't make any sense."

"War doesn't."

"Neither does a healthy nineteen-year-old boy dying from pneumonia."

"It was a real bad case of pneumonia, though," Thomas muttered. "The kid was having so much trouble breathing, he was blue for days."

Robert tossed his shovel to the ground. "Show our private some respect."

Thomas sneered. "Or what?"

"Settle down, Lieutenant," Phillip Markham hissed under his breath as he knelt to smooth away a chunk of earth. For some reason, he was still recovering from a bullet's graze. While some days it seemed like it pained him something awful, for once he didn't seem to be suffering too much. "If you don't lower your voice, you're going to get our fine Yankee hosts to put us in lockdown." Phillip's light blue eyes glared as he continued, as always their voice of reason. "That would be a real shame, 'cause we've got a body to bury." Looking up at Devin, he said, "I think the grave is deep enough, Captain."

Devin nodded. "Let's do this, then."

Devin, Thomas, and Robert carefully picked up Rory's body and lowered it into the ground.

After Rory was settled, they surrounded the grave in somber silence.

When Devin was able to push through the lump that had formed in his throat, he led them in prayer.

After another moment of silence, Thomas and Robert picked up shovels and began the painful work of covering Rory's body.

Devin and his major, Ethan Kelly, stood to one side and watched. Devin figured he'd now stood in respectful silence dozens of times since the war began. It never got easier.

When the grave was finally filled, they started walking back to their two-story barracks. Now that the dreaded chore was done, their mood seemed better.

"I'll write Rory's mother tomorrow," Devin said as they went inside. "Let's hope and pray this will be the last note of its kind that I'm going to have to write anytime soon."

"I'll do my best to stay alive," Ethan quipped.

"Me too," Phillip said with a ghost of a smile. "Don't forget, I've got Miranda."

Pure relief filled Devin. That comment had been exactly what they needed to get back on track. Phillip's devotion to his pretty brown-haired wife was legendary—and the source of much ribbing.

"Oh, we know you have Miranda, Phillip," Ethan teased. "You never let any of us forget you've got a beautiful woman waiting for you at home. You lucky dog."

"I received not one but two letters from her today. So yes, indeed, I am lucky." He stretched his arms. "Actually, I'm blessed beyond measure." As always, Phillip never pretended he felt anything but enamored by his wife.

Devin had always thought it was rather an endearing trait in their best sharpshooter.

But Robert was still staring at Phillip in confusion. "You never complain, Lieutenant. You never say anything except you're biding your time until you see her again. I don't see how one woman can make all the difference."

This time, Thomas grinned, showing a full set of exceptionally fine white teeth. His smile was undoubtedly his best feature and he used it to his advantage every chance he got. "If you don't know how one woman can ease a man's burdens, then you've got problems, Truax! Shoot, I'd say you've got more problems than being locked in a POW encampment in the middle of Lake Erie."

Ethan smiled. "I don't mind admitting that I'm looking forward to my fiancée, Faye, easing my burdens the moment I see her again."

Devin tucked his chin so Robert wouldn't see his grin. He'd never had a sweetheart, but he reckoned Ethan and Thomas had a point.

Unfortunately, Robert didn't care to see it. "I'm just saying, a man needs more than the comfort of a good woman. No offense, Markham."

Phillip grunted but didn't say a word.

Devin didn't really blame him. He'd seen a tintype of Phillip's wife. She was lovely, everything a man would want to fight for.

But, Devin supposed, he could see Robert's point. If a man didn't have a good woman waiting for him or a home to return to, there was a strong possibility of feeling out of sorts with their mission. Especially now that it seemed the war was almost over and all points were turning toward the inevitable loss for their side.

Perhaps they did need something more. Something more than dreams and elusive promises. Something dear to hold on to and grab hold of. Something to live for. "How about we make a pact, then?"

Ethan looked at him curiously. "What you got in mind, Captain?"

"Just something to make sure we remember."

Thomas raised a dark eyebrow. "Remember what, Cap?"

"To remember when one of us is sitting in the dark and wondering why he should live to see another morning."

"Bring it on, then," Ethan said. "I could use some of your words of wisdom."

"How about we make a promise right here, right now, to live for each other?"

"I'm already doing that." Thomas grinned. Looking at his major, he said, "I'm already keeping you warm at night, aren't I?"

"Don't remind me," Ethan said with a scowl. "You snore like a banshee." They all slept two by two. It was too cold otherwise.

Devin stood up, warming to his topic. "Come on, men. I'm serious. I suggest that from now on we do everything we can to help each other survive."

"We are in prison barracks, sir. Unless we get pneumonia, we'll live to see the end of the war."

"No, I'm not talking just about now. I'm talking about in the future too. Even after we get out of here."

"Sorry, Cap, but I don't follow," Thomas said. "After we get released from here and the war's over, I'm not gonna have one thing to do with a uniform."

Thomas was truly like his name. He needed a literal, tangible reason to believe in something. Otherwise he couldn't see it.

"Back in Gettysburg, we were once a band of eight. Then we lost Tucker and Simon. This morning, we were six. Now we are five. I propose, gentlemen, that when this war is over, we keep a promise to ourselves. Let's promise to always look out for each other."

"Always?" Robert asked.

"Yep. Even five years from now. Even ten. I think we're going to need to know that no matter what, we have each other."

Ethan nodded. "You might have something there, Cap. I like it."

"I don't," Robert said as he picked up a stick and tossed it into the dwindling fire in their old stove. "When the war is over, we're not going to need to be looked after. Everything's going to be fine again."

"Will it?" Thomas muttered.

"All I'm saying," Robert said, "is that most of us will have lives to go back to. We'll be free. We won't be worrying about dying or someone attacking us in our sleep. It's going to be better."

"I hope it is," Devin said. "But if it's not, let's promise we'll still have each other."

"I'm in," said Thomas. "This promise is as good as any, I reckon."

"Me too," Ethan said.

Phillip nodded. "I'm in too. But, uh, can I ask . . . if something happens to me, would one of you look after Miranda?"

"You'll get back to her," Ethan said.

Phillip nodded, but still looked alarmed. "Just in case I don't?" Phillip pressed.

"If you don't survive," Devin said, "I promise one of us will make sure Miranda is all right. Gentlemen, do you promise?"

Ethan pulled his shoulders back and looked at Phillip straight in the eye. "Upon my honor as a gentleman and a Southerner, I will make sure your wife is taken care of, Lieutenant."

At last Phillip breathed a sigh of relief.

Feeling satisfied, Devin finally looked at Robert. "Are you in?"

After a pause, Robert nodded. "I'm in, Captain. No matter what happens, I will honor this pact."

"Good."

Each lost in his thoughts, no one uttered a word until the last of the fire died out.

But as he thought about what would happen when the war ended, Devin knew they'd all be going back to a world different from when they first put on their Confederate uniforms. It was likely that their troubles would begin anew.

Some of them wouldn't even have their farms and houses, thanks to the Yankees' penchant for burning down everything in their path.

Yes, Devin Monroe feared that, after the war, when the world was at peace but so terribly upside-down, they were going to need each other even more.

1

Galveston, Texas
January 1867

At times, the pain was so intense, she wanted to die.

With a new sense of resolve, Miranda Markham skimmed a finger along the second-floor windowpane just outside her bedroom door. As she did, frigid drops of condensation slid across her fingers, moistening them, transmitting tiny bursts of pain along her skin. The glass wasn't thick, surely no more than a quarter inch. It seemed, to her eyes at least, that the frame was rather rickety as well.

It would be so easy to break.

Miranda wondered what it would feel like to perch on the edge of the windowsill like one of the gulls that rested on the weathered wood from time to time. She wondered what it would feel like to open her arms. To finally let herself go, to lean forward into nothingness.

To be free.

Perhaps she would feel nothing beyond a cold numbness, accompanied by an exhilarating rush of fear . . . followed by the blessed relief from pain.

Did pain even matter anymore?

The iron latch was icy cold as she worked it open. Condensation sprayed her cheeks as the pane slowly edged upward. Tendrils of hair whipped against her neck as the winter wind seemed to beckon.

She breathed deep.

If she could just garner what was left of her courage, why, it could all be over. Within minutes, in seconds, even, she'd no longer be awake. No longer be reminded. No longer be sad.

She'd no longer be afraid to rise each morning.

And wasn't the absence of fear, that intangible notion of confidence that children enjoyed and the elderly remembered, worth everything?

Reaching out, she clasped the metal lining of the frame. Felt the iron bite into her palm as she edged closer. At last, it was time.

"Mrs. Markham? Mrs. Markham, ma'am? Where should I put the new boarder until you are ready to talk with him?" Winifred called up from the base of the stairs.

Slowly . . . too slowly perhaps . . . one corner of Miranda's dark cloak of depression lifted. She realized she was still standing on the landing at the top of the stairs, the window open.

Winifred's voice turned shrill. "Mrs. Markham, do ye hear me?"

Miranda dropped her hands. Turned. "Yes. Yes, of course." Peering through the maze of mahogany spindles, she looked down. Blinked as her home's long-time housekeeper came into focus. "A new boarder, did you say?"

Winifred stared back. "Yes, ma'am. 'E's here a wee bit early. A Mr. Truax, his name is. Mr. Robert Truax."

Though the name sounded familiar, Miranda couldn't place it. Why couldn't she?

"Madam," Winifred began again, her voice holding the slightest tinge of impatience now. She was a reluctant transplant from England and seemed to always stare at her surroundings with varying degrees of shock and dismay. "Madam, don't you remember?" Winifred added, raising her voice just a little bit higher, as if she were talking to a child. "We got the telegram yesterday that said he was arriving today."

She didn't remember much after receiving another threatening letter in yesterday's post. "Yes, of course."

"I been working on his room all morning, I have." Looking pleased, Winifred added, "It sparkles and shines, it does."

"I'm glad," she said absently.

Until and unless Phillip's family found a legal way to run her off—or made her miserable enough to leave on her own—she was in charge of the Iron Rail. It was her house, and with that came the responsibility of at least pretending she cared about the running of it. With a vague sense of resignation, she turned back to the window. Set about cranking it shut before locking it securely.

"Mrs. Markham, he's cooling his heels in Lt. Markham's study. What shall I do with him?" The housekeeper's voice now held a healthy thread of impatience. "Do you want to do your usual interview for new guests, or would you rather I take 'im straight to his room?"

Miranda truly didn't care where the man went. Any room would do—the farther away from her, the better. But she had a responsibility to the staff to at least meet the man she would be allowing to lodge in the house for a time.

Phillip would have expected her to do that. Summoning her courage, she said, "Please escort him to the parlor. I'll be down momentarily." Stepping forward, she smoothed the thick wool of her charcoal gray skirt.

She avoided glancing at her reflection as she passed a mirror.

Though she was out of mourning and no longer wore black, no color appealed. Hence, gray. Though they'd never said so to her face, she'd overheard her four employees talk about her appearance more than once. The general consensus was that the hue didn't suit her any better than unrelieved black. Actually, Cook had remarked more than once that she resembled a skinny sparrow.

Continuing her descent, she said, "Please serve Mr. Truax tea. I believe we have one or two muffins left from breakfast as well?"

"We do. Since you didn't eat."

Miranda almost smiled. "Today it is most fortunate I did not."

Grumbling, the housekeeper turned away.

When she was alone again, Miranda took a fortifying breath. Realized that a fresh scent wafting from the open window had permeated the air. Salt and sea and, well, something tangy and bright.

It jarred her senses, gave her a small sense of hope.

Perhaps today was not the day to die after all.

By the time Miranda went downstairs, she'd made the poor man wait for almost fifteen minutes.

Yet instead of looking irritated, he stood and smiled when she entered the room, bowed slightly, as if she were wearing cerulean instead of gray. Just as if the war hadn't come and gone.

As she studied him, all traces of oxygen seemed to leave her. Robert Truax was terribly handsome. And for some reason, she thought perhaps she should recognize this man whose name had also seemed familiar. Tall, finely muscled, and—dare she admit—exuberant? So different from most of the men living on Galveston Island. Most of the men looked hard, either from their years fighting the Yankees or from a lifetime sailing the open seas. Rarely did any of them smile at her. She was not only Phillip Markham's widow, but she now had the dubious reputation of housing strange men under his family's roof. Neither attribute endeared her to the general public.

As she crossed the room, Mr. Truax stood quietly. As if he had all the time in the world to stand at attention.

His good manners embarrassed her. She shouldn't have been so negligent. "Mr. Truax, I am terribly sorry to have kept you waiting." Since she had no excuse, she offered none.

"I didn't mind. I've been looking at your books. And your housekeeper brought me some tea." He flashed a smile. "With cream."

Cream was a rare treat for most people. These days, with so many having so little, she'd almost forgotten their blessing. "Yes. We, um, have a cow."

His grin widened. "Seems she did a real fine job of it today."

The artless comment was unsettling. His accent was also unfamiliar. It lacked the usual soft r's and smooth cadence of south Texas. "You are not from around here."

"You are correct, ma'am. I am not. And this is my first time in Galveston. However, I don't hail from too far away. I was raised in Ft. Worth." He paused. "Then, of course, serving during the war took me all over the country. I spent a portion of it in the North. I think my accent might have altered after being around all those Yankees for so long."

She winced. Remembering how much Phillip had hated to talk to her about the war, she quickly said, "Please forgive me . . . I shouldn't have pried."

"You didn't pry, ma'am. You may ask me anything you'd like. I'm not a man of secrets."

He was disconcerting, that was what he was. Attempting to regain control of their conversation, she gestured to the crimson-colored velvet settee. "Please, do sit down."

He waited until she sat on the brocaded chair before he took his own seat at the end of the settee closest to her. But instead of leaning back against the cushion, he turned to face her. Leaned slightly forward. So close, she noticed he smelled of mint and leather. So close that their knees almost touched. It was unseemly and rather too forward.

However, she couldn't think of a polite way to withdraw.

"Mrs. Markham, where did you imagine I was from?"

She noticed his gaze had turned a bit more piercing. She also noticed she was finding it increasingly hard to look away. "It doesn't matter."

"But still, I'm intrigued."

She couldn't tell the truth. She would never tell a man that he sounded like a Northerner. To say something like that would be close to unforgiveable.

Almost as unforgiveable as what people said her husband did.

She cleared her throat. What she needed to do was complete their interview, put him in Winifred's capable hands, and retreat to her bedroom. "Mr. Truax, I like to know a little bit about the people staying in my home. Could you tell me about yourself?"

"Not much to tell, ma'am. I grew up in Ft. Worth, spent a good four years in the army. Now I am in Galveston to see to some business."

His answers seemed purposely vague. "Perhaps you could share the nature of your business?"

"It is of a personal nature."

"And for that you will need to stay here . . ." She tried to recall his telegram. "For one whole month?"

"I believe so. It might be longer. We'll see."

"How did you hear of my boardinghouse?"

His dark gray eyes somehow became even more unfathomable. "People talk, Mrs. Markham. What I heard brought me here." He paused. "That isn't a problem, is it? I mean, you do have a room open, don't you?"

His piercing gaze was more disconcerting than

her in-laws' frequent unannounced visits. "Of course we do. It is simply that there are other, better establishments on Galveston Island that I feel would be far better suited for your kind." She smiled. He stilled.

"Did you say 'kind'?"

Her cheeks heated. "Most men of worth stay at the Tremont, for example. You look as if you have money to spend. Most of my boarders don't."

He crossed one leg over the opposite knee. Infiltrating more precious space. "Actually, a friend told me about your boardinghouse. He said it was clean and reasonably priced. The perfect place for a weary soul to find solace." He brazenly met her gaze, then let it drop. "I could use some solace, I think," he added, his voice sounding troubled.

His tone caused goose bumps to form on her arms. What could he mean? More important, why did she care? She averted her eyes, not liking her body's response. How could she be this aware of a man who wasn't Phillip?

"This house has a good reputation, ma'am."

"I see," she said. Because she felt some response was necessary. However, his words were disconcerting. They'd all recently survived a war. Barely. No one's personal reasons for anything meant much these days.

Furthermore, she doubted her house would have garnered any type of good reputation. Most people felt that her husband's sins stained her own reputation. And, of course, the old, drafty house she'd lived in since her marriage to Phillip.

Before she could comment, he shifted and spoke again. "I really do need a room. And I would like to get settled, if you would have me."

If you would have me.

His words reverberated in her mind, causing her hands to shake. Phillip had said those exact words when he'd asked her to marry him.

I'd like to be yours, Miranda . . . if you would have me.

She clasped her fingers together.

"Tea?" he murmured.

"What? I mean . . . beg pardon?"

He gestured to the china pot and pair of cups. His almost empty. Hers hadn't yet been filled. "May I pour you a cup of tea, Mrs. Markham?" A dimple appeared. "It's cold as Hades in here, if you don't mind me saying."

Before she thought better of it, she wrinkled her nose. "I've never heard that expression before."

"Oh?"

"Yes. I mean, I thought it was hot in Hades." Feeling awkward, she bit her lip. Why had she even uttered such a thing?

Instead of replying, he lifted the teapot. The fragile china, marked with a profusion of poorly painted pale pink roses, looked absurd in his masculine hand.

"I'll pour, Mr. Truax."

"It's already in my grip, though. So may I pour you some tea now? I don't dare drink another drop without you."

Oh, those words. That direct, heated look. It was nerve-racking. Whoever spoke so freely? So openly?

"Mrs. Markham?" He set the fragile teapot back down on the small table in front of them.

It was all Miranda could do not to grimace. She needed to focus. To be the lady he assumed she was. "Yes. I mean, sir, I'll pour. That's a lady's job." She blinked in frustration. "That is, I'm sorry you are chilled." She didn't dare offer further apology. The reason for the cool rooms was obvious. All of them had so little now. And living as they did in Galveston?

Timber for fireplaces wasn't an easy commodity.

Miranda picked up the teapot. But from the moment she held it aloft, it was obvious her tremors hadn't abated.

He noticed.

"Let me help," he murmured. Gently, he curved his fingers around her own and supported the bottom of the pot with his opposite hand. Easily, he guided her, pouring hot tea into one cup, then the other.

His hands were comforting. His rough, calloused palms reminded her that he was so very different from her. Those hands were wide enough to completely cover her own. And warm enough to tease her insides—like heated caramel syrup. For a moment, she was tempted to close her eyes, to imagine a man's arms holding her once again. Warming her. It had been so long.

She trembled.

After setting the pot back on the table, he leaned closer. "Ma'am? Are you all right?"

"I'm sorry." She forced a weak smile. "I guess a ghost crossed my path."

Instead of grinning, he merely stared at her, his manner filled with concern. "Are you feeling better now?"

She nodded. "Yes." Oh, but she felt so strange!

She watched as he poured a liberal dose of cream into his cup and sipped appreciatively. "I do love hot tea. It's been ages since I've had any."

"Why is that? I thought you folks in Ft. Worth had most everything you needed."

"Not everything, ma'am."

His presence still confused her. "Mr. Truax, when, exactly, did you arrive in Galveston? Did you arrive on the ferry from Houston this morning?" She couldn't recall if the boats ran this early.

The secret amusement that had played around his eyes faded as his expression clouded. "Yes."

"And what business have you had before coming here?"

"Work that has taken me all over the state."

28

Work? He sounded as if he'd been on a mission.

What kind could that be? Was he a soldier still? Yet he wore no uniform. He said he needed rest, but he didn't look weary.

"I hate to point out the obvious, but you haven't yet actually told me my fate."

"I beg your pardon?"

"Did I pass the test? May I stay here with you, Mrs. Markham?"

She blinked. Perhaps it was her imagination, but she kept getting the feeling that he was talking in riddles. Almost as if he knew something she didn't.

The idea was disturbing. She should probably ask more questions. It wasn't safe for a woman to be living with people she didn't know. Especially not a strange man who smiled too much and evaded questions like they were intricate steps in a quadrille.

However, it didn't really matter, did it? Her reputation was in shreds and it wasn't like she didn't have rooms to spare. She had far too many empty rooms.

But most of all, overriding everything was the fact that she was too tired and too numb inside to really care. Numbness, she had learned, was the key to survival. And if she were going to decide to live, she needed to survive in this house as long as she could.

Eager to end their conversation, she at last answered. "Yes, Mr. Truax. You may stay."

A dimple appeared. "I'm so glad. Thank you."

They stood up. "Winifred, my housekeeper, will give you a key and show you to your room when you finish your tea."

"I have already finished," he said lightly, illustrating that she'd very likely been staring at him, lost in thought for longer than she realized.

She really should be doing better with him. After taking a fortifying breath, she got to her feet. "Mr. Truax, I just realized I haven't yet given you a tour of the house. Or told you about mealtimes. Or explained our fees."

"I'm sure we'll take care of everything in time, ma'am," he replied, his voice gentle. "And don't you worry none. Fact is, I don't need very much at all. Why, I'd bet a three-cent piece you'll hardly know I'm here."

When he left the room to find her housekeeper on his own, she sat back down.

As she sipped the rapidly cooling tea, Miranda knew one thing for certain. It was extremely unlikely that she would forget Robert Truax was there.

2

Robert was never comfortable in a tailored suit. Growing up the way he had on the streets of Ft. Worth, he'd been lucky to have a shirt on his back, never mind anything that actually fit him. After he entered the service, his uniform had been cut for the active life of a soldier. The fabric had been thick and hardy, turning soft after many washings. The cut had been generous through his chest and shoulders too. A man needed room to point and shoot.

A lot had happened in the last seven years, however. When the war broke out, he'd been one of the first to enlist. Given the circumstances of his youth, he was tough. He was good at street fighting and had little to no fear for his person or his life.

Those qualities, while not serving him all that well in the businesses of Ft. Worth, were highly valued in the military. He worked hard to gain acceptance and be valued. It became apparent that, whereas he had no reason to return home, he had every reason to excel in his unit.

It seemed his soul had been aching for a life filled with purpose.

Perhaps because he was so eager—or maybe it was because he was so obviously lacking—he'd gotten a good education from both his fellow enlisted men and his officers. Bored men greatly improved his literacy and taught him to write. Lazy supply officers taught him rudimentary math skills.

Eventually he'd garnered the attention of Captain Devin Monroe and the officers in his unit. Over time, they more or less adopted him, teaching him manners and correct grammar.

After Gettysburg, he fought hard enough and displayed sufficient skills to become an officer. A second lieutenant. Later, when they were captured and moved up North, Robert concentrated on making the best of the experience.

Consequently, he was probably the only man to feel he came out of the prisoner-of-war camp in better shape than when he entered. Those men had not only continued his education in history, science, and literature, but they'd managed to teach him how to waltz one very long stretch of days when the temperatures loomed around zero and the snow and ice covered the ground in thick blankets.

He'd also made some close connections. Soon after their release, he'd gone to work for a locomotive company. The owner had been looking for someone with Texas ties to help encourage new business.

Just as he had in the military, he'd quickly risen through the ranks and reaped the financial rewards. And though most men might not consider him wealthy, he now was blessed with far more in his pockets than he'd ever dreamed of—and he looked the part as well.

When his former captain had asked a favor, it had never occurred to Robert to refuse. He owed that man and his former unit both his life and his peace of mind, so he left the locomotive company's employ and came here.

Most days he didn't think much about how his clothes fit. That moment, however, as he followed the curmudgeonly housekeeper up a flight of stairs into a surprisingly well-kept and spacious room at the far end of a long hall, he was sure the collar of his close-fitting shirt was in danger of choking him.

That was what he deserved, he suspected, for lying through his teeth to a beautiful widow who looked so fragile that a strong wind would likely toss her off her feet. When he quickly realized Miranda Markham had no idea who he was—perhaps Phillip had never mentioned him in his letters?—he followed through with his intent to keep his connection to her husband to himself. His plan might be more successful that way. Mrs. Markham seemed like she was barely hanging on.

However, though he had the best of intentions at the moment, he felt lower than he could ever recall. Well, not since he'd followed his captain out of the prison he'd shared with his four best friends in the world, leaving Phillip and so many others in unmarked graves in the small cemetery just outside their barracks.

The housekeeper fingered the coverlet on the bed. "I trust everything is to your satisfaction, sir?"

He didn't bother to look around. In truth, his surroundings didn't interest him as much as the woman downstairs did. It was true, as well, that rooms and amenities meant little to him now. If he was warm and dry, he would be a far sight better than he'd been on Johnson's Island. "It is. Thank you."

Her expression flattened. "I'll be seeing you, then. Let me know if you'll be needin' anything." She took a breath. "That ain't to say that I can find it, but I can try," she said as she started toward the door.

"Times still hard here?"

She drew to a stop. "War ain't been over that long."

"I meant in this house." Of course, the moment he said the words he wished he could take them back. The woman had had to open her house to strangers. Things were obviously not good at all.

She turned, umbrage in her posture. "Mrs. Markham runs a respectable establishment, sir. I don't expect you'll be finding anything remiss."

"Of course not. I suspected nothing less."

She nodded. "Good. I'll expect you ta remember that."

"Shame she lost her husband," he interjected quickly. He needed information and so far she was his best and easiest option to get it. "I mean, I assume she is a widow."

"She is." After eyeing him for a long moment, she said, "Lt. Markham died near the end of the war." Her voice lowered. "He perished less than a month before Lee surrendered at Appomattox."

"Shame, that," he said lightly.

"It was worse than a shame, sir. It was a tragedy."

"Indeed."

He considered his ability to even say two words to be something of an accomplishment.

Because the fact was, he remembered Phillip's death well. Too well. Phillip had lingered, fighting the inevitable with each breath. Robert had painfully watched him fight that losing battle, helpless to do anything but watch him waste away for days. On his last day, Robert had held his hand for hours, attempting to give him some degree of warmth in a very cold existence. Then, after he'd left his side and Devin Monroe had gone to take a turn, Phillip had passed on.

"He died in a Yankees' prison barracks, he did," the housekeeper blurted. "He would write Mrs. Markham letters from there, trying to sound positive, but we all knew he weren't doing well."

Robert had watched Phillip write those letters. They all had. But because he didn't want anyone in Galveston to know that yet, he kept his expression impassive. "Oh?"

"Oh, yes. He died up in Ohio, he did." She grimaced. "Poor man, forced to live and die on an island in the middle of Lake Erie. Don't seem natural, if you ask me."

He agreed. "I would imagine any prison would be a hard place to live. Or die."

After eyeing him carefully, she said, "I should probably let you know that if you stay on Galveston Island for any length of time, you're going to hear a lot of talk about Lt. Markham and even more talk about Mrs. Markham herself. Some of it is ugly." She closed her eyes. "Actually, the majority of it is ugly."

He knew she was warning him for his own good. He was more than willing to heed it. "I've never given much credence to idle chatter."

"If you are living here, that would be good to bear in mind," she advised. "Sometimes life interferes with all our best intentions."

Robert felt as if the walls surrounding him were closing in. Remembering the drafty barracks, how cold it had been in the winter, how endless the days had lasted, he felt a thin line of perspiration form along the middle of his back. "Some might believe there's more glory from

36

dying on the battlefield, but I imagine there's just as much honor dying in prison."

She lifted a graying eyebrow. "You really think that, don't you?"

"I do." It took everything he had not to embellish his statement. He wasn't ready to discuss his own imprisonment. Still less ready to remember his comrades' pain, suffering, and eventual death. The memories were too crystal clear—the damp smell of their cells, the faraway look in his commander's eyes, the long hours spent in boredom.

Those memories, it seemed, were reserved only for the middle of the night.

With a new awareness in her eyes, Winifred looked him over. She seemed to hesitate, then blurted, "Since you're going to be hearing things anyway, you might as well know that folks not only say he died a coward's death in that Northern prison, but he also died while being interrogated and gave secrets to the enemy."

Only by digging his fingers into the palms of his hands was he able to remain impassive. "I don't understand."

"I know. It don't make no sense at all. If he died while being questioned, it would mean he kept his secrets, don'tcha think?" Before Robert could comment on that, she continued on in her loquacious way. "Sir, anyone who knew the lieutenant knew he would no more share precious secrets with the enemy than he would have harmed a hair on Mrs. Markham's head. He was a good man."

Phillip had been better than that. He'd loved his wife, yes. But he'd also loved the men he'd served with. He'd been loyal to the cause. Even more than that, he'd been loyal to the men he served with and led into battle.

As far as he was concerned, Phillip Markham had been the best the South had to offer. Anyone who said different was surely a liar and a scoundrel.

"So you don't believe he did share military secrets?"

She shook her head. "No, sir, I do not, and neither does Mrs. Markham. Even if one didn't call into account the fact that he'd been injured, captured, then hauled up to the middle of Lake Erie, therefore not able to share anything of use, he weren't that kind of man," she murmured, her English accent sounding more pronounced. "That said, if he did say anything he shouldn't, I'm of the mind that he should be forgiven, don'tcha think?" She stared at him, her pale gray eyes practically daring him to refute her.

Or, perhaps, she was looking for hope instead?

Robert stayed silent.

He wasn't sure who should be forgiven. They'd all committed atrocities in battle. They'd all done things in captivity they'd never imagined they would do before they'd donned a uniform.

Visibly uncomfortable with his silence, the housekeeper spoke a little faster. "I mean, six months before General Lee signed that treaty, well, things were already a foregone conclusion. No Yankee cared about what a Confederate lieutenant had to say. And especially not one locked up on an island." She looked at him worriedly. Practically begging him to reassure her. "Don'tcha think?"

She was wrong, of course. Their enemy had cared about everything they knew. Then there were guards who cared about nothing other than recriminations.

Though they were treated with a light hand compared to the atrocities of Andersonville or even in some of the other Union prisons, their guards hadn't been especially kind to them. Why, once word got out about the horrors of the treatment in the Confederate prisons, their rations had been cut in half. Hunger and cold had been constant companions.

Robert now knew any confinement was debilitating. "I couldn't begin to guess."

She waved an impatient hand. "Whatever the reason, it would help Mrs. Markham if you kept the gossip you hear to yourself. I promise, nothing you could say will sway the gossip-mongers, and it ain't anything she hasn't heard before."

"Understood."

39

Her face cleared then, seeming to come to a decision. "We're pleased you're here, whatever the reason, Mr. Truax. We serve supper at six and breakfast at seven. Don't be late."

"No, ma'am."

"Charmer," Robert heard her say under her breath as she walked out of the room.

The moment the door closed behind her, he strode to the desk, found a letterhead, envelope, ink, and quill, and sat down to collect his thoughts. Though he would have preferred to simply tele-graph his progress, he couldn't risk anyone discovering his real mission. His job was to get to know Phillip Markham's widow, ascertain how she was truly doing after her husband's death, and make whatever changes he could to ease her life. Then he was to leave and go on about his life—unless Monroe summoned him for another assignment.

This duty had seemed so easy when he learned its details from their former captain. His mission had felt cut-and-dried. He'd been certain he would have been able to remain carefully distant, even if she had known from the beginning that he served with Phillip. He'd imagined he would feel nothing more than pity for her. After all, she was merely one of hundreds—if not thousands— of women struggling to reconfigure their lives without husbands by their sides.

But from the moment she'd entered the room

and he'd caught sight of her beauty and heard her slow drawl, he'd been mesmerized. Then he'd noticed that her eyes were a curious shade of blue—almost lavender in color. And that they were framed by dark circles, illustrating her lack of sleep and an abundance of worry and stress. His heart had been lost.

Miranda Markham was a woman in need of a savior. And though he was no heavenly angel, he was determined to do what he could to make her life easier. The first step in making that happen was to gain her trust. A tall order when he was beginning with a lie.

With bold strokes, Robert wrote that he had arrived, made contact, and would be in touch with an update soon.

For the first time since he'd come to terms with the outcome of the war, Robert had a new goal, a reason to step out into society, and, for once, to look forward to another day.

"He's a right one, he is," Winnie declared when she stepped inside the kitchen. "At least six feet of muscle and brawn, all wrapped up in a handsome package."

Belle Harden glanced up from the pot of chowder she was stirring. "Who is?"

"Our new boarder," Winnie said as she trotted into the room, looking much like a pigeon. She was round and gray haired. By turns sharp and

41

nurturing. Belle had loved her from the minute Winnie had invited her in to have a bowl of soup at the end of the war.

Within an hour of Belle's stepping into the kitchen, Winnie had procured her a job in the expansive mansion, known to everyone near and far as the Iron Rail. At first she worked for room and board, but once Mrs. Markham opened for business as a boardinghouse and business was good enough, Belle received a small salary It was enough to save and fuel her dreams of one day working in a dress shop. To do that she was going to need money to pay for her own room. Until that time came Belle planned to stay in the confines of the Iron Rail and help out as much as she could.

After all, Mrs. Markham needed them.

Brought back to the present by Winnie's bright expression and even brighter tone of voice, Belle put down her wooden spoon. "How did Mrs. Markham receive him?"

"About the way you'd expect. She looked like she could hardly do anything but summon the energy to walk down the stairs to greet him in person." Winnie's warm expression fled just as quickly as it had come. "She's in a bad way today, Belle. If she doesn't improve soon, why, I don't know what we're going to do."

"There's not much we can do. There's only four of us—you, me, Cook, and Emerson." She didn't add that Cook and Emerson were recently married, and while they did a fine job with their duties— Cook in the kitchen and Emerson filling every job from handyman to coachman when needed— they spent any moments to themselves wrapped up in each other.

Winnie said, "We can start by trying to convince everyone who has been so unkind to her to let the past lie buried in Ohio like it should."

"That would be a hard thing to do given the fact that Mrs. Markham owns this here house and any number of people want it out from under her," Cook said.

"Not everyone," Emerson pointed out. "Only Mr. Markham's mother and sister."

"And every third ship captain who sails through and sees the dock," Cook added. "Why, a man could sail here from any part of the world and walk right into the house without anyone knowing the difference."

"I wonder why she doesn't simply give in," Belle said. "It would make things a bit easier."

"Maybe, maybe not. She likes this house and everything it reminds her of," Winnie said. "If she left here, it would be like she left Mr. Markham too."

Emerson grunted. "You women are far too sentimental. It's not just the memories keeping her here. We all know she needs the money. Plus, running a boardinghouse keeps her occupied."

Cook guffawed. "I can think of any number of things to keep a woman occupied besides opening up her home to strangers."

Pulling out a fresh rag, Emerson continued to polish silver. After carefully holding up a tray and looking for signs of tarnish, he placed it in one of the many cabinets underneath the counter. "Winnie, have you seen any more of those letters lately?"

"I found one she received yesterday in the trash this morning."

"I don't understand how Sheriff Kern can't do anything to stop them," Belle mused. "They are terrible."

"It ain't like they're signed, Belle," Cook said. "All we know is that they are local."

"Well, that eliminates no one. Whoever started those tales about Mr. Markham did a good job. Nobody hardly speaks to her anymore."

Winnie poured herself a fresh cup of hot tea. "You should say something to someone."

"Me? I don't think so."

"Why? Everyone seems to like you."

Belle knew the men who liked her were secretly hoping she was a sporting girl. The good men, the churchgoing men, didn't give her the time of day.

The women who were of Mrs. Markham's class didn't even see her. To them, she was yet another young woman of questionable means cleaning rooms and peeling potatoes.

"I don't know who you think I'm friendly with, but I surely don't carry that kind of weight in this town," Belle replied. "And beg pardon, but you three don't either."

"Maybe not," Winnie agreed. "But Sheriff Kern might listen to you. I think he's sweet on ya."

Belle shook her head. "I don't think so." Sheriff Kern had moved to Galveston in the summer of '65 and quickly been appointed sheriff. At first everyone thought it was because he was friends with the Northerners put in charge of their island. In no time, he'd corrected that misunderstanding. He told everyone that he had been loyal to the South and that it was simply his experience in the war that had enabled him to be appointed so quickly and easily.

Most people took him at his word, but Belle had never been positive he was telling the truth. After all, he never talked about the war or where he'd served.

Blowing out a deep breath, Cook blurted, "All I do know is that Mrs. Markham needs a champion, she does. Someone somewhere needs to step up and help her before she loses hope."

Belle completely agreed. But she also knew it couldn't be her. She needed this job. The last thing she wanted to happen was to be let go for being impertinent, and denied a little recommendation to boot. "Someone will, I bet."

"I hope that someone does soon." Winnie's lips

pressed together tightly. "I swear, every time I think about the way her supposed best friend Mercy Jackson turned her back on her, I want to spit nails."

"When I spied her pointedly ignoring Mrs. Markham on her last visit to the bank, I considered whacking that woman on the head with a saucepan, I did," Cook stated. Glaring at Winnie, she said, "Don't know what possessed you to mention that vixen's name in my kitchen. You're liable to make all the milk curdle, you are."

"I'm simply saying Mercy should be acting a little bit kinder to poor Mrs. Markham, seeing as her man came back from the war with hardly a scrape. She should be acting more like her name, you know."

"If I know anything, it's that pain comes in all sorts of names and appearances," Cook said. "All of us know that. Especially Mrs. Markham."

And, Belle realized, especially herself too. She also had suffered during the long, bloody War of Northern Aggression. All she could hope for was that no one would ever discover the things she'd had to do to survive.

If anyone here found out, well, even these women in the kitchen would no longer give her the time of day. She'd be out of a job and out of a home.

And once again, she'd have nothing. Nothing at all.

3

It was a journey she hated, but it had to be done. Every Friday Miranda made her way to the downtown business district, most of which was located on the Strand. It was a pretty area, and flourishing even after the war. So much so, many folks called it the Wall Street of the Southwest.

Miranda only thought of the walk as something she had to get through as best she could. She walked quietly, striving to attract no attention to herself as she passed the row of Victorian office buildings, most of which had survived the war intact, thanks to their brick structure and cast-iron fronts.

She would cross the small grassy expanse that filled the center of it, bypassing any number of horse-drawn carriages, groups of freedmen, exhausted from long hours working in the cotton warehouses, and noisy dockworkers eager to collect their pay. Then, at last, she would enter the bank. Once inside, she would stand in line and pretend she didn't feel everyone's eyes on her. As she was both ignored and observed, she would stand as straight and tall as her five foot six inches would allow. And act as if she didn't hear the whispered comments about Phillip and the woman they all thought she'd become.

The line would feel endless, even if there was only one person in front of her. Her nerves would grow taut, and she would coax herself to pretend nothing was amiss, that her skin hadn't turned cold or her breathing hadn't turned shallow.

Then and only then would it finally be her turn with Mr. Kyle Winter, the teller. He'd look down his nose at her while he collected her week's deposit. He'd double- and triple-check the amount, making her wonder if he'd believed her husband had been both a thief and a traitor.

Just when her nerves would be stretched so tight that she feared she would either collapse in dismay or give in to weakness and allow her tears to form, Mr. Winter would nod. Smile crookedly.

"Your business is concluded, Mrs. Markham," he'd say. Then he would look beyond her to the next person in line, triumph lighting his eyes.

She hated every minute of it.

All four of her employees had offered to do the errand in her place. Miranda knew it would probably do everyone, including Kyle Winter, a service if she accepted that help. But she also knew no good would come from avoiding the chore. If Phillip could go off to fight, get injured, and eventually die in his captors' prison, she could survive one grueling half hour a week doing her banking business.

At least, she hoped so.

With a sense of doom, she put her carefully counted money in her wallet and placed it in her reticule. "You can do this, Miranda," she muttered to herself. "It's only a trip to the bank. Not a battle."

Feeling a bit better after her talking-to, she reached for her favorite black wool cloak lined with a dark mauve satin. At least the beautiful cloak would give her some comfort. She was just about to slip it over her shoulders when she heard her new boarder's footsteps on the stairs.

"Going out, Mrs. Markham?" Robert asked.

"Yes."

"Allow me," he said as he took the cloak from her hands, gently covered her shoulders with the wool, then circled around her to fasten the closure at her neck. "Will this be warm enough? The wind is particularly powerful this afternoon."

"It is January," she stated. Which, of course, didn't answer his question.

He smiled pleasantly. "Where are you off to this afternoon?"

"The bank."

"Is that nearby?"

"It's on the Strand. Only a fifteen-minute walk."

He looked around the foyer. "I don't see a maid," he said, sounding concerned. "Are you going by yourself?"

"Yes. Of course."

"Surely not."

"No one puts on airs like that here in Galveston." She tried to smile.

But instead of looking reassured, he only looked worried. "May I accompany you?"

"Accompany me?"

"I'd like to. If I may."

Obviously he was worried about her safety. "There is no need."

"Perhaps. But may I?"

"Why do you want to?" she asked suspiciously.

"I'd enjoy getting the opportunity to walk by a lady's side for a spell," he answered easily. "Plus, I'm trying to get the way of the land. Per se."

"While I can understand that, I don't need any help." She also was in no hurry to see his expression when he realized just how vilified she was. Once he understood that, there was a very good chance he would remove himself from her home, and then she wouldn't even have a deposit to make.

He continued to look at her directly, his gaze steady and sure. Somber. "Even if you don't need any help, it would still be my honor to accompany you. May I? I promise, I'll be a perfect gentleman."

There was something startling about the way he was staring at her so solemnly. Almost as if he cared about her. Almost as if he already knew how difficult her weekly banking journey was for her to take.

How could he have any idea? And even if he did, why would he care? They were strangers. There was little chance they'd even become acquaintances. After all, when his business was concluded, he would leave. It was likely she'd never see him again.

But as she looked at him, noticed how sincere he looked, she found herself thinking it would be nice not to have to make this weekly journey by herself. "Mr. Truax, if you would care to accompany me, I would be obliged."

His lips curved upward. "Thank you, ma'am. You honor me."

With effort, she bit back a smile. His words were so gallant, so different from the way most people spoke to her, she'd almost felt giddy. "You, sir, are quite the gentleman."

"Hardly," he said as they exited the old house. "I'm afraid my skills in that area are rather rusty."

"That's all right, seeing as how my skills are virtually nonexistent."

"Tell me about the square. What is its name again?"

"It is called Recognition Square."

He looked rather unimpressed as he eyed the small expanse of land lying just off to the side of the main thoroughfare. "It seems to me that it's a rather big name for such a humble area."

"Yes. Um, well, I suppose it is." For a split second, she was tempted to apologize for its state. Why, she had no earthly idea. She'd neither named the square nor spent time there. Feeling uncomfortable, she pointed to the stately Victorian on their left. "That house over there is owned by the McKenzie family. They hail from Scotland."

Mr. Truax didn't even look. "What is it recognizing?"

"Recognizing?" she repeated.

"Yes. The square."

With a start, she realized she'd been staring at his expression—and maybe his dark gray eyes— for far too long. "Oh, the, um, dead." She pointed to the monument that had been recently erected on the far side of the square. "Both the name and the monument are to honor the heroes fallen in the war. It was just completed and dedicated two months ago."

"I'm surprised the Yankees let you erect such a thing."

"I was, too, as a matter of fact. However, to be fair, we, um, don't get a lot of reconstruction supervision around these parts. And a few of the wealthier shipping merchants paid for it." Allowing a bit of humor to touch her, she added, "The Yankees seem to prefer to oversee the city dwellers."

"I see."

She doubted he did. She didn't, not that it

mattered. Their town had been filled with Union soldiers by the end of the war. When the fighting had stopped and the treaty had been signed, Galveston had reinvented itself, becoming a rather booming port city with a decidedly ribald atmosphere. Anything could happen in Galveston, and often did.

Now, except for the monument, all that reminded one of the war was a sense of injustice, a loss, and the vacant stares of a great many widows like herself.

His expression turned sympathetic as he offered her his arm. "Come, show the monument to me."

"I'd rather not."

"It won't take up too much time." Gesturing toward the stone, he said, "I see a great many names carved here. At least fifty, or thereabouts."

"There are seventy-five," she blurted before thinking the better of it.

"Seventy-five fallen. A shame. Where is your husband's name? I understand from your housekeeper that he was one of our cause's heroes."

Such a simple question. It was a shame she didn't have the correct answer. "I am afraid I can't show his name to you."

"Why not?" As if he'd just realized he'd been holding up his arm for a full moment, he let it fall to his side. "Are you worried we'll cause a scene? If so, I promise I will be on my best behavior."

"No. I, um . . ." Why was she being so hesitant? Phillip's name's absence on the monument wasn't a secret. Why, any person in the town would most likely be thrilled to share the awful truth. "Phillip is not listed," she said at last.

His expression seemed to harden, but that was likely her imagination. "But he was a Confederate soldier. An officer, yes?"

"Yes. He was a lieutenant."

"And he died during the war."

"Yes. In captivity. He was a prisoner of war on Johnson's Island."

"Therefore, his name should be listed here. Honored." His tone held a new edge to it.

It took her off guard. "Yes," she said hesitantly. "But, well, there are some, I fear, who feel that he died betraying the South. The townspeople elected not to include him."

His expression turned murderous. "That is most unfortunate, ma'am."

She didn't quite understand why he even cared. "Yes. Yes, it is." Just then she noticed several people staring at them curiously. "We best go. We're causing a scene."

But he didn't budge. "How would we do that? We are merely standing here. Reading the names of the fallen heroes."

She didn't miss the sarcasm in his voice. Or the fact that his tone had risen enough to carry.

"Please, Mr. Truax. I am still unsure as to why

you decided to accompany me. But since you did, I must ask you to abide by my wishes. I rarely leave the house and of late I never am accompanied. Your appearance and anger are going to cause further talk about me. And though it pains me to admit this, I have been a target for gossips and conjecture. I'd rather not give them any more ammunition."

He backed down at once. "Of course not. Please forgive me." Looking a bit abashed, he said, "Like I said, my manners have become quite lackluster. Any refinement I've ever had has taken leave."

"There is nothing to forgive. I simply need you to see how things are."

"I hope your circumstances change soon."

She did, too, but she doubted they would change. Well, at least not for the better.

The rest of the way to the bank, Miranda tried not to be aware that his hands now remained clasped behind his back. That he was keeping a respectful distance from her side. That he remained stoically silent.

The first thing Robert noticed when they entered the ornate building was that it was in far better shape than most likely any other bank building in the state. The woodwork gleamed. The brass fittings on the drawers and cabinets sparkled. The marble floor looked shiny enough to eat off of.

In short, it could hold its own against any grandiose building in Philadelphia or even New York City. Which, of course, was impressive, given the fact that they were in the post-war South and living in the throes of Yankee Reconstruction.

However, even the building's imposing beauty paled compared to the second thing Robert took note of. And that was the way the teller eyed Miranda with a combination of disrespect and lewd appreciation. It was blatant. Bordering on how many men had eyed the sporting girls when they'd come to their camps during the war.

Robert was shocked, seeing as how Miranda was everything the camp's fallen angels were not. But what was more surprising was how everyone in the building allowed the man's behavior to go on. Did no one see or hear how a bank employee was speaking to her? Or was it simply that no one cared?

Before his eyes, Miranda retreated into herself. She quietly stood in the short line and waited far too long to be served. A few ladies held glove-covered hands to their mouths and smirked.

Robert's jaw clenched as he understood that the teller's behavior was an intentional oversight. He was playing a game at Miranda's expense. Only when the man noticed Robert watching him coldly did he call Miranda forward.

"Mrs. Markham, if you're ready?" His voice was laced with sarcasm.

She started. And, Robert was dismayed to see, a hot flush rose up on her neck. "Yes, sir." Before she stepped forward, she looked back at him in some sort of apology. "I'll be right back, Mr. Truax."

It took everything he had not to step in front of her and guard her from everyone else's interested eyes.

But that was neither what she needed nor why he was there. "Take your time, ma'am," he said gently. "I've got all day."

However, when she moved toward the teller, and Robert noticed that the smarmy man boldly scanned her body as she approached, he realized it was going to be impossible to remain off to one side.

Instead, he followed, stopping just short of her. Close enough to hear every word spoken but far enough to provide the illusion of privacy. When a man behind him started to speak, obviously confused as to why Robert wasn't waiting his turn, he looked over his shoulder and glared. Now every person in the building was aware that Miranda Markham was no longer alone.

A new, uneasy silence permeated the room.

She glanced his way nervously, then timidly opened her reticule and her wallet and laid a small stack of money on the counter. "I have a deposit, Mr. Winter."

Instead of taking the bills and collecting it in an

expedient fashion, the teller sighed. And started counting the bills out loud.

Stopping.

And then beginning again.

He looked up once to peer at Robert.

"I guess some people don't care where they stay. They'll even consider the Iron Rail." He paused, glancing at her with a wicked gleam in his eye. "Kind of makes me wonder what services you offer there." He smirked again and glanced up at her face.

Obviously, Mr. Winter was double-checking to see if his words had made a direct hit.

Robert clenched his fist as Miranda said nothing.

Looking pleased with himself, the teller jabbed again. "Do you ever tell your guests about your husband? About what he was really like?" he continued, his voice oily. Slick. "Do you ever admit to those folks what he did? Or do they simply prefer you to keep silent?"

Robert tensed as he prepared himself for Miranda to berate the man for his poor manners. After she had her turn, he was looking forward to speaking a few choice words himself.

However, she only inhaled before speaking. Her voice trembled but was thick with emotion. "I simply wish to conclude my business, Mr. Winter."

"Do you? What is your hurry? Do you have new boarders to entertain?" He leered at her.

Robert had had more than enough. Gently, he took her arm and moved her away from the teller's window. "Mrs. Markham, perhaps you'd like to sit down while I take care of this for you?"

"Mr. Truax—"

"It would be my honor, ma'am." He kept his voice hard. Firm.

When at last she nodded and moved to do as he bid, the teller sputtered. "I can't allow that."

Once he was satisfied that Miranda was out of earshot, Robert pressed both hands on the counter in front of him and leaned close. "I know you can allow me to see to her business. And once more, you will allow it," he said. "Furthermore, I suggest you conclude Mrs. Markham's business
in a more expedient fashion."

"Who are you?"

"No one you would have ever heard of. Simply a friend."

Winter's expression was filled with derision. "I see. You're one of her men."

"No. You do not see." Lowering his voice, he said, "It has come to the notice of several people that Miranda Markham has been in need of scme protection. I have come to offer that. You would be wise to change your attitude toward her."

"Because?"

"Because I am not helpless. I am not demure. I am not used to men in ill-fitting, cheap suits telling me what to do," he continued, his voice rising. "Most of all, I am most certainly not used to explaining myself."

The teller inhaled sharply. "Are you threatening me?"

"Sir."

"Pardon?"

"You forgot to add 'sir.'" When the teller gaped, Robert added, "If you are going to ask me a question like that, be sure to address me properly." After the briefest of pauses, he murmured, "Now give it another try, Mr. Winter."

For the first time, Mr. Winter looked shaken. "Are you threatening me, sir?"

"I don't make threats. I make promises." He lowered his voice. "As of today, Mrs. Markham's circumstances have changed. You would do well to take note of that."

Mr. Winter's eyebrows rose. "Yes, sir."

"I'm glad we see eye to eye. Now, if you would, finish the lady's banking needs in a more expedient fashion."

Immediately, Mr. Winter looked down to his hands, which were now clutching the crumpled bills. After smoothing them out, he began counting them, all in lightning-quick motions. After writing the amount in a ledger, he tore off a receipt. "Here you are. Sir."

"I'm glad we understand each other now." Robert took it, then turned back to Miranda, who was perched on the edge of one of the dark wooden chairs. "Mrs. Markham, are you ready to leave now?"

"Yes, I am." She rose gracefully, then took his elbow. She looked wary, but her eyes were shining.

Robert wondered if that new gleam was from happiness, unshed tears, or amusement. He hoped it was the latter. He would like to think she had enjoyed seeing that little worm of a teller finally get his comeuppance.

As he guided her out of the ornate building, Robert didn't look at the teller again. He didn't make eye contact with any of the men and women who had been eavesdropping curiously.

But most important, he made sure not to look at Miranda. There was only so much a man could handle at any one moment. He wanted to enfold her in his arms and promise that she would never be treated so shabbily again.

Furthermore, he knew if he saw that it wasn't amusement shining in her eyes but new pain, he would be very tempted to go back into that building and punch that teller for his insolence.

But that was not what she needed. She needed a protector, not a bully. And for her to accept his protection, she needed to first trust him. That meant he couldn't do anything to make her fear him.

He couldn't afford to do that. She couldn't afford that.

When they stepped outside, the cold air slapped their cheeks, making his eyes water and, as he saw when he finally looked down at her, her skin flush.

He wished he had a soft scarf to wrap around her.

She paused on the steps and breathed in deeply.

"Are you all right, Mrs. Markham?"

As she turned to him, he noticed her eyes were no longer shining but were a clear blue. "I believe I am. Thank you for what you did in there. Mr. Winter has always been rude, but he has never said such things to me before."

"You never need to thank me for defending your honor."

"He looked browbeaten."

He wished he could have simply beaten the man. "Mr. Winter was insolent and disrespectful. He needed to be reminded of his manners."

"I believe you did that."

He couldn't resist smiling. "I think so too." He gestured toward the street. "Shall we?"

She nodded, leaning into him when he rearranged his hands so one was resting on her back while the other was gripping her elbow.

He liked how she was depending on him to help her.

He probably liked it too much.

But at times like this, he missed the easy retribution that he'd learned on the streets of Ft. Worth. There, violence wasn't a last resort; it was the norm. Men didn't hold their tongues; they spoke their minds and made sure each word was sharp.

Reputation was everything, and a healthy dose of intimidation was often employed.

He had known that life and had been good at it. Robert also realized right then and there that if there came a time to unleash his baser qualities, he would look forward to it.

Perhaps far too much.

4

From the time he'd returned Miranda to her home, Robert fumed about his visit to the bank with her. At first, he'd been so angry about Winter's treatment of her that he'd been tempted to return to the bank and show the man what happened when someone was rude to a woman Robert cared about.

Just imagining how good it would feel to knock some sense into the clerk had made Robert smile. But of course, no doubt Miranda would not appreciate the use of such violence on her behalf.

He made do with going for a long walk before supper, stopping and chatting with assorted passersby on the Strand and around the port. He'd learned a great many things about the island, its part in the war—and the rumors swirling about Phillip Markham and his widowed bride.

After supper, when Miranda had actually apologized for making him witness her abuse, he'd gotten angry all over again. He'd paced back and forth in his room, silently fuming. Over and over Robert reminded himself that he was no longer a daredevil soldier in the wilds of

Arkansas. Instead, he was a gentleman whom Miranda needed to trust. That helped a bit, though punching a hole in the wall or ripping something into shreds was tempting.

Now, in the dim, winter morning light, Robert realized what the correct course of action needed to be. He needed to write that letter to Captain Monroe.

With a new intent, he sat down at the small corner desk, dipped his quill into ink, and began. After writing a few lines about his travels and the state of Miranda's boardinghouse, he got to his point.

The situation here is beyond disturbing, sir. In fact, it borders on disbelief. The woman is treated like a pariah. She is avoided by practically every man and woman in the city, both because of rumors that Phillip was a traitor and because they think her boarding-house is not a respectable establishment, though it most certainly is. It is as if everyone feels the need to make sure she is held in contempt, which makes no sense. Phillip told me she was from a good family and that their courtship, while impetuous, was not out of the ordinary.

He paused, letting his quill drip ink onto the corner of his paper. Only a quick dab of blotting paper prevented it from bleeding onto the rest of the page.

After reviewing what he'd written and being satisfied that he was neither exaggerating nor presenting Miranda Markham's situation too lightly, he continued.

Furthermore, from what I understand, no one has any true knowledge of what Phillip Markham actually did other than "giving the enemy secrets." It's all innuendo and veiled accusations. However, those allegations have already done terrible damage to our friend's reputation.

He gripped the quill, holding it so tightly he feared he was in danger of snapping the instrument in two.

He forced himself to inhale. Exhale. Repeat the process.

Gathering his wits, he added:

I will attempt to further investigate this matter and discern how these rumors started. I will also do my best to try to alleviate some of Mrs. Markham's worst fears.

I'll write again in a few days.

He reviewed his words one more time, then signed his name. Next, after blotting the page, he carefully folded the paper and stuffed it into the awaiting envelope.

It was time to post it and move forward.

If he thought too much about his words, he would be tempted to tear the missive and rewrite it. But that would prove to be unnecessary and foolhardy. There was really nothing else to say and not much else to report. If he added too many of his thoughts or emotions, the captain would suspect that he had already begun to become too involved in the woman's life.

And that was not why he was there. No, it was far better to let the letter speak for itself and concentrate the rest of his energies on calming down and appearing detached.

Yes, that was how he needed to be. Detached.

At last satisfied that he had regained his composure, Robert carefully splashed water on his face, rolled down his shirtsleeves, slipped on his coat, and headed downstairs.

As he walked across the foyer, he passed a maid. She was small in stature, slim and petite. She was also on her hands and knees, scrubbing diligently at a scuff mark on the floor. Unable to help himself, he paused to watch her, enjoying how her black dress and crisp white apron coordinated with the black-and-white floor.

As if she noticed his regard, she stopped and stared up at him. "May I help you, sir?"

"No. Thank you." He turned on his heel and

walked out the door before he did something foolish and started asking about her employer's mood that morning.

Now just past noon, the sun lay nestled in a mass of low-hanging clouds. Rain was in the forecast, he supposed. Perhaps it would be welcome. Though the temperatures were hovering around the forties, the air was thick with a strong, clawing humidity. His shirt stuck to his back and his lungs felt parched.

The humidity brought back memories of marching for hours in the Georgia heat, the red dust staining his uniform and black boots. Instinctively, he reached for his collar, his fingers fumbling with the starched seams, reaching for the button before remembering that he was no longer in a snug uniform. He was also no longer in a Yankee prison camp. He no longer had to fear running out of breath.

Would he, too, be forever marked by his months in captivity? Inwardly scarred from the traumas that had befallen him, that had befallen all of them?

Shaking off the doldrums, he crossed the road and headed toward the mercantile. He assumed he could post a letter from inside. Then perhaps he could find a place for some lunch and a drink.

A striking young woman with golden hair and wearing a well-tailored shirtwaist greeted him as he approached.

"Sir. How may I help you?"

Her voice was lilting. Melodic and surprising to find in the city. Since he'd arrived, a haze of depression had seemed to encompass almost everyone he met. Though it was no different from the atmosphere throughout much of the South, he'd naively expected something different in Galveston.

After all, it had survived the war better than most places. Its port was bustling, and it was the ranking port when it came to exporting cotton. The crowded warehouse district was full of it, and he'd heard that the business provided many men, both white and freedmen, with work.

So different from the parched plains of northern Georgia when he'd marched and fought there that one awful summer. There, pain and suffering and deprivation were daily occurrences.

In spite of the direction his thoughts were heading, he found himself smiling at her. "I need to post this letter, miss. Would you be able to assist me?"

A dimple appeared in her cheek, giving that final touch of ingénue and beauty that he hadn't even believed she lacked. "Of course." After taking the letter from him, her blue eyes examined him curiously. "You don't sound like you're from here."

"That's because I am not."

The dimple disappeared as a new suspicion

69

appeared in her eyes. "You from the North, sir?" Her voice now sounded brittle, as if her composure could easily break.

"No."

"Forgive me. It's just that you sound different." He knew his captivity on Johnson's Island had altered his accent. Maybe it had altered many things about him. "I'm from all over," he said simply.

Then, because he knew his answer told her nothing, he smiled again. Though this time, his smile was forced, brought forth for him to get his way. As much as he was eager to be done with the girl's company, he wondered if she might be the person he needed to discover just how Miranda Markham was doing among the people with whom she surely did business.

"I see," she said, her eyes lighting with interest, just as if he'd uttered something of value. "I've never met anyone who was from all over before."

Her gentle flattering inspired his vanity. He'd never been a man especially in need of female appreciation, but he couldn't deny that it did his soul good to realize he was not without certain charms.

Or perhaps it wasn't his charms. She was likely very skilled in conversation.

The thought amused him.

Remembering his goal, he lowered his voice. "More of us are from nowhere than one might assume," he murmured. He knew, of course, that this answer, too, told her nothing. Therefore she had nothing to remark upon. "How much?"

"Two bits." She smiled, revealing her one flaw, a set of crooked teeth. "Are you here for very long?"

"A month. Maybe longer."

"Oh? Where are you staying? At the Tremont?"

"No. At Mrs. Markham's house, the Iron Rail."

She blinked. Then visibly straightened. "Forgive me for being so blunt, but you really shouldn't be there."

"Why is that?"

She looked ready to blurt something, then glanced away. "It's just that the Tremont is far nicer. You should consider relocating."

"Relocating sounds like a lot of trouble. I'm sure Mrs. Markham's boardinghouse will suit me fine."

Her expression darkened. "You won't find many here of the same mind. Trust me, sir. You should take heed to what I say."

"You sound sure of yourself."

"I am. And you should listen. It's for your benefit, you see."

Seeing as he had no one standing behind him, Robert took the bait. "Why would you say such a thing? Is it because of the rumors surrounding her husband?"

"You've heard of them?"

"It's hard to be in Galveston five minutes and not hear them."

"There is a reason for that. He was a traitor." She lifted her chin. "As far as most good people are concerned, Miranda Markham should have done the decent thing and left Galveston Island. She could have sold her house and left the rest of us in peace. Not set up a boardinghouse."

"You'd ask her to leave her home? That sounds exceedingly harsh."

The girl looked as if she considered arguing that point, but instead simply stared steadily at him. "Sir, you have not paid me yet. Do you intend to?"

He dug in his pocket and pulled out the coins, slapping them on the counter with, perhaps, a bit more force than was actually needed.

She palmed them with alacrity. "Good day, sir."

He tipped his hat before turning, realizing several men and women were now behind him.

Had his skills deteriorated so much that he hadn't even been aware he was surrounded? The thought was disconcerting. If the captain had been around to see that, the man would have boxed his ears good. The childish punishment would have been no less than he deserved too.

With effort, Robert hid his chagrin and nodded at the four or five pairs of eyes watching him suspiciously.

It was time to exit the building, take a stroll back to Recognition Square—or whatever the

Sam Hill that place was called—and make himself focus. He needed to get his head back on straight and become more alert. He needed to concentrate on the reason for being here. The multiple reasons for being here. Then, once he was firmly reminded of that, he needed to make a plan.

"Excuse me, sir?"

Robert looked to see a dapperly dressed man, perhaps five years younger than him, staring at him intently. He was standing a good two yards away, almost as if he didn't trust Robert enough to venture closer. His denims were new, his chambray shirt worn. On his feet was a fine pair of brown leather boots, the likes of which Robert hadn't seen in ages. Not since he'd witnessed a trio of cavalrymen taken to their barracks back on Johnson's Island. A Yankee soldier had claimed one of the men's boots in exchange for a freshly washed blanket. While Robert had burned atthe indignity of it, the cavalry officer had merely shrugged, saying there wasn't a great need for good riding boots at the moment.

Hating that the memories he'd held at bay for so long seemed to be creeping back into his head like forgotten relatives who refused to stay away, Robert cleared his throat. "Yes?" he finally muttered.

Looking pleased that Robert had acknowledged him at last, the man stepped forward. "My name is Jess Kern, Mr. Truax."

The name meant nothing to him. But then, as the man's intent dark eyes remained steady, a sudden memory returned. "You were there," he said. "You were at Johnson's Island too."

Looking pleased to be remembered, Kern nodded. "I was. Though not too long. Only a few months." He added, "I was captured in January of '65."

Robert remembered his long captivity in terms of how cold he'd been. "Just in time for the lake to freeze."

"We marched on the ice from Sandusky to the barracks."

Robert felt chill bumps form on his skin just from the memory of it all. "January was a difficult month on the island."

Kern shivered dramatically. "If I close my eyes, I can remember the chill that permeated my skin. Some nights the men in my unit huddled together. We told ourselves it was for company, but it was certainly for warmth."

They'd done that, too, though he and his comrades had been there long enough to not need reasons to share cots. They simply were glad there was someone near enough to take the edge off the constant ache.

Those memories were so clear, so piercingly real, that he had to close his eyes to forget them.

"There were a lot of men there. Over two

thousand at the end of the war. I'm surprised you recognized me."

"Everyone knew who you were."

Robert lifted his chin. "Why is that?"

"You were with Captain Monroe." Looking a little sheepish, Kern said, "He was a formidable figure, even though he was only a captain."

"He was a formidable figure." Looking at Kern intently, he added, "He still is." No man would ever get far if he dared to say anything bad about his commanding officer.

Kern's eyes widened. "Hey, now. No need to get riled up. I meant that as a compliment. After all, there were generals in camp with us."

"There were." They'd been impressive. Some had been West Point graduates. Yet even those men had treated their captain with a combination of awe and respect.

Eager to find a few minutes of solitude, he stared at his interloper coldly. "You have the advantage of me. While we might have both had the misfortune to be detained in the middle of Lake Erie, I do not know you. Furthermore, I am afraid I don't take pleasure in remembering my time in captivity."

Something uneasy flickered in Kern's eyes. "No, I don't reckon you would."

That told Robert nothing. Losing patience with the man's lack of information, he bit out, "Any particular reason you wanted to say hello?"

"There is." After another brief moment, the corners of the man's lips turned up. "Though I told you my name, I should also let you know I'm the sheriff here." He paused, presumably waiting for Robert to give him his due.

However, Robert could find no reason to respond to the lawman. He'd done nothing wrong and was far beyond feeling impressed by men wielding authority, especially men in power with such a lazy drawl.

Therefore, he merely stared.

A flash of awareness filled Sheriff Kern's features before he attempted to smile again. "Don't want to trouble you, but I'd like a few minutes of your time. If I may."

All of Robert's defenses went on alert. The lawman knew his name and had sought him out away from Mrs. Markham's boardinghouse. Both things gave him pause. "Is there a specific reason you've sought my company, Sheriff?"

"Yes."

Impatience gnawed at him as he realized the sheriff had no intention of providing any information without Robert investing a considerable amount of time and energy. "I am at a loss for what we could possibly have to say to each other."

"I aim to rectify that if you would kindly spare me a few moments of your time."

Robert knew he had no choice. He was going to

have to listen to this man no matter what. But still he muttered, "I don't believe I've done anything here in Galveston you might find fault with."

"Neither do I—especially since you have been here barely more than twenty-four hours." After another weak attempt of a smile, Sheriff Kern said, "I promise, this won't take up much of your time."

Robert searched the man's features. Noticed the freshly shaven cheeks, the earnest look in his eyes. His solid stance. Then, upon further examination, Robert saw a hard glint in his eyes, a faint scar marring one of his dark eyebrows.

And an air about him that warned most everyone to give him respect. This man might not have fought in the war for years like the rest of them, but he was no tenderfoot. There was a will of iron lurking behind his easy, relaxed expression and slow Texas drawl.

And in that hint of iron, Robert found a measure of respect for him. The sheriff grew in his estimation. "Where would you like to talk?"

"Not here. It's too public."

"No offense, but I'd prefer not to meet in your offices." A lawman's offices were always barely one step away from his holding cells, and Robert had no desire to ever be that close to a set of iron bars again.

"None taken." Sheriff Kern looked amused. "Perhaps you would join me on a walk? I could show you the sights. Galveston is a progressive city with a lot to be proud of."

Satisfied that Kern didn't seem to be harboring any ulterior motives, Robert gestured to his right. "I was about to revisit your square."

The lawman frowned. "Ah. Well, if you don't mind, I'd rather not go there right now."

"Anywhere else in mind?"

Looking as if he'd just discovered oil, his expression brightened. "I know. There's a place at the end of one of the docks that I find particularly pleasing. How about there?"

Robert was officially intrigued. "I can't think of a better spot I'd like to see."

Kern turned on his heel and started down a nearby alleyway that Robert hadn't even noticed. After a moment's hesitation, Robert followed, wondering all the while if he was about to be set up to be ambushed.

Though it was midday, the alley was dark and narrow and smelled like forgotten trash and desolation. It was also damp and held a peculiar chilliness, in direct contrast to the relative warmth on the public square. Here and there sat poor lost souls—some men, some women holding a child or two. Their disinterest in both the sheriff's approach as well as the unfamiliar stranger's appearance spoke volumes. They'd been through much and didn't hold out hope for anything to change.

Just as Robert slowed to stare in wonder at one of the women who looked like little more than skin and bones, he heard the rustling and squeal of a rat racing across his path. He released a low cry of alarm before he could stop himself.

Kern glanced over his shoulder with a chuckle. "There are more rats here in Galveston than people. You'll get used to 'em."

Robert sincerely hoped he did not. "You need some cats."

"Not for those rats. They're big as coons and mean as snakes. I wouldn't put any creature I liked in their paths. But don't worry, Billy'll catch him sooner or later. He always does."

"Billy? He your rat catcher or something?"

The sheriff let loose a bark of laughter, its sound reverberating around the brick walls of their enclosure. "Heck no. This ain't England. He's just an old codger man with a way with rodents. He says they're good eating."

"You haven't tried?"

Sheriff Kern visibly shuddered. "To my good fortune, I have not. Even when times were tough around here, they were never that tough." As they exited the alleyway, Kern gestured to the harbor looming ahead. " 'Course, I'd rather eat a fish any day of the week. What about you, Lt. Truax?"

Robert was momentarily taken aback by the title. It seemed that the sheriff, for all his good-ole-boy persona, was actually far sharper than he let on. He wondered how he'd discovered his rank in twenty-four hours. Or had he known on Johnson's Island? "I've had rat," he said at last. "But only once. It wasn't a meal worth repeating."

"Don't imagine it was. Fan of fish?"

"From time to time."

"I'll see if my sister, Diana, can cook up some while you're here visiting. She has a way with catfish and frog legs."

"I'll pass on the frogs, if you don't mind."

Kern grinned. "You're kinda particular for a man who has spent time in prison."

He was particular because he'd spent time in prison. Instead of sharing that point, Robert kept his silence as they walked toward the harbor. The few men loitering around watched them with silent, steady expressions. Sheriff Kern ignored them, his lanky, relaxed way of walking giving the impression that they were strolling along a boulevard in Savannah.

Not along the rundown docks of the former Confederate port.

His guard relaxed when they at last approached a pier. The air smelled both of the sea and the fetid remains. A cross between fish and decay and coal and debris. The scent was acrid and strong. And though far different from the smells he remembered coming off Lake Erie around his prison, not completely dissimilar.

The memory, like all the others, threw him for a

tailspin. He inhaled the cloying air, attempting to locate something fresh weaving in the middle of it. Anything to clear his head yet again and bring him back to the present.

As his vertigo dissipated, he breathed deeply and cautioned his body to remember that he was no longer at another's mercy. No more bars separated him from freedom.

He wasn't cold. He wasn't shooting his mouth off about things he had no knowledge of. Phillip Markham wasn't dying next to him.

Once he got his bearings again, he realized the dapper young sheriff was staring at him with concern. "Mr. Truax, you've grown pale. Is something distressing you?"

It seemed he could either pretend he had no past or admit what was really the matter.

His instincts told him telling the complete truth at this point in his mission would be exceedingly foolhardy, not even to a lawman. "My body seems determined to take its time getting acclimated."

Instead of letting his comment pass, the other man looked at him curiously. "To what do you need to become acclimated? The ocean? Or the South?"

Despite his vow to remain distant, Robert felt his eyes flash in annoyance. "As you well know, I was an officer in the Confederate army, sir. I have no need to become acclimated to the South."

When Kern took a page out of his book and

merely stared steadily at him, silently daring him to reveal his dark secrets, Robert gave in and admitted the rest. "As much as I don't care to think about our time in captivity, sometimes the memories still inundate me."

Kern winced. "I dream about all that water that surrounded our encampment. In my dreams I relive the feel of the ice under my worn boots and my fears about being forced to march on it during the spring thaw. I think those pieces of ice floating in it scared me more than anything."

Robert couldn't believe they were currently making small talk about his months in captivity. Discussing the weather like it mattered. But as he involuntarily shivered, his body recalling the chill against his skin that he could never seem to completely forget, he nodded. "I was always cold. And damp." And though the sheriff hadn't prompted any more confidences, he found himself continuing to talk.

"Every once in awhile, something triggers my body, and for a brief amount of time I imagine I'm back. A loud crash, or the smell of burning fibers. Cold, damp air."

"It seems no matter how one might wish otherwise, the past always treads on our present."

Kern's tone wasn't light. Instead, it gave Robert a reason to believe he wasn't the only man present suffering from the war. "Do you, also, have demons that you find difficult to escape?"

"I do."

"I must admit I'm surprised. You don't look old enough to have fought, let alone been sent to Johnson's Island."

"Toward the end of the war they didn't just send officers. Anyone would do."

The younger man's simple statement shamed him. "Forgive me. I didn't mean to negate your experiences."

"There ain't a thing to forgive. We've all experienced loss, sir. Only some of the things, I think, are harder to imagine than others."

Robert blinked. It seemed this young pup had more to him than he had anticipated. The other man's acceptance of Robert's weaknesses felt like he was being exposed. Opening a wound, leaving himself bare for further viewing. For pain.

And though one might argue that uncovering such a wound might eventually give a man the hope of healing, Robert wasn't exactly ready for that. No, it would be far easier to live with the dull ache that filtered through his heart and soul.

At least he was used to that.

Obviously seeing that Robert was done sharing his experiences, Kern cleared his throat again. "Well, we are here. How about we take a seat at the end of the dock?"

The dock looked rickety. "You sure it can hold both our weight?"

"Only one way to find out, Lieutenant," Kern called out as he walked to the end of the pier and sat down with little fuss or fanfare.

Wondering how his errand of posting a letter had come to a sojourn down memory lane with a youngish sheriff with a penchant for good humor, Robert followed the sheriff's lead and made his way down the pier.

When he reached the edge, he sat down. The wood felt warm underneath him. And with his legs dangling over the water, he felt both younger than he had in years and curiously ancient. He couldn't remember the wood ever feeling so unforgiving when he had been younger.

"What did you want to speak to me about?"

"Miranda Markham."

Robert held his temper with effort. "Don't tell me that you, too, seek to warn me about her?"

"Definitely not. On the contrary, I was hoping you could tell me more about your relationship with her."

"We have no relationship. I am a guest at her boardinghouse."

"Is that right?" Kern's lips pressed together. "That's all?"

"Do you expect more? I only met her yesterday morning."

To Robert's amazement, Kern relaxed. "I see."

Again, he was feeling like he'd stepped into the middle of a maze for which there was no way

84

out. Tired of such foolishness, he hardened his voice. "What, precisely, do you see?"

The muscles in Kern's throat worked a bit. "Nothing."

"Except?"

"Except that Mrs. Markham attracted my notice from my first day here over two years ago. I suppose I feel a bit protective toward her."

"If you do, I would venture that you'd be the only one. The few townspeople I've met seem to treat her as a pariah."

Kern stiffened. "I know. I don't understand it myself."

"It's my understanding that many believe her husband is responsible for betraying the Confederacy."

"I've heard that too. But beg pardon, I don't know how that rumor started, though it was about a year ago. It coincided with her opening the Iron Rail as a boardinghouse. And furthermore, even if her husband did betray the South while in prison, he was only a lieutenant. And he was only imprisoned at the end of the war. What could he have possibly said that would have made much of a difference?"

"Any idea who is responsible for the rumors?"

"I can only surmise that it is the same person who sent her a threatening letter."

Everything in Robert froze. "What letter? I haven't heard anything about that."

"Mrs. Markham brought it to me the day she received it, just after she opened the Iron Rail for boarders. It was an ugly piece of work," he said with a grimace. "The author threatened to reveal missives supposedly in Phillip's handwriting, ones that supposedly proved he had been a traitor."

"That means nothing. Anyone could say the missives were in his hand."

"I agree. I told her to ignore it as best she could. There was no way to trace where it came from and therefore it would be better to simply dispose of the letter and forget it ever came."

Robert was incredulous. Sheriff Kern seemed to be telling him that Miranda's concerns meant nothing. "Is that how you handle most problems that come your way? You simply tell the victim to forget about it?"

"Of course not. However, I didn't see any other course of action. There was nothing I could do and she was terribly agitated. I decided to err on the side of caution. After all, Mrs. Markham had already been upset by her husband's imprisonment and death. She was barely out of mourning. No reason to make her suffer more."

Though Robert wasn't sure he would have given her the same advice, he wasn't exactly sure he would have said anything much different either.

"If you weren't worried about her, then why are you so concerned about her now?"

"She hasn't seemed well. Actually, it looks to

me like she's fallen into melancholia. She looks like she's lost weight and she hardly leaves her house now."

"I am not sure why you sought me out."

"I heard about your walk with her yesterday. I heard that you stood up for her with that weasel Winter." Kern turned his head and stared at Robert directly. "Beg your pardon, but those actions are not things a man who just happened to be in Galveston would do."

"They might be."

"No, I don't think so. Mr. Truax, I'm going to be honest with you. Mrs. Markham knows I served in the war; everyone in town knows that."

"But?" Robert pressed.

"But I've never told anyone I was on Johnson's Island when Phillip Markham was, not even his wife."

"It seems to me that news might have eased her in some way."

"I don't think so." He shifted, his expression pensive. "Fact is, I didn't want to add to her pain when I didn't really know anything about what happened to the lieutenant. I don't have any proof to refute the rumors about him." Before Robert could comment on that, Kern turned his head to stare at him directly. "Say what you want, but I don't think it's by chance that you're here. I think you knew her husband because you both served under Devin Monroe."

"I did know Phillip Markham. Furthermore, I sat by his side in his last hours."

Kern relaxed. "Was he actually the kind of man Mrs. Markham believes him to be?"

"Yes. We talked a lot, you see." Actually, there hadn't been much else to do. But every time they'd complained about their lack of activity, of their inability to help their comrades still battling across frozen fields, Captain Monroe had chastised them. All they needed to concentrate on was living. Survival—that was the key to life in a prison camp. Nothing else mattered.

They'd known it, and the soldiers guarding them had known it too. As the battles became even more one sided and rumors flew about Lee's eventual surrender, even the guards had lost their interest in keeping a vigilant guard. All of them were missing their sweethearts and families.

Why, they'd even all shared stories about their homes one long snowy evening, all of them huddled around their meager stove, burning scraps of wood and one soiled blanket.

Of them all, Phillip had spoken the most lovingly of his wife. He'd talked about her beauty. About how strong she was, how she'd never even led him on a merry chase when they'd been courting. She'd simply gazed at him with her blue eyes and asked if she could trust him.

They'd all gazed at him with mixed emotions. For Robert, jealousy combined with a healthy amount of incredulousness had filled him. He had never heard of a woman so well regarded. Actually, he'd been more of a fool than that. He, in all his inept naiveté, had doubted their lieutenant's word. He'd also been resentful of a man who had been so blessed, not only with good looks but property and an adoring wife.

It had seemed like too much. Too much when he'd had so little.

Two days after they'd all sat around the fire and listened to Captain proclaim they needed to look out for each other after the war, Phillip's wound took a sudden turn for the worse. His arm began to swell.

Twenty-four hours after that, he'd spiked a fever and his injury became visibly infected. Then, unfortunately for all of them, he lingered. For weeks. Gangrene settled in. And with that came pain for Phillip and the helpless knowledge for the rest of them that they could do nothing of worth for him.

His death had upset them all. Even the guards stood in silence while Robert and the rest of Phillip's comrades buried him. Their pickaxes and shovels had clanged against the frozen ground. Jarring their muscles and helping to take the sting off tears.

They'd all been hurting about the injustice of it all, and none more than he. Because he had been so full of himself. Instead of agreeing that Phillip had been blessed, Robert had thrown it in his face.

And Phillip had no doubt died thinking Robert hadn't believed in him.

"When I heard you were being so kind to Mrs. Markham, I wanted to touch base with you," Kern explained. "If you hear that she's had another threat or if she confides that anything else worrisome has happened to her, will you tell me?"

Robert wasn't following. It was a lawman's job to help, not stand back in the shadows and wait. "Why haven't you asked her yourself?"

"Because I let her down before," he explained. "She doesn't trust me."

"Why not?"

"I told you. I denied her request for help. I didn't investigate the letter."

"She may not trust you, but she doesn't know me."

"Then get to know her." Kern's cheeks flushed. "After all, she's a beautiful woman. A beautiful woman in need of a man to care for her. A woman like that shouldn't be living alone. It ain't right."

"And you'd like to be the man to offer her companionship?" Robert made sure he infused his words with a healthy amount of sarcasm.

The sheriff drew himself up to his impressive height. "Suppose I did. Do you have a problem with that?"

Robert knew he shouldn't. From what he'd learned so far, Kern was truly concerned about

Miranda. He cared enough about her to approach Robert and make his concerns clear.

And hadn't that been what Devin had asked him to do? Yes, he was supposed to discover why Phillip's widow was having such a difficult time. But he was also supposed to try to help her, to perhaps be her friend. She was lonely. A good, caring man who would happily face the gossips and the naysayers was a blessing. Someone worth holding on to.

But though all those reasons made sense, Robert couldn't do it. At least, not yet. "I know nothing about you."

Kern's eyes narrowed. "I didn't realize my background or interest was any of your business."

"I've made it my business."

"I don't know why. I was under the impression that you didn't know Mrs. Markham before you came here."

Robert's earlier doubts about Kern were becoming stronger. The man spoke in circles. "I'm starting to think I might know Miranda Markham better than most," he stated with a new edge in his voice.

"Is that right? Even though you've only just arrived on Galveston Island?"

"I have learned she is a gently bred lady who has already had her fair share of pain . . . and that she is in dire need of a protector."

"That occurred to me as well, Lieutenant. That

is exactly why I asked you to talk with me," he continued, his expression hard. "Therefore, sir, if you know something about her to help me in my goal, I respectfully ask you to share. I don't cotton with cowardly fools who prey on the weakness and fears of women."

"On that, we are in agreement."

Kern nodded. "Good to know. Now that we have that settled, if you learn of even a hint of who was behind the letter she received and who started the rumors about Phillip Markham, I hope you'll share that information with me as well."

"Nothing would make me happier than to give you that name."

"I'd be obliged." Slowly, he added, "Finally, like I was saying, I have an interest in Mrs. Markham that is aboveboard and completely respectful. I hope you do not intend to stand in my way."

"I don't intend to, but like I said earlier, I don't know you yet. I don't plan to make any promises."

"Take your time," the sheriff said easily. "Unlike yourself, I have all the time in the world to win her trust."

Robert nodded, then turned away and started back to the Iron Rail. But as he walked, he realized that much had already changed in his heart.

5

It made no sense. In just four days, Robert Truax had managed to become a prominent fixture in her life.

Miranda figured the reason for this was that she simply did not have enough to occupy her mind. Most days, she mended linens, planned menus, welcomed her few guests, and kept up with correspondence. Conversations with her staff were pleasant but impersonal.

None of those tasks took much time or thought. Until Mr. Truax's arrival, it had been a struggle to merely get through each day without succumbing to depression, especially since she had been forced to open the boardinghouse to survive and the rumors about Phillip had started. Moreover, she had felt empty inside. Devoid of any joy or goals.

And she had received the last letter.

Now, however, wherever she was, Robert found her. He engaged her often, sometimes talking of nothing more than the weather or some interesting tidbit he'd discovered about one of the buildings or Galveston Bay. He asked her questions. Made jokes and asked her opinion. In short, he gave her no choice but to interact with him.

After the first couple of times, she'd dared to respond. Every time she did, Robert would look pleased.

She'd likely smiled and even laughed more in the past week than she had since Phillip died. So much so that she found herself forgetting to mourn for him, and she was even able to put her worries aside for hours at a time.

Miranda knew she'd be a liar if she said this transformation in herself didn't feel strange. On the contrary, she worried about what was going to happen when Robert left and the support she was gradually getting used to accepting vanished.

Would she delve back into her dark depression? Would the blackness consume her, finally pressing in deep enough to give her the courage to open that windowpane again?

The idea was frightening.

"Knock, knock."

Looking up from her desk—and her musings—she saw Robert standing in the parlor's doorway. He wore dark denims and black boots this morning. He had on a dark brown shirt and a thick vest as well. He looked almost like one of the cowboys who came onto the island from time to time, intent on sampling the wares of fallen women in the warehouse district.

His dark hair was curved behind his ears and he was freshly shaved. And he was watching her closely. Once again there was no judgment in his dark eyes. Instead, only a lazy appreciation that she would have to be dead not to appreciate.

"Good morning, Mr. Truax. I trust you slept well?"

A half-smile formed on his lips. "I did, thank you. And you?"

"Me? Yes, I did sleep well, thank you." To her surprise, she realized she wasn't lying. She had fallen asleep soon after she'd slipped into her bed and had enjoyed a lengthy, peaceful slumber. She'd slept better during the last two nights than she had in the previous two months.

Realizing he was still standing in front of her waiting, she smoothed the fabric of her pale lavender gown. No gray today. "May I help you, sir? Or did you simply stop by to say hello?"

His smile grew as if the question amused him. "I came for a reason, of course."

She got to her feet. "Yes?"

"I had a hankering to take another walk on the Strand today."

Though she still wasn't sure what that had to do with her, she responded. "Oh! Well, I hope you have an enjoyable time. As you have already seen, we are fortunate to have a great variety of shops, restaurants, and businesses to sample. Many claim it is Galveston Island's crowning achievement."

She didn't think it was quite that, but it was a lovely area. Many of the fronts were ornate and built in the Victorian style. Furthermore, each was showcased in its own right. "My husband told me many of the buildings are made of cast iron and brick because the architects hoped the expensive building materials would help withstand the storms and hurricanes that wash ashore fromtime to time."

"I didn't merely come to inform you of my plans, ma'am," he said with a meaningful look. "I had another goal in mind."

"Oh?"

"You see, I am standing here in the hopes that you would consider accompanying me."

She stilled. Not since before the war had she gone for a simple stroll by a man's side. When Phillip got leave one summer, they had walked down on the Strand, stopping for ice cream. Once, they'd dined out, just like some of the ship captains who arrived from all over the world or the cattle barons who vacationed in the Tremont.

And though Robert had walked with her to the bank, this offer was different. She was sure the whole experience would be different, and she wasn't exactly sure how she felt about that.

No, to be fair, she wasn't sure how she would be able to do such a thing without having it affect her. Or, for that matter, what would everyone say? Of course, did it even make a difference?

Even thinking about the distaste she would encounter from passersby, she tamped down her wishes. "As you know, the Strand is nearby, sir. I doubt you'll have difficulty locating whatever shop you are hoping to find."

He chuckled. "I'm not worried about getting lost, Miranda. I am asking because I would enjoy your company."

"My company?"

"Yes." He looked at her curiously. "Surely you can understand that I would want to spend an afternoon with a beautiful woman?"

He thought she was beautiful. It had been a long time since she'd thought of herself as attractive, as anything other than a shell of the person she once was.

And though she knew she should ignore his flowery words, her insides warmed and that same cautious burst of nervousness mixed with butterflies settled in her stomach. "Thank you for the compliment and the invitation, but I am afraid I cannot do that."

"Why is that?"

Yes, why was that? Scrambling for a real reason, she ventured, "Well, first of all, it wouldn't be seemly."

"Why not?"

Oh, his questions! Some days she was sure he had a never-ending supply locked in his head. "It wouldn't be seemly because we are both unmarried. That is obvious."

But instead of looking as if he understood her

point, he looked amused yet again. "Perhaps that might have mattered if we were eighteen, but we are of age, ma'am." He paused. "I am thirty and survived a war. And you, well, you are a widow," he added. "I consider both of us past the age of needing to justify our actions to anyone."

He was right. He was thirty and she was twenty-six. Both of them had a number of experiences that could neither be ignored nor simplified.

But it was because of those events that she was reluctant to make a stir. Because she'd rather be blunt than simply refuse him and inadvertently hurt his feelings, she said, "Mr. Truax, the truth is that while I would enjoy accompanying you, I don't know if I could survive the talk that would ensue."

"Do you truly think two people walking out together would cause so much notice?"

"If it was you and someone else, no. However, I am afraid everything I do now causes notice." Hating how terribly pitiful she sounded, she added, "Other than Mr. Winter, you might not have noticed anything out of the ordinary when we went to the bank, but—"

All traces of amusement vanished as he stared hard at her. "I noticed," he interrupted.

She wasn't sure if she was glad he understood or if she was now more embarrassed than ever. "I've begun to hate leaving the house."

"We need to put a stop to that."

"There is nothing one can do."

"I disagree." He stepped forward. "Ma'am, I think it's time you ignored the looks and the criticism and enjoyed your days. We need to get you out more. Go on the offensive, per se."

"Spoken like a true military man."

He shrugged. "I am used to finding solutions to problems, ma'am. It is second nature."

He was so sure. So confident. Miranda was tempted to simply agree, to let him make decisions about what was best for her.

If he was going to stay, she might even give in enough to let him.

But eventually he would be gone and she'd be back to being alone. When that happened, she would have to bear all the consequences, and no doubt they would be dire indeed.

Not wanting to let on just how much his kindness meant to her, she kept her voice light. "Sir, I must admit to being tempted. But again, I must decline. The talk would be even worse than normal after last week's visit to the bank."

"Because?"

"Well, Mr. Winter has undoubtedly already turned your defense of me in the bank into something ugly."

His expression turned ice cold. "He wouldn't dare."

"Oh, I am afraid he would. I know we've already talked about this, but there are rumors circulating about Phillip. His reputation isn't ensuring my protection, and for some reason, Mr. Winter in particular has an interest in me."

She paused, mentally preparing herself for Robert to take back his offer to go on the Strand.

But instead of retreating from this latest bit of news, Robert stepped closer. And with that increased proximity came an increased awareness of his scent. Sandalwood and soap. The combination shouldn't have been appealing. She found it masculine and irresistible.

Her attraction to it—and the man it belonged to—also worried her. She'd promised to love Phillip forever. Until Mr. Truax appeared in her parlor that first day, she'd had no doubt that she would never love again. Would ever even look at another man.

But now she was discovering that was not going to be the case.

"Miranda," he drawled, "how about if I promise you that when I leave, no one will dare to disparage your character ever again?"

"I doubt such a promise can be made."

"Let me prove you wrong."

"Sir, trust me when I say it is better that I keep to myself."

"You can't imagine your life being much different because you have given up." His voice hardened. "It's time to try harder."

He was baiting her. Goading her.

It wasn't fair and she knew better than to let him.

But sometimes even she wasn't capable of continually saying no.

And sometimes she didn't even want to.

Robert hadn't been lying when he told Miranda he'd been his unit's problem solver during the war. Whether it was a by-product of living a childhood devoid of assistance or he simply had been blessed with a devious mind, Robert Truax had always been able to obtain anything he or his friends needed. He could pick locks. He could lift produce without notice. He could charm old women and crusty men and bitter scoundrels.

Monroe had called him a master manipulator. Phillip Markham had said he was far too conniving. Other men had called him names that weren't half as kind.

Robert had never cared. He'd liked being useful and he liked being able to depend on his brain to survive. He had secretly felt it was a far more gentlemanly way to go through life than the way Sgt. Thomas Baker had, which was to use his bulk and his fists to convince others to follow his lead.

However, though he'd been on many missions and had stolen, lied, and grinned his way toward food, shelter, ammunition, and even medical help, Robert wasn't sure if he'd ever had to be as patient and persistent as he had to be with Miranda.

Her stubbornness would give a mule a run for its money! He'd never been so glad he was as stubborn as she was.

It had all been worth it, though. Now he was reaping the rewards. He was walking along Market Street with Miranda on his arm. She was wearing an attractive wide-brim hat and a navy day dress that favored her blue eyes. She'd also forgone layers of petticoats and had opted for one of fashion's newer looks, the bustle. She looked very fine.

He soon found out she hadn't been exaggerating. His escorting her to the bank and the mercantile had not been so bad, but today one would have thought they were notorious bank robbers or visiting royalty, the amount of attention they were receiving. At first he'd glared at anyone who dared to stare at them too long.

But he soon discovered Miranda also had a certain number of skills. She was a master of walking along and mixing in with crowds. She could talk to him without making eye contact with anyone surrounding them.

And she could look at ease and serene even when it was obvious that people were whispering about her.

He instinctively knew she hadn't been born with such skills or had even practiced such behavior in her childhood. When she let down her guard, Miranda seemed bright and vibrant. That was who Phillip had spoken about with such care. Robert believed her husband would have been truly dismayed to see the way she was forced to behave now.

After she led him into a sweetshop where he bought some hard candies, he walked with her down the street until they were looking only at the ocean beyond them.

The air was ripe with the scent of salt and ocean and decay and mildew. The combination was unusual, but it wasn't unpleasant. It was also decidedly distinct. Right then and there, Robert knew if he ever smelled it again, he would instantly think of this moment with her.

He was about to comment on a flock of seagulls circling a shrimp boat when he noticed Miranda had her chin slightly lifted. She looked bright and alive and vibrant. Beautiful.

"You like it here in Galveston, don't you?"

She laughed. "I suppose I do. Even though I've had so many difficult days here, there is something wonderful about standing here at the pier. I enjoy the water."

"You don't mind the fishy smell?"

She laughed again. "Not so much. I've grown used to it, I think. The air is odorous, but it is pungent and fresh too. And if I stand still, I can feel faint droplets of water from the ocean. And taste the salt. I don't think I'll ever forget the combination of it all, even if I move far away from here and live for thirty more years."

Her comment made him curious. "Where did you grow up?"

"In a small town west of Houston. We had a ranch and my father ran his uncle's mercantile." She sobered. "Everyone is gone now, of course."

"And you met Phillip there?"

"Oh, goodness, no. Phillip would have ridden right by my dusty town without a second look," she said without a trace of embarrassment. "Actually, my cousin Carson joined the army around the same time Phillip did. Somehow they bonded during basic training and Carson's letters were always filled with stories about Phillip."

"So you started writing to him?"

"Not at all. Phillip and I met when I went with some other cousins to a dance in Houston."

"It must have been quite a dance," he teased gently.

"Oh, it was. Phillip had recently graduated from West Point and was in his uniform. He looked resplendent."

Her words were sweet, her voice softly lilting.

No woman—no person, really—had ever spoken to him or about him that way.

Robert carefully bit back the sharp taste of jealousy that coursed through him. "I imagine he was quite a sight to see."

Still looking moony, she sighed. "He was. But everyone was dressed to the nines." Giggling softly, she said, "My mother and aunt had outdone themselves, outfitting my cousin Beatrice and me." She giggled. "We arrived at that dance in beautiful dresses."

"What did yours look like?" he asked, hoping to keep that soft smile playing on her lips.

Her voice took on a dreamy quality. "Mine was white with pink bows along the bodice and the capped sleeves. I also had the most beautiful long white gloves. And a bonnet with silk roses! It was gorgeous and so, so heavy!"

Though it wasn't that long ago, she was referencing a time that most every Southern man tried to forget. The memories were too sweet. "I'd almost forgotten about hats like that."

"Bea and I had our fancy bonnets and our princess dresses. We were sure we were the most fetching young ladies in attendance. Why, we were sure we were sporting the biggest hoop skirts this side of the Mississippi."

He laughed. "I most definitely do not miss those skirts."

"Because they got in the way of everything?"

"Because a man could never get close enough to the woman he was flirting with," he teased.

When she laughed again, he smiled at her. He liked seeing her like this, so carefree and happy. He liked it almost as much as the idea of her being all dressed up in a white dress and gloves and dancing with Phillip for the first time.

"I bet you took his breath away, Mrs. Markham."

"Maybe I did," she mused. She bit her bottom lip. "I'm sure I couldn't say."

"Surely your husband paid you many compliments."

"He did. But he was the person who looked so dashing." Her voice went soft as she rested her elbows on the wooden railing. "He was handsome and tall and so very kind."

"He sounds like a true gentleman."

She sighed. "He was. Even with everything that's happened since, with all the rumors and innuendos and pain, I've never regretted falling in love with him."

"I would wager that he would have been happy to know that, ma'am." The moment he said the words, he tensed. No doubt they sounded too familiar for a man who was a stranger to say.

But instead of looking confused, she simply shrugged. "Maybe."

She looked away from him then and stared back out at the gulf. Below them, water lapped at the wooden pilings under their feet. The faint echoes of fishermen coming off boats floated toward them, their sharp orders and barks of laughter and raucous conversation mixing in with the shrill cry of the seagulls overhead.

"No . . . I mean, I know so," she said after several minutes. "We were a love match. He would be pleased to know that my love for him has never wavered."

He made no reply. Instead, he leaned his forearms on the weathered railing and simply let the moment wash over him. After years of barely surviving, it seemed especially sweet.

Far too soon, Miranda stepped away. "I think we had better get back, Robert. I'm no longer a child or a young bride. I have things to do."

"Yes, it is probably time we returned." He had been too entranced by her for his own good.

As they started walking, she said, "I'm sorry, I chattered on about myself this whole time."

"I enjoyed your chatter."

She smiled. "No, I meant, I bet you probably have your own stories to tell about those dances. Do share."

He laughed. "I most definitely do not have any stories about officer dances."

"No? Why not? I was under the impression that all officers were expected to attend those assemblies."

"They were, but I did not enter the army as an officer, Mrs. Markham. I could never have afforded that." For the first time that afternoon, he felt a small burst of pride. He could never compare to a gentleman like Phillip Markham, but he wasn't without any redeeming qualities.

"Robert, you earned your rank?"

"I did."

Her eyes widened. "I've heard that is hard to do."

"It would have been near impossible . . . if we hadn't been at war." He shrugged. "My captain needed men unafraid to take chances. I was fearless."

Thankfully, she didn't ask him to divulge stories about the battlefields. "So you mean to tell me you never had a sweetheart? I'm sure you eventually attended a dance. They were all the rage here."

He debated about how much to tell her, then realized it was of no consequence what she thought. It wasn't as if he ever had to worry about truly impressing her. No matter who he was or what he'd done, he was never going to be good enough for a lady like her.

Especially not after she'd had a husband like Phillip Markham.

"Miranda, when I first entered the army, I had no manners to speak of. I was as unruly as a bobcat in the wild."

She looked skeptical. "I am positive you weren't quite that bad."

"I was. My only redeeming qualities were my size and my lack of fear. My officers taught me discipline and deportment while my captain and men like your husband taught me everything else." Thinking of how awkward and frustrating those lessons had been for all involved, he shook his head. He thought he would never conquer proper table manners.

"It is actually because of them that I'm even fit company for a woman like you," he added.

She tilted her head to one side. "Robert, why was that? Did your parents not teach you those things?"

"I had no parents to speak of."

Her eyes widened. "Who raised you?"

"Experience, I guess." He didn't want to sound too ramshackle, but he didn't want to sugarcoat his past either. Miranda had been too brave, too vulnerable about her faults and hurts for him to attempt to hide his past. "My mother died in childbirth and my father . . . well, he took off as soon as he could. Though some of his neighbors helped me out from time to time, for the most part I grew up on the streets in Ft. Worth."

She looked shocked. "I . . . I'm sorry."

He was too. For most of his life, he'd always felt rather bitter about the things he didn't have and the care that had never been given. He'd wondered how the Lord could have overlooked the basic needs of a young child. Surely he couldn't have been that much of a brat?

But now he realized all of that had brought him to this place and this moment. He was walking sedately next to a true lady. She was holding his arm and he was not only protecting her but making her happy.

"Don't be sorry, Miranda," he said lightly. "I am not."

When she blinked, then cautiously smiled, he smiled too.

And realized he'd told her the truth.

Captain Monroe would have been pleased.

6

Two days after their walk on the Strand, Miranda was still reliving the outing. She found herself dwelling on the feel of Robert's arm under her hand. Of how safe she felt by his side—as if no one would dare to slight her out of fear of incurring Mr. Truax's displeasure. For a few hours, she'd allowed herself to forget all about her problems. She'd forgotten her pain, pushed aside her worries, even managed to stop thinking about what would happen when Robert left and she was alone again.

Instead, she had let herself remember the feel of the ocean breeze on her skin, the scent of the wharf, the antics of the pelicans and seagulls. She'd smiled more than she had in months.

For a little while, she'd simply been a woman on the arm of a handsome and attentive gentleman.

Last night she'd fallen asleep remembering their conversation about their childhoods. Somehow, remembering how idyllic hers had been while Robert's had been so painful had helped her heal even further. It seemed she'd needed to remember that no one ever had an easy life. Instead, there were gaps and curves and dips and valleys. Men and women of strong grit survived instead of giving up.

She certainly liked the idea of being a survivor.

Indeed, that small outing had changed her in ways she hadn't expected. As had the man himself.

Today the house had felt abnormally silent without Mr. Truax. Cook had informed Miranda that he'd left shortly after breakfast, saying he would likely not return until close to nightfall.

But even though she'd known not to expect him, throughout the day Miranda still found herself looking for a sign of her new boarder. In spite of her best efforts to remind herself that one lovely walk didn't mean they would go out on another outing anytime in the near future.

But as she walked down the empty hallways, it was apparent that Mr. Truax was not only still not about but he hadn't been for some time. He was an unusually messy boarder. He left his papers and his handkerchiefs and his books all over the place. She and Belle and Winifred had even started placing everything they found in a little basket in the dining room. That way he could deposit his articles back in his room easily.

And since he was paying extra to have his room cleaned, Miranda had also learned he was just as messy in his room. Clothes were left on the floor, his bed was a constant rumpled tangle of sheets and blankets, and blotting papers were strewn about his desk and on the floor underneath.

More than once Miranda had wondered how an officer in the military could have such untidy habits. Now, though, his basket was empty and the table and chair where he ate his meals were absent of his usual disarray.

Picking up the empty basket, Miranda realized she missed the clutter. Missed all signs that made Robert unique. How could one man make such an impression on her, and so quickly too? She'd hosted many guests in the mansion over the last year. For one man to mean so much, well, it hardly seemed fair.

"Oh! Hello, Mrs. Markham," Winifred exclaimed as she entered the dining room. Right away her gaze zeroed in on the basket in her hands. "Is everything all right?"

"Yes, of course. I, um . . . well, I was just thinking I should put this someplace out of the way."

"No real reason you should, if you don't mind me saying so. We both know we're gonna be filling it up with Mr. Truax's items soon enough."

Hastily, she set the basket down again. "Yes. I imagine so."

But as if her housekeeper was used to her making no sense, or maybe because she didn't know Miranda had ever acted differently, she smiled brightly. "It's right quiet without him here, don'tcha think?" Winifred asked as she pulled out a rag from one of her pockets and started wiping down the shelves on the top of the server.

She was too embarrassed to lie. "Yes. He not only is rather messy, he's loud."

"I don't mind a man making a noise every now and then myself. Makes me think of my pa. When he got to talking, well, no one else could ever get a word in edgewise."

"My father was quieter, but I know what you mean. Thank goodness for Emerson or we'd be a quartet of women."

"This is true." With a wink, she said, "I won't tell him that, though. It'll cause him to get a big head, it will."

"We can't have that."

Winifred giggled. "Anyways, Cook told you Mr. Truax left just after breakfast, saying he had several people to meet and might not be back until nightfall, didn't she?"

"Yes, she did. I wonder whom he needed to meet," Miranda mused before she stopped herself. All sorts of activities and projects came to mind, all of them nefarious.

"I expect he'll tell us when he returns," Winifred said, her voice suspiciously bright. "He's a friendly sort, he is."

"He is, indeed." Needing to get her mind off the man before she was reduced to watching for him out the window like a lovesick girl, Miranda picked up the stack of letters Winifred had left neatly folded for her on a small table by the door. "I'll be in the parlor sorting the mail, then."

Winifred paused in the doorway before taking her leave. "How does some tea sound to ya? Belle can bring you a cuppa."

"Yes, thank you." A cup of piping-hot tea was exactly what she needed to get through the rest of the day. It would settle her nerves and hopefully rejuvenate her enough to sort the day's mail in lightning speed.

Moments later, Belle arrived in the parlor with a cup and teapot, along with a freshly baked scone. "Hot tea and a currant scone, ma'am."

Miranda smiled at her. Today Belle was wearing a light gray dress. It should have made her look washed out and tired but, as everything did on her pretty maid, it only seemed to emphasize her beauty. "Thank you, Belle."

"Oh, you're welcome." Smiling at the plate she'd just set on the corner of Miranda's desk, she added, "You're in for a treat, Mrs. Markham. The scones are especially good today."

"I think we say that every time Cook bakes."

"I guess we do." She shrugged. "But it's better than thinking they could always be better."

Miranda chuckled. "Indeed. Thank you for bringing me this treat." Belle set about straightening the room, and after taking a fortifying bite of the scone and a bracing sip of

115

tea, Miranda pulled out her letter opener and began slicing open the envelopes.

The first five were reservations, two others were bills. One was a letter of appreciation for a restful visit.

And the last was another threat.

Hating the sight of it, her hands shook as she pulled out the letter. The handwriting was familiar. The letters were ill formed and slightly block-like. Though she wanted to do nothing more than crumble the offending paper away, she forced herself to read it.

I know what he did. I know he betrayed the South. I know how you have been dishonoring his memory. And I can prove it all. Soon, everyone will have the proof if you don't leave Galveston and never come back. I've been warning you for a year, and my patience is gone. Your time has run out.

Her hands were trembling so much that the paper fell through her fingers. Panicked, she grasped for it but knocked the tea over instead. Hot liquid splattered over the desk and on the rest of the correspondence.

Miranda jumped to her feet to escape being burned. That action caused the rest of the letters to drift to the floor.

Tears pricked her eyes as every worry she'd pushed aside came back, tenfold. The return of her fear was almost as frightening as the letter itself. She had thought the letters couldn't be any more threatening, but it seemed she was wrong. She'd thought she was done being afraid of everyone in Galveston, but that fear was still there. Alive and well. Stronger than ever.

But what if the rumors were true? Even if they weren't—and she was desperately clinging to that belief—what if this monster had falsified documents that made it look like Phillip was a traitor? It had to be someone who hated her enough to torture her and blackmail her into leaving her home. Did she dare to contemplate who that might be?

Belle rushed to her side. "Oh, Mrs. Markham! Are you all right? Did you get burned?"

Miranda worked her mouth but, try as she might, no sound came out.

"Here, come sit down, ma'am. I'll get this cleaned up in no time."

Miranda said nothing as Belle wrapped an arm around her shoulders and guided her to the chaise lounge in the corner. "Here, ma'am. You just rest for a moment."

"I . . . I am fine, Belle. Yes, as you said, it's merely tea. I don't know how I managed to spill it. I'm not usually so clumsy."

"We know you ain't clumsy at all, Mrs. Markham. It was just an accident. That's all. Everyone has them."

Relieved that Belle wasn't making a fuss over her anymore, Miranda attempted to smile. "Yes, they do. I guess it's my day."

"Wish my day didn't come up quite so often," Belle said as she wiped up the tea with the tea towel. "I'm forever knocking into things."

As Belle continued to prattle on, Miranda closed her eyes and tried to breathe deeply.

"Now that it's all spick and span again, may I bring you some more tea, Mrs.—" She abruptly cut off her words with a gasp. "Oh no. You got another one of them."

Miranda popped open her eyes. When she realized Belle was staring at the letter on the floor like it was about to gain legs and jump out at her, a terrible realization settled inside of her. "What did you say?"

Belle stood up slowly. "Beg your pardon, ma'am," she whispered, her cheeks turning bright red. "I didn't mean to look at your letter."

"My letter?" She cleared her throat.

Wringing her hands, Belle whispered, "I am sorry I said a word. I promise, it won't happen again."

It was a sweet apology. However, it most certainly wasn't a retraction. "You, um . . . you have been aware that I've been receiving letters like this? Threatening letters?"

Belle swallowed. "Yes, ma'am."

Shock, mixed in with a bit of paranoia, set in.

For a split second, Miranda considered the possibility that someone on her staff might very well be behind them. It would be so easy for them to make sure she received them on a regular basis.

But then, as she remembered how hard they all worked, how much they put up with her, with their mistress's mood swings and self-doubts and, yes, self-loathing, Miranda knew no one who acted like they did could be so duplicitous.

"Belle, when did you first discover them?"

Her maid's eyes darted around the room. Settling on anything but herself. "Well, ma'am, I don't rightly know. I couldn't say for sure."

"Please, do try to remember. It is important to me."

"Yes, ma'am." Looking truly miserable, Belle swallowed hard.

Miranda knew she needed to get control of her patience. "I promise, I won't get mad," she said as gently as she could. "I simply want to know. And it must be said that I feel I deserve an answer."

"Yes, Mrs. Markham. Yes, you do." But instead of blurting out the information Miranda had asked for, her maid was chewing on her bottom lip.

With a sigh, Miranda got to her feet. "Belle, I am doing my best not to lose my temper, but I have a feeling that I'm about to lose that battle. Answer my question, if you please."

At last, Belle visibly steeled her spine and took a fortifying breath. "To be real honest, I don't recall that single moment when I discovered you were getting those awful letters. It was more like I simply became aware that you were receiving them."

"Simply aware? That makes no sense."

"Well, um, it kind of does. Because, you see, we all know about them."

Miranda didn't know if she was more shocked, embarrassed, or bemused. She never would have thought that something she had tried so hard to keep hidden would be common knowledge . . . and that her servants were attempting to keep their own secrets too.

However, she could almost hear her well-bred mother's voice in her ear, reminding her that servants know everything that happens in a house and a good mistress made sure that nothing untoward happened. "We? All?"

Belle shifted uncomfortably, looked down at the soiled towel in her hand, and deposited it on the tea-filled plate. "Well, me, Winnie, Cook, and Emerson know about the letters."

"All of you do." She raised her brows. "And not a single one of you decided to speak to me about it?"

"As a matter of fact, a couple of times one of us made that very suggestion, but then the others knocked that idea down. You see, we all kinda figured it would be best if you thought these letters were your secret."

"Because?"

"Because we all saw how upset they made you," Belle said. Looking decidedly more uncomfortable, she added, "We thought if you believed no one knew, then you might not worry about them so much."

All this time she'd been living in fear of Belle or Winifred discovering the letters, fearing that once they saw she was being targeted by a stranger they would finally decide to quit. Every time a letter arrived she would break out into a cold sweat, force herself to read it again and again, and then become so desolate and afraid she'd hide in her room until she could act in a calm and genteel manner.

But it seemed all that hiding had been for nothing. She never expected they would look through the things she threw away.

"I see." Once again Miranda felt as if she'd stepped into a play about another person's life. Here she'd spent months doing her best to pretend she was okay. That life was normal. That she had no cares beyond the Iron Rail and missing her husband.

But it had all been a lie, and once more it had been a useless one. She could have saved all that energy.

She wasn't exactly sure how she felt about her big secret being not so secret after all.

She didn't feel embarrassed. Instead, she felt a curious sense of relief. As if she could maybe— just maybe—not be quite so alone anymore. That would be so nice.

"I am glad this is out in the open now," she said at last. "Thank you for telling me the truth."

Belle looked extremely distressed. "I really am sorry, ma'am. Both about the letters and about knowing your secrets and never saying a word. I never thought you'd be so understanding."

How did one respond to that? "Perhaps we should simply drop this subject."

"Yes'm." Belle nodded. Then blurted, "You see, I don't think any of us wanted to make you more upset than you already were."

"Pardon me?" Just how pathetic had she been?

Belle winced. "I know you don't like to speak about your personal life. I mean, I know we aren't supposed to talk about you. On account that you employ us and all—"

"You are right. Most employers value their privacy."

"But, ma'am, well, I just want to say that I've felt real sorry for you," Belle continued in a rush. "I mean, those letters are cruel, that's what they are."

"They have been difficult to read." Raising a

brow. "I am guessing you felt the same way?" She didn't mean to be sarcastic and unkind, but this conversation was becoming increasingly uncomfortable.

Belle's eyes widened. "Oh, I haven't read them!"

"No? I thought you could read."

"Oh, I can!"

"Then?"

"It's just that . . . I mean, I've only read one," she sputtered. "Emerson, Cook, and Winnie told me what the others said."

"So all of you have taken to reading my disposed correspondence without my knowledge and then discussing it in secret?"

Miranda truly had no idea how to handle this. She fervently wished her mother were sitting next to her. Then she could have educated Miranda about the best way to handle this sticky situation.

Whatever she would advise had to be better than what Miranda was contemplating, which was to call all four of them to the parlor, chastise them soundly, and then promptly fire them all. Servants who disrespected their employers' privacy were worse than useless.

But of course, they had been some of her only defenders in the city. If she let them go, who would even consent to work for her?

She sagged as tension filled her neck and shoulders. What she wouldn't give to go back in time to just an hour ago, when she was still reveling in yesterday's walk in the Strand!

"Mrs. Markham, please don't be upset. It's just that, well, Winnie found one on the floor about a year ago. She'd been in the hallway when you'd opened it. You'd cried out and ran upstairs to your room. It was obvious you were upset."

"Yes." Unfortunately, she remembered that day well. It had been the second time she'd received a letter. She'd been forced to accept that whoever was behind the threats wasn't going to go away. And she never realized she hadn't thrown the letter away.

One of Belle's hands was twisting the edge of her white apron now. "Mrs. Markham, I'm sure Winnie only meant to pick up your letter. I'm sure she didn't actually mean to read it, but . . ."

"But she did." With a sigh, Miranda sat down at her desk chair. "I suppose I don't blame her for that. It was human nature."

"Yes." Belle nodded. "It was that. Exactly."

"I suppose she couldn't resist telling the rest of you about it, either." Miranda supposed she would have been tempted to do the same.

Belle winced. "It wasn't like that. We don't gossip about you. And I promise, no one has said anything to anyone outside the house." She bit her lip then.

"But?" Miranda asked, wanting to get the rest of this awful story out in the open.

"But, well, it's just that we're all real worried about you. Like I said, those letters are cruel, especially with you being a widow and all. And with Lt. Markham's mother and sister nagging you something awful."

Ruth and Viola did nag her something awful. The description was so fitting, she almost smiled. Why, if she didn't know how much they had cared for Phillip, she would suspect them of spreading rumors about him and sending threatening letters to get her out of this house rather than depending on their lawyer to find a way.

Yes, Phillip had known his mother and sister loved him, but he was reluctant to spend much time with them because of their dispositions. He was just as happy when they decided to move to Houston rather than live in the mansion with them.

Wearily, she ran a hand along the muscles supporting the back of her neck. They were bunched and knotted. In need of a small massage.

It was moments like this when she missed having a husband. Someone to share her burdens and take charge. Someone to help her figure out how to speak to servants about letters she wished she hadn't received. Someone to help her talk about things no one was supposed to know about in the first place.

Yet, on the other hand, she no doubt wouldn't

have received such letters if Phillip had still been alive.

Because she was alone, she was at a stranger's mercy. He could freely play with her emotions, threaten to harm her reputation, practically do whatever he wanted because he knew he could.

She wasn't from Galveston. She had no family or long-standing support system here to help her through trying times. And Phillip's mother and sister still resented her keeping the house and not giving it back to the Markham family.

All she had was a large house that she'd inherited on a prime piece of real estate. She had that, which many valued highly, and the name of her husband.

Which, until recently, had kept her feeling secure. Now that so many people had besmirched his name, Phillip's reputation didn't keep her safe anymore.

"I don't know what to do," she finally admitted. "I've tried to be strong, but someone desperately wants me gone. But if I leave, I have nowhere to go and no way of surviving or making a living." She couldn't emphasize enough how much that idea scared her. "I did tell Sheriff Kern about the first letter, but he brushed off my worries as a feminine drama."

For the first time since their conversation began, Belle looked certain. "That was wrong of him."

"I thought so too. But he made me so worried, I was afraid to go back to him."

"Beg your pardon, ma'am, but I don't reckon admitting you are afraid or need help is a sign of weakness. I think it simply means you're like the rest of us."

"Thank you for that, Belle. I have to tell you that though this conversation is difficult, I'm thankful to be able to discuss the letters with someone."

She sighed in relief. "I'm thankful things are out in the open now, too, ma'am."

"So, um, if I was your sister, what would you advise me to do?"

"You need to get help," she replied instantly. "And though all of us here would be happy to help you do whatever needs to be done, I think you need to go back to ask Sheriff Kern for assistance."

"But what if he doesn't listen to me?"

"Then go talk to him again."

"Yes, I suppose you're right." She bit her lip. "Now I wish I would have saved the letters. Then I could prove to him how vicious they have become."

"You don't need to worry about that. Winnie saved them."

"Of course she did."

"I think you really should talk to Sheriff Kern, ma'am. The sooner the better."

Before she lost her nerve, Miranda nodded. "I

think you're right. Belle, please go to the sheriff's office right now. When you get there, ask Sheriff Kern to pay me a visit at his convenience."

"Are you going to write this down? I could hand him a note."

Miranda shook her head. "No. I'd rather not have anything more in writing. Simply tell him it's about the letters and that you and I've talked." Aware that Belle wasn't exactly comfortable with the errand, Miranda added, "While I realize visiting the sheriff's office is not the easiest errand to run, I can assure you that Sheriff Kern is polite and gentlemanly. I'm sure this visit won't take up much of your time."

"It ain't that, ma'am."

"Are you concerned about what to say? Simply tell him I've received more letters and I would like to speak to him without the whole city knowing I am in his office. He'll understand that."

"Yes, ma'am."

"Thank you, Belle. I appreciate it."

Looking a bit more confident, Belle smiled. "I'll go speak with Sheriff Kern straightaway."

"Thank you. When you return, I'll probably still be here in the parlor. If not, please look for me. I'll want to know what he says as soon as possible."

"I'll do that." Just before she turned to leave, Belle smiled. "This is nice, isn't it?"

In her opinion, the conversation they'd just shared had been one of the most difficult in recent memory. "I'm afraid I don't understand. What is it that is nice?"

After visibly weighing her words, Belle said, "I think it's going to be a real good thing when we all know you are no longer at this coward's mercy. And that it's going to be nice to know all of us can now speak freely about your letters. It's nice when secrets are unveiled, I think."

Though she had no idea what was in store for her future, Miranda had to agree. No matter what happened, anything was better than being at a stranger's mercy.

Anything had to be better than that.

7

The moment after she closed the door in the study to allow Mrs. Markham some privacy, Belle scampered down the hall, hurried down the stairs, ran out to the walkway, threw open the door, and at last burst into the kitchen.

When she saw Winnie, Cook, and Emerson all look up in alarm, she grinned. "Oh, good. You all are here."

Instead of smiling in return, Cook frowned. "We're here, but you aren't acting like you belong here, attending to your duties. What has gotten ahold of you?"

"Mrs. Markham."

Cook dropped the heavy knife she'd been holding. It clattered onto her work surface with a noisy clang.

Emerson glared. "Belle, some complete sentences would be real welcome right about now."

"Yes. Of course." Forcing herself to calm down and try to make a lick of sense, Belle took a fortifying breath. "When I served tea to Mrs. Markham, she was opening her mail."

Cook shrugged. "And?"

"And inside one of the envelopes was yet another one of those letters!"

"Oh my word."

"She gasped when she saw it and spilled her tea."

Cook wasn't even pretending to cut vegetables now. "Did she burn herself?"

"No, but to be honest with ya, she was so upset I think even if she was burned she wouldn't have noticed."

Emerson stood up from the chair he was sitting in and began to pace. "I'd like to wring up that coward by his neck, I would."

"I would help you too," Cook said.

Winnie stared at Belle impatiently. "Well, don't keep us in suspense. What did you do?"

Kind of enjoying the fact that she had their undivided attention, Belle drew out her answer. "Well, I would have ignored the letter, her manner, her tears, everything. You know, like we always do."

"But?" Winnie asked sharply.

Belle knew that tone. It meant Winnie wanted some answers and she wanted them fast. Feeling a bit uneasy again, Belle sputtered, "But . . . well, I made a mistake. Before I knew what I was saying, I told Mrs. Markham I was sorry she received another one."

Cook's eyes widened. "Please say you did not do that."

"I'm sorry, but I really did. I couldn't help

myself." When three disbelieving pairs of eyes stared back at her, Belle backtracked. "Well, I mean, I know I should have been able to, but I couldn't hold my tongue. Before I knew it, I was telling her I was sorry. Then, next thing I knew, Mrs. Markham was asking me all about what I knew about the letters she'd been receiving."

"And then?" Winnie asked.

"And then I went and told her I've known about them for some time. And, that, well, you all knew about them too."

Emerson moaned, Winnie was visibly gritting her teeth, and Cook . . . well, Cook pressed a hand to her chest and glared. "You just had to go and bring the rest of us into it, did ya?"

"I didn't mean to," Belle replied, knowing deep in her belly that her explanation could use some work. "But Mrs. Markham wanted some answers. I couldn't ignore her questions. And I'm not good at lying. I am sorry."

"I suppose we should all be glad you aren't a liar," Winnie stated. Looking at the other occupants in the room, she shrugged. "No use crying over spilled milk. What's done is done."

Emerson whistled softly. "It's done all right. We're all going to get fired. We might as well sit down with a cup of tea and prepare ourselves."

Cook left her cutting board and stood next to Emerson. "My daughter lives in New Orleans. We could go there, I suppose."

Winnie frowned. "I got nowhere else to go."

Belle cleared her throat. "I don't think we're about to get fired."

Emerson folded his hands across his chest. "Because?"

"Because Mrs. Markham just asked me to go to Sheriff Kern's office. She wants me to ask him to come here, to pay her a call." Daring to smile, she added, "I think she's finally going to tell him everything."

"Do you think so, truly, girl?" Emerson asked.

Belle nodded. "Mrs. Markham even said she was glad her secret was out in the open. She said she'd been afraid we would all leave if we found out about these letters."

Winnie shook her head. "Our lady is a lamb. Doesn't she realize she's not the one who has done something wrong? It ain't her fault some mean coward is sending her ugly letters."

"She seemed a lot better when I left her just now," Belle said.

Cook clasped her hands together. "Praise God! Maybe things are finally going to get better for Mrs. Markham. I was beginning to think he wasn't listening to my prayers."

Winnie made a shooing motion with her hands. "Well, off with you now before she up and changes her mind."

Belle decided right then and there that she didn't need to be told twice. She'd already disobeyed

Mrs. Markham by tarrying in the kitchen. After running to her room to put on a real dress and not her faded work one, she refashioned her hair. Finally, she put on her best bonnet. It was felt and navy and had dark purple ribbons around the brim.

After slipping on her cloak and pulling on gloves, she decided she now looked suitable enough to visit the sheriff's office. She told herself she had gone to so much trouble because she wanted to do her employer proud. Not because she was about to have a conversation with the most attractive sheriff in the great state of Texas.

Fifteen minutes later, Belle was sitting on a hard wooden chair inside the sheriff's small waiting room and doing her best to avoid the dark stares of not only Sheriff Kern's deputy, but also two men who appeared especially weather beaten and rough.

All three of the men had raised their brows when she'd asked to speak with the sheriff and looked at one another in disbelief when she'd refused to explain why she needed to see him.

When she resolutely refused to answer any questions, Deputy Banks told her to sit down and then went about his business.

The other two men, however, merely turned so they faced her and looked at her with increasingly lewd expressions. She felt exposed and at a disadvantage. And, frankly, wished she was sitting anywhere else but where she was.

Her only consolation was that she was the one sitting in the waiting area and not her employer. Imagining gentle, shy Mrs. Markham being subjected to such disrespect was difficult to contemplate. Belle might be small but she knew she was far tougher. She'd also had plenty of experience with men who had next to no manners and little respect for a woman like her.

But as the minutes passed, some of her confidence faded. The men's too-forward stares were making her uncomfortable. She could practically feel their bold, assessing eyes drift over her body. Their disrespect made her feel like she used to when she stood by her mother's side back in Louisiana.

After her mother died, Belle had promised herself she'd do everything in her power never to be at such a disadvantage again. If she hadn't promised Mrs. Markham that she'd contact the sheriff, Belle would have stood up and walked away.

But Belle had promised, and she was willing to do whatever it took for her employer to feel safe. Therefore, she had no recourse but to sit with her hands pressed in a tight knot on her lap and pray for Sheriff Kern to arrive sooner than later.

But as the clock's minute hand continued to move at a glacial speed, the tension in the room rose. Belle could have sworn the very air she was breathing had become thicker.

Though she was trying hard not to look at them, she could still feel the men's appraising leers.

After another five minutes passed, one of the men kicked a boot out. The sudden motion forced Belle to turn her head their way.

"Where do you work?" one asked, his voice sharp and staccato, betraying that he was a Yankee.

The wariness she'd begun to feel was replaced by fear. "That is none of your business," she replied when it became apparent she had no choice but to answer him.

He lumbered to his feet. "Ain't no shame if yer a sporting girl," he said. Almost kindly. "All I is aimin' to know is what house you're a part of." He leaned closer, bringing with him the faint scent of fish and onions and stale clothing. "That way I'll know whether to bring a quarter or a dollar."

She was both appalled and saddened by his comment. Pity for the soiled doves who frequented the port and warehouse district overwhelmed her. It made her ill to think that a man like him could have his way with a woman for less than the cost of a meal.

Against her will, memories of the men who frequented her mother's room hit her hard, causing her mouth to go dry. "I am not a . . . a prostitute."

"But you could be, if you had a mind to it," he

said, as if he warmed up to the idea. "Shoot, a pretty thing like you? Chances are good you could earn a decent living on yer back. Heck, you could even buy a better hat."

She folded her hands tightly in her lap and remained silent. Where was Sheriff Kern? And why couldn't Mrs. Markham have simply written a note that needed to be dropped off?

He grunted. "What's wrong with you?" He scowled. "Can't you talk?"

She didn't want to talk to him. Feeling more anxious, Belle glanced at Deputy Banks. Waited for him to intervene. Unfortunately, he was leaning back in his chair eyeing the interplay with a bored look.

The swarthy man's voice turned rougher. "Or do you consider yerself better than the likes of me?"

Worried that he was going to approach her if she didn't respond, she spoke at last. "I am waiting for the sheriff. That is all."

He coughed. "Where I come from, women know their place. They don't ignore a man when he's speaking to them. They know actions like that have consequences."

His threat did not fall on deaf ears. She believed he would happily retaliate for her rudeness if he felt he could. The fact that not for Winnie and Mrs. Markham taking her in Belle could be at the mercy of a man like him made her tongue sharper than was wise.

A sudden memory returned of her mother pretending that the men who called on her actually cared, and Belle's anxiety transformed to fear.

But she wasn't weak. Not yet. Forcing herself to look far braver than she felt, she raised her chin. "Where I come from, women do not speak to strangers."

The man's friend chuckled. "She's a fiery one, she is, Jeb." Standing up, he stepped in her direction. "Don't be acting like you're a real *lady*, now, 'cause we all know you ain't that." His assessing look turned into something else. "Now, why don't you answer me? Who are you?"

She looked at Deputy Banks yet again. Surely he was going to help her now? If not for her, for her mistress?

After the span of a heartbeat, he colored. "Sit down, Henry. Belle here is right. You ain't got no call to be speaking to women like that."

"Or what?" the Yankee asked, just as the outer door swung open at last. "What are you gonna do, Banks? Tell me I gotta start bowing and scraping to all the girls that walk through yer door?"

She and the three men inhaled sharply as Sheriff Kern entered the room with none other than Mr. Truax on his heels. It was obvious to all that they'd heard the Yankee's words—and Deputy Banks's allowing of it.

Deputy Banks jumped to his feet.

Both of the other men took their seats, looking cowed and bedraggled all of a sudden.

Belle breathed a sigh of relief. Maybe she was going to be all right after all.

"Miss Harden, good afternoon," Sheriff Kern said politely. "May I help you?"

"Good afternoon, Sheriff. I, um, was hoping I might speak with you for a few minutes. If you wouldn't mind."

"Of course I don't." Glaring at the two Yankees and his deputy, too, he gestured toward his office. "Why don't you go into my office? I'll be there directly. I must attend to a piece of business first."

"Hold on," Mr. Truax said. "Belle, is everything okay at the Iron Rail?"

She shook her head. "I don't believe so, sir."

Sheriff Kern raised his brows. "Is this an emergency?" He turned to Banks. "Why didn't you assist her?"

"She said she would speak only to you."

"You knew I was having lunch. You should have gone to get me."

"I couldn't leave her alone in here. Sir." Reddening slightly, he said, "Besides, you know what everyone says about Mrs. Markham. It ain't like Belle here is working for a real lady."

One of the Yankees grinned. "So that's why the girl didn't tell us who employed her. There's only one person around Galveston Island who is even less welcomed than a couple of Yankee

139

dock-workers! No wonder you didn't want us to know about you."

Sheriff Kern looked from Belle to Mr. Truax to his deputy. Then he scowled. "Robert, why don't you join Miss Harden and me?"

"I think that would be a good idea." Without sparing the deputy or the two men another glance, Mr. Truax strode toward Sheriff Kern's office door, gallantly opened it, and waved on through. "Let's go inside, Miss Harden."

"Yes, sir." She stepped inside Sheriff Kern's office, glad to be out of that awful front room and away from the terrible men.

But now that the time had come to speak to the sheriff, she realized he was simply not going to let her share Mrs. Markham's message and leave. No, he was going to want her to share everything she knew. And when she did that, Belle was going to have a whole new set of worries on her shoulders.

She was going to need to find the right way to tell the sheriff and Mr. Truax everything she knew . . . all without betraying Mrs. Markham's privacy.

Was that even possible? And how did Sheriff Kern and Mr. Truax know each other anyway? They seemed too comfortable with each other to have just met.

As she gingerly sat down on the padded leather chair Mr. Truax held out for her, Belle exhaled.

Then, as they waited for Sheriff Kern to join them, she at last did what she should have done in the first place. She prayed that she'd find the right words to do the most good.

8

At this point in his life, Robert Truax knew some things to be true. One, C.S.A. bills were worth less than the paper they were printed on. Another was that regrets were a waste of time, as was foolishly hoping that something good would last forever. Nothing was always good and nothing ever stayed the same.

Robert knew better men than he had died far too young. He also knew men who were not as honest as he was would live far longer than he would.

And finally, he knew Belle Harden was currently scared out of her mind.

Once they were alone in the sheriff's office with the door shut firmly against prying ears, he said, "Tell me, are you frightened because of the news you are about to share or because of something those men did?" Already thinking the worst, he added, "Do you need me to deal with them?"

She shook her head. "No, Mr. Truax. I am fine."

Each word sounded so brittle that he was surprised she didn't break down right there in front of them. "We both know that is not the case."

"I am tougher than I look, sir."

"You are all blond hair and blue eyes. You look like an angel. You do not look tough at all."

"That may be true. But still, I wasn't scared." When he merely stared at her, silently willing| her to stop lying, she bowed her head. "Well, I will admit to feeling a bit frightened before you and Sheriff Kern came in."

Few things made him more upset than men ganging up on helpless women and children. He'd seen men prey on the weak all his life and had been their unwilling victim more times than he cared to remember. When he was seven, he'd promised himself that one day, when he was old enough to protect those weaker than him, he would.

For the most part, he'd done just that.

Now, knowing that this young woman had been afraid while waiting for the sheriff in the waiting area outside his office—one of the few places in Galveston where a woman should feel safe— well, it irritated him to no end.

"What did they do?" he asked as calmly as he was able. She didn't need him to make things worse or more frightening than they already were.

Belle folded her arms protectively across her chest. "Nothing you need to worry about, sir."

"Miss Harden, although we don't know each other much, I hope you will trust my reputation as a former Confederate officer to know that I only mean to help you."

"I trust that, sir. However, I promise that my problems should not be your concern."

When the door opened and Sheriff Kern strode in, looking vaguely put-upon, Robert unleashed his frustrations on him. "What kind of deputy did you hire, Jess?"

Giving him a sardonic look, Kern paused. "A rather weak one, it seems," he said lightly. "He can't seem to understand that he's in the office to help people, not make friends."

Crossing the room, he reached for Belle's hand. "Belle, Chet said those men did nothing more than ask you rude questions. Is that the truth?"

"Isn't that enough?" Robert interjected. "A woman should be able to come into this office without being afraid she is in danger of being accosted."

"I completely agree." Kern's expression turned hard. "He made a mistake and I told him so. That said, he's also in a difficult position. His older brother works with the shipping companies and brings in a lot of business to the island. Because of that, it's in Chet's family's best interests to get along with our city's visitors."

"If that is the case, then he shouldn't be deputized," Robert said bluntly.

Wearily, Sheriff Kern nodded. "You aren't saying anything I haven't thought more than once myself."

"Please, may we not talk about this any longer?"

Miss Harden asked. "There was no harm done, and it was nothing that I haven't encountered before."

"Which is a problem," Robert said.

"We both know I'm not a lady. I'm made of stern stuff." She drew a breath. "Plus, I would have been willing to put up with all sorts of things to help Mrs. Markham." Looking from one to the other, she continued. "Mrs. Markham is why I am here."

"What happened?" Robert asked, already mentally planning the quickest route back to the Iron Rail. "Is she hurt?"

"Not exactly."

Robert stood up. "What does that mean? Does she need medical attention?"

Belle shook her head. "No, sir. It's nothing like that."

Sheriff Kern walked to the front of his desk and perched on the edge of it. Staring at her intently, he said, "What, exactly, is it like?"

But instead of relaying the problem, she continued to hedge. "Mrs. Markham asked if I would come here and ask if you could pay her a call soon. At your convenience, she said to tell you."

Too agitated to sit down, Robert leaned against the wall and studied the maid closely. "What has happened? She seemed well enough yesterday."

Kern ignored him. Instead, he was staring at

Belle intently. "Do I need to walk over there this minute?"

"It's not an emergency. At least, I don't think so. The fact is, Mrs. Markham has been receiving a lot of terrible letters. Threatening ones."

"I was aware that she received a letter. She showed it to me."

"Oh, no, sir. It wasn't just one."

"Really? How many has she received?"

"Lots."

Robert felt as if ice were flowing through his veins. "Define 'lots'."

"At least one a week."

Robert pushed off from the wall. "Kern, you made it sound like the letter was a one-time occurrence. Have you been ignoring her?"

"I have not, Truax," he bit out. After taking a breath, he stared at Belle. "Did she receive a letter today?"

Belle nodded. "I think you should visit her soon. Very soon."

"Have you seen any of these letters?"

She nodded again. "They are bad. Real mean. Some are so threatening it's a wonder she doesn't faint."

"What do they say?" Robert asked.

"They say bad things about Mr. Markham, like the rumors that have been going around for so long. Most also promise that something bad is going to happen if she doesn't give up the Iron Rail."

Robert was so agitated, it felt as if his spine were about to snap. "When did today's letter arrive?"

"This morning. I brought her some tea, and then she was opening her mail." Looking increasingly distressed, Belle said, "I don't know what it said, exactly, but it was bad enough for her to spill her tea. Sheriff Kern, what are we going to do?"

"*We* are not going to do anything."

Looking alarmed, Belle gripped the armrest of her chair. "No, we must—"

"*I,* on the other hand, will. Now, please, Miss Harden, don't trouble yourself any further."

Sheriff Kern's expression softened as he stared at Belle, making Robert realize that while the sheriff might think he had a soft spot for Miranda Markham, he had true feelings for this petite woman sitting across from him. Kern was gazing at her the way Phillip had gazed at the tintype of his wife.

"I'll pay a call on Mrs. Markham today and see if she'll let me see the letters. Then we'll see if we can get to the bottom of this." After a pause, he murmured, "I promise, Belle. I will not let you down."

Robert knew this to be true. After he had finally decided over lunch to take Jess into his confidence about his mission, he knew him to be a man he could rely on.

"It doesn't matter if you let me down, sir. I can

handle it. But I really hope you won't let Mrs. Markham down. If you do, I simply don't know if she'll survive." She stood up, and with a flick of her wrist shook out her skirts and petticoats. "Thank you for seeing me, sir."

Robert walked to her side. "Allow me to walk you back."

"That's not necessary."

"Yes, but it would be my honor."

She smiled softly at him. When she glanced the sheriff's way, her gentle smile turned into a cautious look. She abruptly turned and walked out the door.

Looking over his shoulder, Robert caught the reason for Belle's awkward expression.

Sheriff Jess Kern was glaring at him. "Watch yourself, Truax."

"Always," Robert replied as he walked to Belle's side.

As they walked through the front room, he was pleased to see that only a chagrined deputy remained.

When they stepped onto the street, he couldn't resist grinning. Then, because it felt so good, he gave in to temptation and laughed. Loudly and without compunction.

"What is that for?" Belle asked.

"Nothing important. I was only thinking that some things never cease to surprise and amaze me. And that I'm so glad about that."

· · ·

Robert changed his mind about that less than an hour later when he spied Miranda standing at the landing window, her hand pressed against the cold condensation. She looked extremely beautiful. She also looked desperate and afraid.

"Anything special going on out there?" he asked lightly. He hoped he would make her smile. Encourage her to tease him back.

Instead, he'd managed to startle her. "Mr. Truax. Hello. I didn't know you had returned."

"I got here a bit ago. I came in the servants' entrance."

"Why on earth would you do that?"

He debated telling her the truth, then decided there was no help for it. She was likely to find out. "I ran into Belle while I was out. I volunteered to escort her back."

"I see." Her mouth worked, betraying her curiosity. "Did she, um, happen to tell you where she'd been?"

"She didn't need to. I saw her at the sheriff's office."

"Oh?" Her mouth worked again. "Yes. Well, I asked her to run an errand for me."

"I know. Kern said he would be by here before too long."

Her hand dropped from the pane. He wondered if that was because it got cold or that she suddenly realized she'd been standing with it pressed against the window. "I should go freshen up for his visit."

Her words caught him off guard. Did she have feelings for the sheriff?

Jealousy at the thought of her primping for Kern flowed through him. Knowing his thoughts were inappropriate and unwanted, he ruthlessly tamped them down.

He wasn't there to have a liaison or to develop any romantic attachments. No, he was there to help her and fulfill a promise he'd made not only to his captain but to her husband. He'd vowed that he would look after Miranda for Phillip.

That was what mattered. That was all that was important.

With that in mind, he stepped away. "I'll let you get to it, then."

Looking adorably awkward, she went into her room.

When she was out of sight, he crept up the stairs and placed his hand on the pane where she'd had hers.

Looked out.

And wondered what she saw. Had she been looking forward to the sheriff's visit . . . or had she been remembering how her life used to be?

"Well, you were gone a long time, Belle," Cook said. "I trust you were able to speak with Sheriff Kern?"

"I'm sorry it took me so long. When I arrived, Sheriff Kern wasn't in the office. I was forced to wait."

"And when he did arrive? What did he say?"

"He happened to be with Mr. Truax. Both of them talked to me. After Sheriff Kern promised he'd stop by, Mr. Truax walked me back."

Winnie stopped scrubbing a silver tray and looked over at Emerson and Cook. "There's something going on with that Mr. Truax, mark my words."

"Like what?"

"He's not here just to visit and conduct business in Galveston. He's here for a reason, and I think it has something to do with Mrs. Markham."

"Do you think he's someone from her past? Do you think they knew each other?"

"No. But either he knows something he's not sharing or he knows something about her past. I aim to discover what that is."

Emerson grunted. "That's all we be needing, another batch of questions and a mystery to solve."

Belle was about to offer her guess when they heard the light footsteps of their employer.

All four of them turned to her when she entered the kitchen.

"Good afternoon, Mrs. Markham," Winnie said as she dropped a quick, impulsive curtsy. "Is there something ya need? What may I help you with?"

Their employer looked from one to the other to

the other in confusion. "I . . . well, I was wondering where all of you were. The house seemed especially quiet."

"It's my fault, ma'am," Belle said. "I, um, was telling them about my visit into town."

"Oh?" She paled. "What were you telling them?"

This was why it was a bad idea to lie. Instinctively, she knew it was also a bad idea to mention the sheriff or Mr. Truax. Mrs. Markham would misunderstand why she was sharing. No doubt she would think Belle was gossiping about her instead of being concerned.

Therefore, she let the lies continue. "Um, two new ships arrived at the port today," she blurted.

Mrs. Markham blinked. And who could blame her? Now that the war was over, since when did any of them care what ship pulled into port? "Oh?"

"Yes." When all of them were looking at her expectantly, she babbled on. "One . . . um, one looks to be from England. Or France!"

Mrs. Markham tilted her head to one side. "You don't know?"

"No. You see, I couldn't see the flag."

"Then how did you know it was from another country?"

This was terrible. But in for a penny, in for a pound. "The . . . um . . ."

"She was just telling us about the sailors' uniforms, ma'am," Emerson said quickly. Just as

152

if he noticed sailors' uniforms all the time. "They were white."

"I see. Well, as interesting as sailors' uniforms are, I need your assistance, if you please."

Emerson strode forward. "How may we help, ma'am?"

"We have a new guest waiting in my husband's study to be escorted to his room. The sheriff has just arrived as well."

Immediately, the four of them set into motion.

"I'll go out to see to the guest," Winnie said importantly. "Belle, you accompany Mrs. Markham and see what refreshments the sheriff would like."

"Yes, ma'am," Belle said, leading the way out of the kitchen, outside to the short gap that separated the kitchen from the main house, then into the hall leading to the parlor.

Beside her, Mrs. Markham's movements were wooden.

Though it might have been a bit cheeky, Belle asked, "Are you ready to speak to the sheriff now, ma'am?"

"No, but I guess it's time. So I had better be ready." Looking Belle in the eye, she said, "Try as I might, I haven't been able to forget the past. I guess it's time to deal with the present."

Belle thought truer words had never been said.

9

Johnson's Island, Ohio
Confederate States of America
Officers' POW Camp
February 1865

Phillip Markham's state of health was worse.

The gangrene that had settled in his arm had spread to his shoulder. Angry red welts radiated from his wound, ran down to his fingertips and up along the lines of muscle and veins that marked his upper arm.

Fever had set in, along with delirium. The man's only source of relief was the cool compresses they placed on his skin and the water he drank. Robert would have given a mint for a healthy dose of laudanum or a bottle of whiskey. Anything to give Phillip a few moments of relief from his misery.

Yet, true to form, even though Phillip was undoubtedly in extreme pain, he never complained. His stoic determination to even die like a gentleman humbled them all. Especially Robert, who had never claimed to be anything close to a gentleman.

Even their idiot Yankee guards had seemed to pity Phillip. One stopped by daily to see how he was doing. Another guard had even given Thomas a jug of fresh water for Phillip to drink. He'd gone so far as to assure them they only needed to let one of them know when it needed to be filled again.

That, perhaps, was the true testimony to the man Phillip was. Even their enemy knew they had someone special in their midst.

Because they'd known Phillip's time was near, four of them had been taking turns sitting with him. It was degrading enough for one of the finest men they knew to have to die as a prisoner of war. No one wanted him to have to die alone in their barracks.

Robert had been sitting with him for three hours. He'd bathed Phillip as best he could but hadn't been able to coax him to drink any water. Instead, his friend had simply been lying listlessly on a pallet on the floor.

Robert had placed his hand on Phillip's pulse more than once just to make sure the man was still alive.

Now his shift was over. "I'm going to let someone else take a turn with you now, Lieutenant," he said. "You're in for a treat too. Next up is none other than our esteemed captain."

Though he was fairly sure Phillip wasn't even aware he was there, Robert continued. Maybe he was speaking more for himself than for Phillip. "If you can, be sure to give Captain Monroe some grief. He's been altogether too confident and merry of late."

Robert chuckled, his forced laughter sounding hollow even to his own ears. "You know how Cap gets—always thinking daisies are gonna start blooming and tomorrow is gonna be brighter."

When Phillip didn't so much as flinch, Robert knelt down and clasped his thin, lifeless hand. "Don't give up, Lieutenant. I'll be back tomorrow, and you better plan to open at least one of those eyes for me."

Still reluctant to leave his side, Robert pressed his other hand to Phillip's, curving his palm around Phillip's limp one, attempting to impart some of his strength to him.

But still, Phillip's hand only hung limp between his own.

Feeling more depressed than usual, Robert turned away and walked out of the dank and dark room. The moment he stood outside, he inhaled deeply. It was a relief to feel fresh air on his skin and to be away from the cloying scent of Phillip's disease.

Of course, he immediately felt guilty for even thinking such a thing.

After taking a number of fortifying breaths, Robert spied Captain Monroe. His back was facing Robert, his front leaning against a fence.

His arms and elbows were resting on the top rung. For once their captain didn't look like he was plotting or worrying about anyone. Instead, he seemed captivated by the expanse of water that could now be seen, thanks to some recent chinks in their outer fence.

When they'd first arrived at their camp, Robert had been shocked at just how big Lake Erie was. Though he'd learned about the Great Lakes in a geography text, he'd never imagined anything quite so large.

Now he was used to their surroundings enough to feel something of an authority on them. At the moment, white caps dotted the waves.

Robert predicted they were in for another rough night. He'd been there long enough to take notice of the changes in the water's patterns. He hoped a storm wasn't on the horizon. A storm would bring a fresh blanket of snow and hours of pounding ice on their buildings.

It would also make their barracks blindingly cold.

For a moment Robert considered sharing his weather report, then decided against it. No doubt their captain had already surmised the same thing.

He'd just opted to leave and find someone else to sit with Phillip when Monroe turned to face him. "How's he look?" he asked.

Robert exhaled. "Like a man facing death." There was no other way to describe it.

Devin flinched. "Don't expect it will be long now," he said after a pause. "He'll be in heaven before we know it. Too soon."

"Maybe a day or two at the most." Robert was torn between hoping he was wrong and praying he was right.

Cap nodded. "Figured as much." Still looking out at the waves, he said, "Heck of a way to die, though."

Robert had learned from an early age that death was always unpleasant. His experiences on the battlefield reinforced that idea, along with the knowledge that, while death was unpleasant, there were worse ways to die than others.

But yes, Robert understood his commander's statement. Phillip was a good man. A true Southern gentleman. Loyal and true. It was going to be hard to come to terms with the fact that this good man could meet such a painful and dark death.

Just as Robert was about to say something about pain and suffering and how he wished the Lord would decide to go easier on Phillip, Devin spoke.

"Truax?"

"Sir?" Robert realized he had unconsciously stood at attention. "When you sat with Markham . . . did he say anything?"

All of Robert's senses went on alert. There was a new thread in the man's tone that signified his question was important.

After reflecting on the last three hours, he said, "Yes, sir, he did speak. Well, he spoke for a bit the first hour I sat with him, though I couldn't be sure if he was speaking to me or merely talking in his sleep."

The captain tensed. "What did he say? Tell me exactly."

"I don't recall his exact words, sir. They were a mumbled mash."

"Try, Lieutenant."

"He, uh, was talking about Miranda." Though he was a grown man and had grown up on the streets, he felt himself blush. "Something about her skin, sir." He truly hoped Captain Monroe wouldn't ask for more details than that.

Captain relaxed. "Is that it? He only talked about his wife?"

Robert stared at him curiously. "Yes, sir. Isn't that enough? Ever since we've known him, she's been his favorite topic of conversation. He used to talk about that woman most every waking minute."

"I hope that continues to be the case."

His words were cryptic. And though it wasn't usually his place to question his commanding officer, he asked, "What is on your mind, Captain? Does Markham know something you're worried about getting out?"

After looking around their vicinity, Captain Monroe lowered his voice. "Phillip was a skilled horseman. Skilled fighter. "

"Yes, he was." For the most part, they all were. Well, except he'd been one of the few men in his unit who had never ridden a horse before the war. It had caused an endless amount of ribbing.

Monroe shook his head. "No, he was a better soldier than you know. He was a better fighter, better at strategizing, braver than most people would ever imagine. He was educated too. He knew several languages." Devin paused, stared at him. "Did you know that?"

"I knew he went to West Point. But about the languages? No, sir, I did not."

"Fluent in French and Spanish. It came in handy."

"I didn't know about that." Their job had been to kill Yankees, not speak to them.

"That's good. He was charged to keep it a secret."

Robert wondered if his captain was reminding him of Phillip's qualities to illustrate that the wrong man was dying. If so, it was an unnecessary step. Robert already knew he could never compare to the man Phillip Markham was.

"He was an exemplary officer. The Confederacy will miss him." Robert knew most men who knew him would have blinked twice to hear such words flow off his tongue. Robert was a loyal man but never one to speak in such a flowery way.

"No, Robert. You aren't understanding what I'm trying to say. Phillip often went behind enemy lines. He was a spy."

"What?"

"Markham could lose that Texas drawl and charm-school demeanor faster than you could say 'buttercup.' He's received all kinds of commendations for his missions. One of the generals here pulled me aside yesterday and said that some of the information Phillip shared saved hundreds of lives."

To say he was stunned was an understatement. "I . . . I had no idea, sir."

"That is good. Lee himself swore him to silence. He would have been shot for insubordination if he ever talked about his missions."

"He certainly never betrayed himself to me, sir."

Monroe turned to him at last. "To be honest, by the time he came to report to me, he was done with all that. The powers that be were worried he'd be recognized. Because of that, he was placed into the regular cavalry and asked to serve under me."

"He often told me it was his lucky day when he received orders to come to your unit."

His captain waved off that remark. "I didn't know much of what he'd done. All I'd ever been told was that Markham was valued, with a capital *V*. I took that to mean I should try not to get him killed." He flashed a smile, then sobered. "But then one night I learned a lot more about him."

"When was that?"

"It was back when we were in north Georgia. I was visiting a couple of men at a hospital tent, paying respects and so forth, when a major general stopped me. After I sat down next to him, he pointedly asked how Phillip Markham was doing."

Robert stared. "What did you say?"

Monroe smiled slightly. "About what you'd expect me to. The man's question seemed pointed and out of character. After all, it wasn't like we all went about and checked on our men like they were children." Monroe met Robert's gaze, then turned back to stare at the water. "I kind of shrugged and said he was doing all right. I think I said something about him being good with horses or some such nonsense. That's when the blasted general told me about Phillip Markham's true contributions to the war."

"I must admit I'm shocked."

"I was shocked too. For a while there I even found myself strangely tentative around the man. Phillip had been important enough to the effort to earn the rank of a general. He would have far outranked me . . . if he hadn't agreed to keep all his missions a secret."

"I wish he wasn't dying like this. Seems a poor end to such a great man."

Impatiently, Monroe shook his head. "That isn't why I told you this, Robert."

"What, then, was the reason?"

"I've decided to ask this of you, not Ethan or Thomas. I . . . I think you will be able to handle it the best. From now on, you or I need to stay with Phillip until he passes on. *Only you or me.* No one else. He cannot start telling tales about his past escapades."

"He probably won't. He seems—"

Monroe shook his head again. "He very well might. He's going to start forgetting about where he is. You and I have both seen men do that. It won't be his fault. But the fact is, no one can know about what he's done. No matter what you hear him say, you need to keep it to yourself, or if you truly feel you need to share it, speak to me. That is it." His voice turned hard. "And if you aren't able to quiet him, you will need to silence him yourself. Understood?"

Robert felt as if all the blood were rushing from his face. "Yes, sir."

Monroe continued to stare at him intently. "Do you promise?"

"Yes, Captain." Above all, he was loyal to this man and to the cause.

Captain Monroe exhaled. "Thank you, Robert. And don't forget . . . no matter what, we need to continue to stress that Phillip Markham was nothing more than one of my lieutenants who happened to have a good seat on a horse."

"Yes, sir. And, uh, let us not forget he was a gentleman who really loved his wife."

Captain Monroe smiled. "That will probably be the truest thing we've ever said during our time here. Phillip seems to be fairly sure that the sun rises and falls on his Miranda. The man is still smitten after several years of marriage."

Glad to be talking about something that wasn't so uncomfortable, Robert said, "Do you think any woman can be that wonderful?"

Monroe looked at him sadly. "I would like to think there is at least one woman who is. If Miranda Markham loves Phillip even half as much as he loves her, I shudder to think how she is going to receive the news of his death."

Much to his shame, Robert hoped she was desolate. It was going to be difficult to bear if the woman who was everything to Phillip hadn't actually felt the same way about him.

10

Sheriff Kern was standing against the fireplace mantel, Phillip's tintype in his hand, when Miranda entered the parlor.

When he saw her, his expression softened. "Mrs. Markham, you're back."

As she watched him clumsily attempt to replace Phillip's tintype, she couldn't help but smile to herself. His awkward way of moving and conducting himself was rather endearing. It set her at ease, unlike Phillip's perfect manners. His perfect comportment often made her doubt herself.

Briefly, she wished her situation were different. She wished she trusted Sheriff Kern more. She wished they were friends, or at least friendly.

She would give a lot to be able to look forward to enjoying his company after Robert left. It would be nice to have a good friend.

However, it was likely that such a moment would never come. Or at least not anytime soon.

"Sheriff Kern, thank you again for coming so quickly. I do hope I haven't inconvenienced your day?"

"Not in the slightest."

"I am fairly sure you are lying, but I'll pretend I believe you."

Instead of correcting her, he bowed slightly. "May I say that you look quite fetching today?"

"You may." She curtsied slightly, realizing as she did so that she was blushing. The clumsy compliment eased her like little did anymore. Funny how some things that were drilled into a person's head by force and cajoling could ease the greatest tensions years later. "Won't you please sit down?"

When his gaze darted toward Belle, who was standing silently beside her, Miranda felt her blush deepen. "Please forgive my manners. Sheriff Kern, Belle came in to see what kind of refreshments we might serve you. Would you care for tea or coffee?"

"Coffee would be much appreciated, Belle. Thank you."

"Of course, Sheriff," Belle said before turning to Miranda. "Coffee for two, ma'am?"

"Yes. And if Cook has any blueberry bread, that would be good as well."

After another nod, Belle departed.

After gazing at Belle's retreating form a moment longer, Sheriff Kern took a seat across from Miranda and stared at her expectantly.

Miranda knew she needed to get to the point and fast. No matter how kind the sheriff was, he was not going to have time to sit and stare at her while she behaved like a ninny.

"As I said, I appreciate you meeting me here,

Sheriff Kern," she began before sputtering to a stop. Perching on the edge of the settee, she tried to control her onslaught of nerves. It was obvious that she was doing a sorry job of it, however. Her hands were clenched in tight fists and she no doubt looked anything but relaxed.

Sheriff Kern, on the other hand, leaned back in the chair across from her, one of his elbows resting on the arm as though he was simply taking an hour's respite from work. "Do you think we could move to a first-name basis, ma'am?" he said with a small smile. "We've known each other for some time now."

"About a year, I believe."

He raised one eyebrow. "Since that is the case, perhaps you would be so kind as to call me a friend?"

"Yes, of course." Had he just read her mind?

"Therefore, may we be on a first-name basis?" He raised a brow. Goading her on.

There really was no other choice. Though she felt as awkward as a wallflower at her first ball, she smiled softly. "Please, allow me to introduce myself. I'm Miranda."

"Miranda, I am Jess."

She felt herself blushing again. Her reaction was troublesome, indeed. She had never believed a man—any man—would cause butterflies to flutter in her stomach again. But now it seemed she truly was not immune to masculine

167

appreciation. First she experienced this with Robert, and now Jess Kern.

Or perhaps it was simply that she wasn't dead.

If anything, he looked even more relaxed. "I'm glad we got that out of the way."

"I, as well."

He smiled at her again, and then, before her eyes, his whole manner changed. "Miranda, I don't believe you brought me here simply for coffee."

She gulped. It was time. "I'm afraid I wanted to discuss something of a serious nature with you." She paused, mentally trying out several different ways to discuss her problem. She wanted to share her concerns in a quiet, easy way. She wasn't sure if that was possible, however.

But instead of making her wait, Jess said, "You want to discuss the letter you received today."

She exhaled a breath she hadn't even realized she'd been holding. "Yes. Belle must have told you."

He uncrossed his legs and leaned forward. "May I see it?" His voice had become all business.

"Yes, of course. Though, um, I'm afraid I must tell you I've been receiving letters like this with startling regularity."

All traces of ease vanished from his expression. After he read the letter, he asked, "How often have you been getting these letters, Miranda?"

His use of her Christian name jarred her composure. It was going to be next to impossible to tell him anything but the stark truth. "Almost every week." Either Belle had not told him that, too, or he was pretending not to know, protecting her maid from her employer's possible anger for discussing her private affairs. But she didn't care anymore. She wanted it all out in the open now.

"You've been receiving a letter every week. For the past year?"

"Yes. Since, um, around the time I opened the Iron Rail for business."

"So you've received at least fifty letters."

"Yes."

His expression was incredulous. "Miranda, I know I did not take the first letter seriously enough, and I'm very sorry about that. But why didn't you come to me when the letters continued?" His voice was harsh. It was obvious that he was trying hard not to scare her, but he was upset.

"I don't know why I didn't come to you," she blurted, then forced herself to be honest. "No, that isn't true. At first I started thinking that maybe those letters were nothing less than I deserved."

He inhaled sharply. "Why on earth would you think you deserved to be the recipient of such abuse?"

"Because I'm alive, I suppose, and Phillip is

not." Her heart started beating faster. She hadn't allowed herself to verbalize these thoughts before. It was amazing how ridiculous her reasoning sounded. Her husband would have given her a good talking-to for turning those letters into something so convoluted.

Jess's expression flickered from anger to confusion to pity. He got to his feet, turned from her, and paced. Then after a pause, he walked toward her again and sat down. "Phillip was a good man, Miranda. Though I didn't know him, many officers I met in the army knew of him and thought very highly of him. He was well respected."

"He was," she said quickly. "He was a wonderful man. He treated me well. He was better than I deserved." Lowering her voice, she said, "We married in haste, were hardly more than strangers, really. I was so young, and here he entrusted me with so much. No doubt he would wish I was stronger and wiser."

"Stronger?" He cocked a brow. "Wiser?"

Even to her ears, her words sounded convoluted. "Oh, I don't know . . . better?"

Jess shook his head. "No, Miranda. Phillip Markham was exactly who you deserved. You deserved a good man. You are worthy of that love."

Just as she was about to murmur something inconsequential, he continued. "However, even though Phillip was good, I am sure he was not perfect. He had flaws just like all of us. He was no better and no less. And more than that, I'm told he loved you dearly. Nothing would make him more upset than to realize that someone was taking advantage of your widowed state and preying on you. And . . . that you felt guilty about living."

"Perhaps you are right."

"No, I know I am right. Promise me from this day forward you will cease to assume that you deserve anything but happiness."

"I will try, sir."

"That isn't good enough. I promise you, dear, you being miserable will not make either Phillip's reputation or memory better. It will simply make you worried and upset." Looking at her intently, he said, "Will you promise me?"

She nodded. She didn't know if it was a fool's promise, but she saw Jess's point.

His eyes flickered beyond her again. "Ah."

She turned to see that Belle had returned with a coffee cart. And that Mr. Truax was entering the room just behind her.

Uneasiness jangled her nerves as she noticed he seemed as confident as ever.

Confident and full of his own secrets. She suddenly realized the letters had taken a stronger, ugly turn after his arrival. Did that mean something?

Could he have had something to do with them?

"Belle told me you both were in here. I thought I'd join you," he said with a charming smile.

When Jess merely stared at him, not looking pleased by his appearance in the slightest, Miranda drew herself up. "I'm sorry, Mr. Truax, but you will have to excuse us. This is a private conversation."

"I'd like to think I can help you."

"I don't believe you can. It's of, um, a somewhat confidential nature," she replied. Beside her, Jess continued to stare at her boarder.

It was beginning to make her worried.

But instead of abiding by her wishes, Robert simply sat down next to her. Uninvited. Immediately she was surrounded by his masculine scent. Against her will, she was aware of everything about him.

"You see, the fact is, I have knowledge of your problem, Mrs. Markham. I was at the sheriff's office when Belle arrived and I know about your letter."

Sheriff Kern propped one leg on his other and glared. "Truax, I'll take care of this. Watch yourself."

"That is what I'm doing, Jess."

As Miranda stared at the two men, she realized they were speaking to each other with a measure of comfort, as if they had already met. Perhaps even with a compatibility? And why

172

was Robert at Jess's office when Belle was there?

While Jess looked ready to spit nails, Robert lazily leaned back and propped one foot on an opposite knee and smiled at Belle. "Bring me a cup of coffee when you can, would you, please, Belle?"

"Of course, sir," she said easily. Just as if she were used to taking orders from him!

Feeling both confused and frustrated, Miranda watched Belle set china cups in front of her and the sheriff, then pour piping-hot coffee from a pot. Finally, she set out a small plate of Cook's berry bread.

Jess took a sip, while Mr. Truax reached over, rudely picked up a piece of bread, and took a large bite. A faint sprinkling of crumbs littered his vest. He brushed them away.

"Perhaps you would care to explain yourself?" she asked, somewhat caustically.

"I'll be happy to. As soon as Belle returns with my coffee. In the meantime, I think it would be wise for me to see the letter that came today."

Instead of arguing with him, she sipped her coffee as Jess handed him the letter. When Belle returned, she served Mr. Truax, then finally left them.

Through it all, her suspicions grew. Jess Kern and Robert Truax were no strangers.

"You two know each other?"

For the first time since his entrance, Robert looked uncomfortable.

The two men exchanged glances and seemed to come to the same conclusion.

After setting down his fork, the sheriff said, "We actually met for the first time the other day, but Robert and I also have much in common because of the war."

"You mean . . . you two served together?"

"Kind of. We were both in . . . the same place once."

She barely refrained from rolling her eyes. That answer told her absolutely nothing. "Why did I not know this before?"

"It never came up in conversation. You know I only recently arrived here," Robert answered.

She clenched her hands in a last-ditch effort to calm her temper. "Don't prevaricate, sir. You knew the fact that you served together would have been meaningful to me. Yet, for some reason you chose to keep it a secret." Looking from one to the other, she said, "Both of you did. I suspect you actually knew each other before Robert came to town. You've been lying to me about this."

Robert bristled. "I didn't do anything of the kind."

"You did. I was led to believe that you knew no one here. That you were a stranger." Remembering her chatter about the park, remembering how inane, how foolish she must have sounded, she said, "You've probably been here before. You should have told me."

"I didn't lie about that, Miranda. I've never been to Galveston before."

Suddenly hating that she'd been so familiar with him, hating how comfortable she'd felt walking by his side on the pier, she flinched. "You may call me Mrs. Markham."

Looking contrite, Robert nodded. "As you wish. The truth is, I have not revealed everything about my visit."

"Give him a chance, Miranda," Sheriff Kern said.

Glaring at him coldly, she said, "I think it is best if we go back to a more distant relationship, sir."

Hurt flashed in the sheriff's eyes before he nodded. "If that is what you wish, Mrs. Markham."

When she noticed the men exchange yet another cautious glance with each other, her pulse started racing. "Explain yourselves, gentlemen," she bit out, hardly able to keep her anger and dismay at bay.

"I served the Confederacy in the war, ma'am," Sheriff Kern said. "Just as Robert did. And Phillip."

"A great many men served the Confederacy."

"That is true. A great many men also died."

"I am aware of that."

Mr. Truax's jaw tightened, then he said, "Several thousand men were also imprisoned in a camp in the middle of Lake Erie, off the coast of Ohio. It was called Johnson's Island. Most of the captives there were officers but there were also a smattering of privates and grunts like me."

She felt as if the wind was getting knocked out of her. "Johnson's Island is where Phillip was imprisoned."

"Yes, it was. Johnson's Island is also where I was imprisoned, Mrs. Markham," Sheriff Kern said quietly. "Robert was too."

"You . . . you two knew each other there, then?"

"No. We never met there, although Jess told me the other day that he remembers me, and I remember seeing him," Robert said. "All three of us were taken to be prisoners of war in early 1865. There was a large group of us. Some were great men. Even generals. We were bored. And some of us bonded."

"Did you know Phillip, Mr. Truax?"

"Yes, I did."

"You served with my husband."

"Yes. And may I say that he was everything you knew him to be. A true gentleman. Heroic and brave."

Robert had known her husband. He'd known Phillip. He'd seen him before he died.

"How did he die?" she whispered.

"He died in his cot surrounded by friends," Robert said. "He was injured. He had gangrene. It spread. He died just weeks before we were released."

She knew that. She'd received the telegram. "Were you with him when he died?"

"I was," Mr. Truax said, his eyes looking strangely vacant. "Well, I was there shortly after. Another officer was taking a turn by his side when he passed."

Though their words were far beyond anything she'd ever imagined, she forced herself to focus on one thing. "So he didn't die while being interrogated and giving secrets."

"None of us was interrogated," Robert said. "Not really. It was at the end of the war. There was no point."

She gasped. Tried to hold her tears at bay. "But . . ." Her voice drifted off as she tried to wrap her mind around what she'd just learned. "I mean, everyone's been saying he betrayed us all."

"They are wrong," Mr. Truax said without a moment's hesitation. "That rumor is wrong. Phillip betrayed no one. If you only believe one thing I say, ma'am, please know that Phillip Markham died a hero. He was honorable and stoic. He also loved you more than mere words could ever describe."

Tears pricked her eyes. Tears that she'd thought she'd long since stopped crying. The feeling of despair that had clung to her like a heavy, prickly cloak dissipated. It was replaced by something new—a hot, vigilant anger.

She got to her feet. "Why haven't you said anything, Mr. Truax? Why did you not tell me who you were to Phillip when you came? I remember now. Phillip wrote about you, just as he wrote about his other friends. You know how I've been treated here in Galveston. You know how Phillip's memory has been vilified with these lies. How could you have let that continue? How could you have kept your silence?"

"I had no choice."

"Of course you did."

"Ma'am, I did not. I could not betray a confidence."

"What confidence?" she scoffed. "Phillip is dead."

"You don't understand, Miranda. There are things I can't tell you."

"Obviously," she said bitterly.

"There was more at stake than your husband's memory," Robert whispered. "We couldn't betray the cause."

"The cause? As you said, the war is over and we lost. We lost!" she cried out, not even caring that she sounded out of control and shrill. "We lost and so did Phillip."

Sheriff Kern clumsily got to his feet. "Mrs. Markham, please take a chair. You must calm yourself."

She ignored him, still staring in wonder at Robert. "Why? Why did you keep your silence?" She was shaking now. "What confidence are you talking about? The war is over. Nothing that used to matter does anymore."

"That is where you are wrong, ma'am. Every-thing that happened matters. And everything we shared in that god-forsaken camp matters now. It is not forgotten."

Tears now fell unashamedly down her cheeks. "What happened there means more to you than I do? Than what I've been going through? I've been so upset by the rumor everyone's believed . . . I've been hopeless."

"Yes. Well . . ." Sheriff Kern leaned forward, as if he was intending to clasp her hand.

She was very glad he did not. And though it was so difficult, so painful, she forced herself to continue. "I have not wanted to live anymore."

Though both men flushed, neither spoke.

Which was why a sudden, terrible thought entered her mind, took hold, and fairly took her breath away. "Sheriff, are you the one who has been writing me those letters? Are you the one who has been torturing me all this time?"

"Of course not."

But when Kern and Mr. Truax exchanged glances, she felt her insides practically fall apart.

They were still keeping secrets.

And that made her realize her situation wasn't just bad.

It was actually far worse than she'd believed it to be. Maybe far worse than she'd ever imagined.

11

Robert was afraid if he touched her, Miranda would lose the last bit of control she had over her emotions.

She looked that fragile.

She was staring blankly into space. Tears ran unabashedly down her face, unchecked. Robert figured she either didn't notice or didn't care that the tiny drops were cascading down her cheeks. Each one landed on the bodice of her gown and made a small stain.

As he stared at the water marks, the self-loathing he felt deepened.

Across from Robert, Kern stared at her in much the same way Robert was assuming he looked. The sheriff's expression reflected a hundred emotions, each one guiltier than the next.

They needed to do something. Fix this. Fix her pain.

But was there a way to tell Miranda—and Jess —enough about Phillip's undercover work without ignoring Captain Monroe's orders or betraying the very men Phillip had risked so much to protect? Though the war was over, both sides hadn't completely put the battles, injuries, or losses behind them. No soldiers wanted everything they'd done in the name of war to come to light.

As soldiers and officers, they were trained to put their mission and their cause above personal needs. Above any one person's feelings. But their cause had died, along with so many of the men they'd sworn to protect and serve.

And here was a widow who had dealt with the consequences of their actions. In many ways she'd suffered as much as they had.

Was there a way to ease her suffering and make things right . . . without betraying his vow to Captain Monroe? He wasn't exactly sure. All he did know was that he had to at least make an attempt.

"Miranda," he began haltingly. "I know how you must be feeling."

Her eyes flashed. "Forgive me, but you have no idea." Somewhere inside her, she seemed to find the strength to raise her voice. "Ever since I learned Phillip was gone, I've been alone." More tears filled her eyes.

Kern shifted uncomfortably. "I'm sorry for your loss, but of course you are not the only Confederate widow."

"I am not. But I am the only widow in Galveston, Texas, who was burdened with her husband's sins." Looking at Robert with a barely concealed contempt, she added succinctly, "Sins I never believed he had."

"He was a good man, Miranda. What I knew of him, he was brave," Kern said.

She glared at him. "Forgive me, Sheriff Kern, but I don't have any desire to hear you talk about my husband ever again."

Kern flinched. "I never meant to hurt you."

"Yet neither did you help."

"Don't forget, madam, that you kept much of your pain to yourself. I had no idea you had received so many letters."

"I won't forget. How could I ever forget what it felt like to be vilified by my friends? I came here as a young bride, moved into Phillip's house just days before he left for battle, and with his death turned from his bride to his reminder. At first, he was considered a hero like all the other men who fought. But then the lies started, and everyone turned their backs on me."

She drew in a breath, then added, "All because someone made up rumors about him that I now know for certain are not true."

"I will discover who did that," Robert said.

She stilled. "How?"

"I'll find a way."

"Thank you, sir. That explains so much."

Robert knew there was no way he could fully explain either his motives or his reasons. "Let us not dwell on the past, Mrs. Markham. There is nothing we can do or say to make it easier to bear."

"I agree. However, the past is all I have."

He leaned forward. "Not anymore, ma'am. I am here to make sure your future will be far better. Please, trust me to make things right."

But instead of looking relieved, she merely stared at him in loathing. "I don't intend to ever trust you again. You lied to me about who you were as well as your past."

"I did not lie about my past. I told you I served."

"You did not tell me the whole truth about your connection to Phillip. When you arrived, you should have simply told me you served with my husband. I would have been glad to meet you."

"I couldn't. I was bound by my promise to our captain."

"What promise could you have possibly given him that affected me?"

"I was asked to visit you, to make sure you were all right. If you were, I was going to leave and not disrupt your routine."

"My routine. And never tell me who you were?"

He exhaled. "It all sounds convoluted now. All I can say is that my intentions were true. And I will help you now. I promise, I will not leave here until your burdens are lighter."

"Even if I did let you help me, I don't see how

you will ever be able to make my life easier. I don't know how either of you will be able to discover who wrote these letters, who started these rumors."

"We will, Mrs. Markham," Sheriff Kern said. "Whether or not you believe me, I can promise you I intend to keep my word."

"I will earn your trust, minute by minute, hour by hour," Robert vowed. "And while I am working toward that goal, I will do everything in my power to seek out this blackmailer."

"Everything in your power?" she echoed, her voice thick with doubt and sarcasm. "What power could you possibly have?"

At that moment, Robert would have liked nothing better than to share his whole past with her.

Instead, he ached to describe to her in more detail what his childhood was like, to describe just how dirty and hungry he'd been. How lonely. How bitter. How it had felt to join the army and to be so grateful for his meals in basic training that it had caused the other men to ridicule him.

How it felt to fight next to men who believed they were so much better than he was because they were blessed enough to be born to parents who cared.

He yearned to describe the battlefields of the war to Miranda. To tell her the things he'd done.

He ached to share with her the conditions in

their prison camp. The despair they'd all fought. The melancholy, hope, and guilt that filled them, knowing they were merely biding time while their comrades were putting their lives on the line.

Maybe if he shared those things, she wouldn't think he was merely some polished dandy filled with nothing more than empty promises. Maybe then she'd look at him in the eye again. Look at him like he was worth something.

Look at him like he was worthy of her.

But of course, he did none of those things. Instead, he said stiffly, "I would like to think I have some power. But the man your husband and I served under has even more influence than I. I'll send a dispatch to Devin Monroe immediately."

She blinked. "Captain Monroe?"

"Have you heard of him?" Kern asked.

"Yes, of course. Phillip wrote of him. Often." Some of the bitterness that had enveloped her evaporated. "I wasn't aware he had survived the war."

"It is my honor, then, to inform you that he not only survived, but he's made it his calling to ensure that we all survive the war's aftermath. He's the reason I came here to check on you. Once he discovers how terrible your situation actually is, I have no doubt that he will come here to join us."

"But why? Phillip is gone."

"Phillip has passed on to heaven, that is true. But what you might not understand is the depth of his love for you."

"How would you know?"

"He spoke of you often." Feeling a bit bashful, he corrected himself. "Actually, he spoke of you all the time, ma'am. And he made us all aware of you and your goodness." He also told them about her beauty, but he kept that to himself.

Her blue eyes widened. "I . . . I had no idea."

"Before he died, he asked us all to look out for you," Robert continued as he got to his feet. "To my shame, I haven't done much of a good job of that. But eventually I will do him proud."

"We all will, Miranda," Kern said as he stood up. "Somehow, some way, you will be avenged and Phillip's true heroism will be celebrated once again. That is my vow."

Still sitting, she stared up at both of them in obvious wonder. Gazed at them as if she'd never seen them before in her life.

And then, at last, she smiled.

Her smile was beautiful. It was a gift.

Once more, Robert knew it was everything he'd ever desired and never believed he could have. The appreciation of a beautiful woman.

One day, he vowed, he would deserve it.

Bowing slightly, he said, "Again, I am sorry for my deception. I'm going to move out of here, find somewhere else to stay. Perhaps you have a spare room at the sheriff's office, Jess?"

"You don't wish to be around me anymore?" What was she asking?

"Given the circumstances, I think it would be best for both of us if we had some space between us."

"No. Please, don't go." Her tone was desperate.

She'd managed to shock him. "I won't ask for a refund of money," he said slowly.

"It's not the money. It's . . ." She closed her eyes, then stammered, "I simply don't think I can bear to feel like I'm by myself again."

Her honesty was humbling. "Are you sure?"

She nodded. "I have much to come to terms with, but I'd rather have you here than not."

Robert inclined his head. "Thank you, ma'am. I will stay until you tell me otherwise."

"I had best take my leave." Turning to Miranda, Kern bowed stiffly. "Mrs. Markham, I am sorry for my deception. I hope in time you will be able to forgive me."

"I hope so too, sir," she said before he took his leave.

When they were alone, Robert stared at her. Noticed how pale and exhausted she looked.

Wished there was something more to say. But because he felt as if he was out of words, he simply turned and walked with leaden steps to his room.

He needed to go to his desk and write another,

more urgent note to his captain. But at the moment, all he wanted to do was sit and stare out the window and think about all he had almost lost.

Belle approached him just as he reached his room. She looked as hesitant and worried as she had when he'd found her at the sheriff's office. "Belle, what is wrong?"

Her hands were clenching the sides of her white apron. "Mr. Truax, you're not going to leave, are you?" Had she listened to their conversation?

"No, though I probably should. It's improper for me to continue to stay."

"Of course it isn't. Though your reasons for being here might be different, your circumstances haven't changed."

"They have." No, everything had changed. Miranda now thought of him as a liar.

The maid looked skeptical, but still she pressed. "But you're still going to stay."

"I'm going to stay," he promised.

"Good," she said before turning down the hall.

Leaving him with his thoughts.

And he? Well, he now realized Miranda had gotten under his skin. He didn't look into her blue eyes thinking about her husband or his quest to make things right. Instead, he only thought about how he could make a living out of simply gazing into her eyes. Or making them shine.

He no longer sought only to redeem her husband's memory. Instead, when he thought about her, he thought about how gentle she was. How much he cared about her.

He thought about how he wished she was his.

He found himself plotting in the middle of the night ways in which he could try to win her over. Win her heart.

As if he were worthy of such a woman's love.

It was selfish too. Yet again, he was betraying his humble roots. Or maybe it was his selfish, rough nature. He was used to fighting for things he believed in and clawing and grasping at everything he wanted. Somehow in his goal to clear the black mark around Phillip's name he'd interjected his own wants.

This wasn't right in any shape or form. In fact, it was nothing like what he should be doing and everything that was detrimental to both his honor and the honor of his brothers-in-arms.

If Devin Monroe ever discovered just how much he was in danger of losing his heart, he would no doubt demand an apology and expect Robert to bow out of any future missions. Deservedly so.

But until that happened, something had to be done.

He needed to distance himself from her. But more important, she needed distance from him, because if he stayed this close, he was going to find multiple opportunities to seek her out. If he was able to accomplish that goal, he knew he'd use every wile and trick he'd learned on the streets to cajole her to trust him. Eventually, she would grow to trust him. He would take that trust and hold it close.

But he knew himself well. He recognized what he was good at and what he would always be a dismal failure at. Because of that, he knew it was very likely that, sooner or later, he would make an even greater mistake than the ones he was contemplating. He was going to hurt her. Or ruin her reputation.

Or, even worse, she might be so desperate for a kind word, for protection, that she'd grow to depend on him. Maybe even develop feelings.

With him!

If that happened, just like in the thick of battle, he wouldn't hesitate. He'd ask her to marry him. With haste. Because she was, without a doubt, the most enchanting woman he'd ever met.

And if she said yes and they did marry . . . it would be such a mistake. Oh, he'd try his best to be everything she wanted him to be. He'd show her how much he cared for her. He'd profess his love as well.

It would only be later, when the pleasure of

waking by his side faded, that she'd at last look at him with clear eyes. See him for exactly what and who he was and everything he wasn't.

He was a former Confederate officer whose best friends in the world were men he'd met during a long and difficult war.

A man who had learned social niceties from a variety of people, none who would ever be fit company for a lady like her.

She'd see he was a man who was quick to temper and slow to feel remorse. She'd see him for who he was.

And when that happened, he'd see some of the glory fade from her expression. She'd realize that she'd become tainted. And when it was too late, after she'd given him her heart and trust, she was going to wake up one morning and dare to compare him with Phillip Markham.

And the moment she did that, she would realize just what a sorry comparison that was.

He doubted she would ever utter such a thing aloud. Instead, Miranda Markham Truax would most likely keep her regrets and dismay and worries to herself. She'd simply continue to care for him with her head high and her spine straight.

But they both would know.

And then she'd live the rest of their days together pretending she hadn't made a terrible mistake, and he'd spend every moment of it watching her swim in an ocean of regret. It would be tortuous and painful. As painful as getting captured by the enemy and being forced into a Yankee prison camp.

As painful as spending countless days passing time, watching his fellow prisoners write and receive letters home . . . and realizing that he had no one to write to.

It would no doubt be just as painful as watching Phillip slowly die.

That was unbearable.

Therefore, as Robert slowly walked up the stairs, his hand on the gleaming wood banister leading to his room, he came to a decision. He would do everything in his power to uncover the blackmailer, improve Miranda's reputation, and then get out of Galveston.

As soon as possible.

12

How was it that she could experience both devastating heartbreak and exhilarating euphoria in the span of one hour?

Miranda reviewed everything she'd just learned as she paced across the width of her room, paused for the briefest of moments, then turned and paced again.

Never would she have imagined to hear that Robert had actually known Phillip and that he came to see her out of some misplaced vow on her husband's deathbed.

Never would she have imagined that Sheriff Kern, who had practically brushed off her worries a year before, was now offering to be her friend and practically turn the city upside down to find the author of the letters. Both revelations had been such a shock, she felt like crying and laughing at the same time.

However, all that would do was cause her staff to worry about her even more. What she actually needed to do was compose herself and think.

With that in mind, she stopped her relentless pacing and breathed deep. Trying to find comfort in the cool shades of chocolate brown, mint green, and eggshell white that she'd painstakingly decorated with when she and Phillip had first married.

In her naiveté about marriage, she'd attempted to create an oasis of sorts for her husband. She'd had visions of him entering their bedroom, seeing how comforting and beautiful she'd made the room, and somehow feeling refreshed.

In those first days of war, when everyone had reassured each other that their men would be coming home in a matter of days, that there was truly nothing the Yankees could do that their men couldn't do better, she'd sat by the window and waited for Phillip to return.

But as the days turned into weeks and eventually months, she'd known their circumstances were never going to be as easy as she'd hoped and believed.

Later, when Phillip had gotten leave, the man she'd brought to their bedroom was far different from the one she'd first said good-bye to. This Phillip was harder, moody. More sullen and physical. There was a new struggle behind his smooth words and quiet stares that had never been there before, and she hadn't known how to react to it. Small things set him off, sudden movements did too. And when she'd teasingly wrapped her arms around him from behind, he'd turned to her with a curse and almost hit her.

She'd cried out. The look that had appeared on

his face was one she'd never forget. Complete devastation and remorse. That hadn't been hard to accept. Though he'd refused to talk about his life in the cavalry, she'd had a very good idea that war was a terrible, bloody experience. After all, everyone read about the accounts in the papers, heard stories from other men who were far more forthcoming, and, most heart-wrenchingly of all, saw the names of the injured and dead on the lists that appeared in the papers.

So she'd been understanding of his need to keep his secrets. She'd come to realize that he wasn't going to be the same. That war had changed him.

But what had been much harder to come to terms with was the way he'd turned away from her. His smiles had vanished. He'd become silent. And he insisted on sleeping in a separate room, stating that his restless sleeping habits would keep her awake.

No protests from her had made a difference. Neither had her smiles, her understanding, or even her one failed night of seduction. He'd been distant.

The only time she'd found an inkling of the |man she'd fallen in love with had been their last moments together. He'd held her almost painfully close, run his hands over her face, over her hair, over her body as if he needed to remember her by touch alone.

She'd been so grateful for his attention she'd clung to him and allowed him to grip her just a little too hard. Allowed him to mess up her hair, wrinkle her dress. She hadn't cared about anything other than she'd gotten him back for a few precious seconds.

It seemed that she, too, had needed to keep hold of their memories. She'd needed to remember what he felt like against her body. She'd needed to remember everything about him.

And then, of course, all too soon, he was gone.

His loss had been devastating. What had followed had been even harder to live with. Though she'd always been a solitary person, she'd learned that living as a shunned one had been almost unbearable.

And now she learned that, despite his distance, Phillip had loved her very much, so much that he told others about her until his dying days. That was worthy of the euphoria she had felt.

But worse, the cause of the devastation she felt was discovering how many lies she had been told. And the one man in Galveston whom she'd trusted had known they were lies. And now claimed he had to keep more.

She pressed her cheek against the cold window-pane, remembered how cold the windowpane on the landing had felt the morning of Robert Truax's arrival. Back then, the frosty pane had served to wake her up.

Now, however, it merely served as a reminder

of just how much she'd lost and how, for some unknown reason, she was still alone.

"Jesus, why?" she whispered. "I thought you suffered so much so I wouldn't have to. Why do I have to keep being reminded of how hard life is and how fleeting the feeling of security is?"

Closing her eyes, she thought of the verses she'd read time and again. Of how all Jesus' disciples had moved away from him when he was whipped and nailed to the cross. Though she'd never compare her relationships to Sheriff Kern and Robert Truax to Jesus' to his disciples, she couldn't help but feel she had been receiving a hint of what her Savior had been going through. Trusted friends had betrayed him. Trusted friends had chosen other causes instead of Jesus' teachings.

Jesus, of course, had forgiven them.

But now, as she came to terms with the fact that everything she'd believed to be true was once again turned on its side, Miranda realized the unavoidable, ugly truth.

She was not Jesus.

Moreover, it seemed that her suffering was not about to end, either.

Moving from the window, she unfastened her kid boots, pulled down her window shade so darkness penetrated her world, and lay down on the bed. If she couldn't summon up the nerve to end her life, she was simply going to have to escape it for a while.

At least the Lord was still letting her sleep. She took refuge in that and fell into an exhausted slumber.

After Mr. Truax went into his room and Mrs. Markham's room fell silent, Belle wandered about on the upstairs hallway as she contemplated what to do next.

Should she report what she'd heard to the rest of the staff? Surely Winnie and Emerson and Cook would know what to do. However, if she did that, she would be betraying Mrs. Markham's privacy and trust. And though the lady of the house was the primary topic of conversation, it still seemed a betrayal to share something that was most definitely the woman's private business.

But what if she didn't share her news?

Mrs. Markham had looked decidedly depressed and hopeless. Winnie had whispered to her that they all had to be on the lookout for times when their employer got a case of the blues. Because she actually didn't just fight a case of the blues, but battled serious depression.

Winnie had even confessed that once she had seen Mrs. Markham open an upstairs window and lean so far out that she was sure she'd been contemplating a fall.

Was the devastated expression Belle had seen a sign of something horrible about to come?

And what if it was? Miranda Markham's mental state was not any of Belle's business. A grown woman should be able to do harm to herself if she wanted to.

Shouldn't she?

Belle bit her lip. She simply wasn't sure.

As she stared at Mrs. Markham's closed door yet again, she felt her stomach roll into tight knots. How could she live with herself if she didn't do anything?

But . . . what if Mrs. Markham was just fine? The lady would no doubt not thank her for disturbing her rest! And if she had an inkling about what Belle was suspecting of her, there was a very good chance she would get fired. Winnie, Cook, and Emerson wouldn't come to her defense, either. No, they'd let her accept the consequences of her foolish thoughts completely on her own.

But what was the right thing?

She knew. She knew what Jesus would do. She knew what she should do. After all, the Lord never promised an easy life, only that he wouldn't forsake her.

Resolve straightened her shoulders. She was going to have to do this. She was going to have to knock on Mrs. Markham's door and check on her. And if the lady needed her, she was going to have to counsel her. Somehow or some way, Belle was going to need to be the person she'd always hoped to be.

Her mind made up, she turned on her heel and started toward Mrs. Markham's door.

Just as her fist raised, the door behind her opened.

"Belle, what has you in such a dither?" Mr. Truax called out.

"Did I disturb you? I'm sorry, sir," she sputtered.

He ran a hand along his brow, smoothing back a chunk of hair from his face. Revealing his startling dark gray eyes. "You didn't disturb me, but I did hear you mumbling to yourself. It sounded like you were having quite the conversation too."

This was just getting worse. "I'm very sorry."

He paused in mid-nod, then looked at her more closely. "Care to tell me why you are so distraught?"

"Not especially."

"Now I'm afraid you actually are going to have to tell me. I'm intrigued."

"I was just, um, trying to decide whether or not I should knock on Mrs. Markham's door."

"Why would you worry about that?"

"Because . . . I am afraid she is resting?" She couldn't help but pose her statement as a question. Because it was a ridiculous statement, after all. If Belle thought she was resting, then she should leave her in peace.

"You know you are making no sense, right?" He walked toward her. All traces of humor gone from his eyes.

"Yes." She opened her mouth, then shut it just as quickly. Mr. Truax was simply a boarder. She knew she shouldn't bother him with her worries.

But he also seemed to have formed a bond with Mrs. Markham. Did that mean she should trust him?

Folding his arms over his chest, he stared at her intently. "Perhaps you should tell me what you are concerned about."

She bit her lip. Belle knew confiding her worries to a guest was even more of a bad idea than telling Winnie or Cook. However, she also knew Mr. Truax was part of the reason Mrs. Markham was in the state she was in.

A muscle in his jaw jumped. "Let's make this easy, miss. You will tell me what has you concerned. Immediately. And the truth, if you please."

His words might have been cloaked in niceties, but he'd just given her an order. One she didn't dare refuse. "I am worried about Mrs. Markham's emotional state, sir."

He paled. "Say again?"

"I saw her expression when she walked up the stairs," she whispered. "She . . . well, she wasn't in a good way. Sir."

"You mean she was upset."

In for a penny, in for a pound. "I mean she looked hopeless." She licked her lips. "As if she didn't want to live anymore." There. She said it. "We—I mean Winnie, Cook, Emerson, and I—have seen this look before, you see."

Mr. Truax's stunned expression turned hard. "I see. And you . . . ?"

"I was debating whether I should check on her."

His expression became an impassive mask. "Thank you for confiding in me. I'll take care of this now."

"Sir?"

"Go on downstairs, Belle. And please send word to the others that we are not to be disturbed."

Feeling as if she'd just not only lost her job but part of herself, she clumsily curtsied. "Yes, sir."

The moment she started walking down the stairs, she heard Mr. Truax open Mrs. Markham's door. Without knocking.

And then, to her shock, he walked in and shut it behind him.

She would now be left to only guess what he would find on the other side.

13

Some memories of the war were so painful that Robert would gladly trade the loss of one limb if the Lord would remove the images from his mind.

However, since he was pretty sure God didn't necessarily appreciate a man bargaining with him, Robert had long since resigned himself to cope with his flashbacks as best he could. Some methods worked better than others.

After spending too many hours nearly paralyzed by his thoughts, Robert had begun to try to ease those dark thoughts in a variety of ways. So far, the best way he'd found to find relief had been to consciously attempt to never think about the war.

Ever.

After a bit of practice, that method worked rather nicely. Every time his mind would drift toward a particularly horrific event that had played out on the battlefield, Robert would stop himself and concentrate on something at hand. Like music, for example. Or the way a woman smiled at a shopkeeper. Puppies and kittens and babies he saw. Anything that was the complete opposite of the grim realities of war.

But now, as he walked into Miranda Markham's

darkened bedroom, his mind drifted back to one of his most painful nights on Johnson's Island . . . the night after they'd buried Phillip Markham. The burial ceremony itself had been a rather grand affair, given their circumstances. Over a hundred men had gathered together to pray before Robert, Captain Monroe, Thomas, and Major Kelly laid him to rest in the Confederate cemetery.

Captain Monroe, a man always to be counted on for eloquence, spoke about Phillip's love for Galveston Island, honor and chivalry, and of course, his beloved Miranda.

Robert had committed much of Monroe's speech to memory, it had been so beautiful. Their captain had spoken of living life to the fullest, even if it was a shortened one. He'd talked of finding joy in most every blessed event—even those events that didn't seem blessed at all.

And for a while, Captain Monroe's words had given them all a measure of hope and solace. His speech had offered a small amount of understanding in a time when so very little of what had happened to them was understandable.

But then the night had come.

And with that night came silence and men's cries. For Robert, it had also brought with it the realization that never again would he hear Phillip's slow drawl. Never again would Phillip chat incessantly about love and marriage and his beloved Miranda.

Late in the evening, long after midnight, Robert had felt a desolation so strong that it had hurt to breathe. He'd remembered all the men he'd known who had already died. He'd even forced himself to remember the day Rory had passed away.

And then his state of mind had gotten even worse.

For one long, interminable hour, he'd gazed at his sheet and contemplated making it into a rope.

All that had stopped him was the thought of the other men having to bury his body. Digging graves was a grueling and daylong affair. It left one sore and dirty and feeling hopeless. Then, of course, was the pain that he would put his captain through. He'd have to stand up once again and fashion words to comfort the other men.

He'd gone to sleep that night taking some comfort that he was sparing his fellow prisoners that, at least.

Now, as Robert opened Miranda's door, he was instantly inundated with the faint scent of roses that always clung to her skin and hair. Though his instant reaction was to breathe deeply, he pushed that thought away and forced himself to remember that long, painful night when he'd convinced himself to stay alive.

At that moment, even though they were so very different, he realized he felt as one with Miranda. After all, he knew what it felt like to give up hope.

But more important, he also knew the sharp relief that came from making the decision to not give in to despair.

"Lord," he whispered, "please help me out here. Please help me be of use to this woman . . . and not scare her half to death when she realizes I've entered her bedroom unannounced and uninvited."

After waiting a second for the Lord to process his request, Robert cleared his throat. Paused.

His muscles were so tense, he was pretty sure he would be able to hear his heart beating.

When he heard nothing, he cleared his throat. And into the silence, he called out, "Miranda?"

He heard a gasp, then a rustle of taffeta.

Then he could almost feel the tension reverberating from her. "Miranda, it's me. I mean, it's Robert. Truax." He winced. Why was he sounding so tentative now? After all, he came into her boudoir without knocking.

"Robert?"

Her voice sounded confused, not frightened. And not angry. That was something, he supposed. "Yes, it is I."

Through the faint shadows, he saw her scramble from where she'd been resting on top of the bed covering.

And that was when it hit him. She'd been resting, not attempting to kill herself. She'd been asleep and he'd woken her up.

A mere hour after she'd told him he could

stay instead of leave. What had he been thinking?

Robert stumbled backward until his shoulder blades were touching the door. In all of his thirty years, he doubted he'd ever been more embarrassed.

"Why are you here?"

There was only one answer he could give, and that was the truth. "I was afraid for you, ma'am."

She stepped into the light cast by the sheer fabric covering the narrow window next to him. Her dress was rumpled, her hair in disarray. It wasn't loose, but it looked as if a faint breeze could loosen it from its confines.

Her eyes were sleepy looking, her eyelids lower than usual. And her face . . .

He inhaled sharply. There was a sheet mark on her cheek, giving evidence that she'd been sleeping hard.

He had never seen a lady in such a state. Not languid, freshly awoken. Smelling of roses and slumber and still throwing off the faint vestiges of sleep.

His embarrassment faded into longing.

The polite thing to do would be to excuse himself. To turn away. To give her some privacy, or at the very least, the semblance of such. But he found he could no more do that than he could have kept his distance from her if he'd thought she was hurting.

She was everything he'd ever dreamed a fine

woman could be. Beautiful and feminine. Gentle. She encouraged every protective instinct he'd ever had and quite a few feelings of longing that he hadn't known he possessed.

Actually, Miranda was everything her husband, Phillip, had ever claimed her to be when he'd waxed poetic tales about her over the campfires. She was everything he'd said she was and far more than Robert had ever imagined.

And, he realized, she'd taken his breath away.

"Robert, why are you afraid?"

He hated what he was about to say, but he couldn't afford not to be blunt. Looking at her directly, he said, "One of your servants feared for your mental state, ma'am. I decided to make sure you were all right. Perhaps sit with you if you were doing, uh, poorly."

She curved a palm around the top of the wing chair that sat between them. "I don't understand."

He knew she did. Though the light was faint, the rays that did enter the room rested on her face. Illuminating the guilt that shone in her eyes.

"I heard Belle outside your room, ma'am. When I asked her why she was doing that, she confessed she was worried about you. She didn't want to bother you . . . but felt you needed to be checked on."

She shook her head as if she was having trouble

organizing her thoughts. "Mr. Truax, I am so sorry. It seems my servant has overstepped herself. Terribly. I'll speak with her."

"You'll do no such thing."

"Pardon me?"

"You heard me," he said. "She was near tears, she was so worried about you."

"Yes, but—"

"She cares about you, Miranda," he said frankly. "And what's more, she told me only out of kindness to you. You cannot think of punishing a servant for that."

"It was a kindness for my maid to tell one of my guests that she was concerned about her employer's mental state?" Her voice was filled with derision. "Perhaps you were used to such insubordination in the service, but I am not."

Her chin was lifted, her eyes were full of fire. The last of her languidness was now only a memory. She looked indignant and like everything a well-brought-up woman of worth should look like.

But he could tell it was only an act. Her voice was brittle and her posture was so stiff that he feared there was a very good chance she would break.

"Sit down, Miranda," he said harshly.

"It is not your place to tell me what to do. You need to leave."

Ignoring her, he stepped closer. "Madam, I have

been through too much in my lifetime to pretend with you."

"Don't you mean 'anymore'? As in pretend anymore? You lied to me. You knew Phillip. You came here to check on me. Yet, you let me believe you were merely a guest."

"If we're going to say so much to each other, then let us be completely honest," he said, stepping to his left and taking a seat on the small eggplant-colored velvet sofa. "Your husband was a good man. A wonderful man. Furthermore, he was an outstanding officer. He saved all of our lives in one way or another, and observing his death was one of the worst times in my life. But more than anything else anyone will ever know about him, he worshipped you, Miranda."

Her lips parted.

Robert leaned closer, close enough to see the band of dark blue that surrounded her irises. "He. Loved. You," he said slowly, taking care to enunciate each word. "He loved you more than he loved anything else in this world."

"I loved him."

"I know you did. And that is why when it came to our attention that you were not doing well, we decided to pay you a visit."

She sat down. "Who is we?"

"Captain Monroe and me, Miranda. Someone is blackmailing you, threatening you with so-called proof Phillip betrayed the Confederacy if you do not sell this house and leave Galveston."

After a pause, he said quietly, "And I now know that you are at the end of your ability to handle it. Miranda, please allow me to assist you. Please allow me to be someone you can trust. Please allow me to take care of the person who is making you so miserable and ruining one very fine man's reputation."

"Robert, you don't understand. This person is skilled at deceit. If he follows through on his latest threat—even using documents somehow falsified—everyone will believe him, no matter what you say. I will have no choice but to sell this house, and I won't know if I am selling it to the blackmailer or not." Her words were uttered in a halting, clumsy manner.

When he said nothing, only waited for her to continue, she said, "I will lose everything but the money from the sale, which won't be much, given I am branded a traitor's wife. I have little money . . . your help is too late."

"It is not," he replied quickly. Wishing she could trust him, could understand the depth of his regard for her, he added, "I can help you."

"I don't want your money."

"I am speaking about your problems, ma'am. When we discover who has been doing these things, I will ensure that he pays and everyone will know about his lies."

"How could you?"

"That is not something you need be concerned with." The fact of the matter was simply that he knew a great number of ways to bend men to his will. He'd learned many skills when he served, the least of which was strong-arming men to do what he wanted. "Miranda, you need to trust me."

She looked at him with longing in her eyes . . . but it was mixed with doubt. It was obvious that she yearned to trust him but was too afraid. "I trusted the sheriff," she said at last.

"You still can. You can trust Jess Kern."

She shook her head. "You are wrong about that. He lied about being imprisoned with Phillip. It would have meant so much to me to have known that they shared a history, but he didn't care enough about my feelings to inform me of that fact."

"I don't think that was exactly how it went, Miranda."

She continued as if he'd never spoken. "Furthermore, Sheriff Kern never stopped by to tell me who you were when he recognized you."

"Just because he didn't feel he could divulge another man's secrets doesn't mean he won't hold your needs close to his heart."

"Are you on my side or his?" She paused, then asked quietly, "Or are you still more worried about dispelling military secrets than being completely honest with me?"

In spite of himself, he flinched. "We are all on

the same side, Miranda. I promise you this."
Leaning forward, he rested his elbows on his knees. "If you believe anything I say, please know that you can trust Jess Kern, Miranda."

She bit her lip. "All this sounds too good to be true."

Perhaps it was. No doubt something would go wrong in their plan to follow up on their suspicions, and there would be snags.

When she moved to stand and dismiss him, he held up a hand. "I know you would like me to leave, but we still need to talk about the original reason I came in here."

"I cannot discuss that with you."

"I feel differently. Your staff is concerned about you. They are very worried about you."

"I . . ." She swallowed. "My personal problems are not their concern."

It would be so easy to accept her statement. To promise that he would alleviate her worries and then be on his way.

But he had begun to see that he cared about her too much now. She'd become not a mission but a reason to get through each day. In short, she had bewitched him.

Perhaps it was time to see if she, too, was under such a spell. Looking at her closely, he took care to be blunt. Jarring. "I have heard you have been depressed. Beyond depressed." He lowered his voice. "Some might even say suicidal. You said yourself that you have not wanted to live. Do you want to die?"

She gasped, but said nothing.

Robert took her silence as an invitation to push even more. "Miranda, do you, in fact, want to die?"

"I cannot believe you asked me that."

"Yet you didn't answer." Staring at her coolly, he said, "And that, Miranda, is why I am here."

She met his gaze. Stared hard at him. Then got to her feet and strode toward the window and pressed her hands on the cool glass.

If she thought he was going to leave now, then she was sadly mistaken. He was willing to sit on the lumpy settee and stare at her back for as long as it took to get some answers.

After all, as far as he was concerned, that was the real reason he was on Galveston Island. Beyond his loyalty to his unit, beyond his promise to her husband, Robert had agreed to this mission because he needed to know more about himself.

He needed to understand why he'd done the things he'd done and why he'd survived.

He needed to understand why he had been able to get a job and finally flourish while so many men were still suffering from wounds and mental anguish. He needed to understand what was in his soul and in his heart. Only then, at long last, would he be able to find any peace.

14

Do you want to die?

The question was blunt and bordering on blasphemy. It was one she felt no one should ever ask.

Yet Miranda had a feeling she might be the only person on earth who was afraid to answer it.

Which was the problem, Miranda realized. She'd been drifting in and out of her pain for so long, she'd begun to wear her depression like a mantle on her shoulders. After the mind-numbing grief she'd felt from Phillip's death had begun to fade, she'd been at a loss for what to do about her future. For too many years she'd felt confused and adrift.

But she'd had her home. Phillip's mother and sister were bitterly hurt that Phillip had made provisions to ensure she would always have the house as her home and not his family. But then she learned they were working with lawyers to try to contest Phillip's will, and she'd known she must do something.

When Winifred and Emerson, her longtime servants, had suggested that she turn the big mansion into a boardinghouse as a way to solve her financial problems, she'd first been aghast. Phillip would have never wanted her to live with strangers. He had often told her he liked taking care of her and seeing to her needs, much to his mother's dismay.

Miranda couldn't come to terms with the idea of converting his family's home into a place of work. But when their lawyer's letters had gotten forceful enough for Miranda to have to hire her own to fight them, the little money she had left began to run out.

Uncovering a force of will she hadn't even known had existed inside of her, she'd known it was time to take action. Therefore, she'd followed Winifred and Emerson's advice and opened the Iron Rail to boarders.

Oh, but those first few days after she'd placed that advertisement had been nerve-racking! Many of their friends had been scandalized, and acquaintances who had always looked down on her because she was not from Galveston blatantly turned their backs on her. Doubts had begun to set in.

She'd been sure she'd done something unforgiveable.

But then, one Tuesday, two things happened within three hours of each other. She'd received a telegram reserving a room for two weeks. Moments later, a gentleman had showed up and asked for a room for the evening. God had provided.

He'd paid when he arrived and had been both extremely respectful of her and appreciative of the mansion.

Winifred had cooked him a simple supper and Emerson had shined his boots. And in the morning he'd not only left a sizable tip, but promised he would return . . . and spread the word about her charming establishment.

And with his departure, she'd realized there was a chance that she was going to be okay after all. She'd started to think of herself as a survivor. She wasn't broken; she was mending. She was going to make Phillip proud.

However, she soon received her first threatening letter. The words had been ugly and cruel. That note had torn her apart and had reminded her of just how alone in the world she was.

But boarders and guests had continued to come and their company had soothed her soul. Until the letters came every week and the animosity she felt from everyone in her circle of friends had become more intense as rumors about both Phillip and her spread.

She hadn't understood it. Couldn't think of what she had possibly done to deserve such ire, such treatment. Why did everyone believe these lies? She even asked her best friend, Mercy, about it. Mercy had been by her side when she'd married Phillip, had held her hand when she'd first heard that Phillip had been captured.

She'd stayed with Miranda for days after they learned he'd died.

Miranda had turned to Mercy when Mr. Winter had first leered at her and the first time two women she'd known walked by her without acknowledging her. Almost as if she were a fallen woman.

But as she'd confided all her fears and worries to her best friend, a change had occurred. Instead of being supportive and optimistic, Mercy's expression had become shuttered. Instead of offering Miranda advice, Mercy had shuttled her out of her house.

And then had become as distant and aloof as everyone else.

That betrayal had been so difficult, almost as if she were experiencing another death. But this time, there seemed to be no one around her to lean on. Somehow, for some reason, she was all alone.

She'd begun a downward spiral after that, and it had culminated with the morning she'd not only contemplated jumping from the window, but gone so far as to open the pane.

But yet . . . she hadn't jumped.

Did that mean something? Did that mean she cared enough about her life to keep it? Or was she merely too afraid about failing in her suicide attempt?

Only to herself had she been able to admit that she hadn't been sure.

But now, with Robert staring at her, practically willing her to confront the truth, even when it was so shameful that she knew she'd barely been able to admit it to herself, she yearned to say that she did not want to die.

She blinked. Realizing that she felt more certain about that than ever before. She did not want to die. She wanted to breathe and walk and talk to other people and plan.

And even remember.

"I . . ." Perversely, the words felt stuck on the tip of her tongue. It was as if her brain was telling her one thing but her mouth was completely incapable of following its directions.

Still Robert watched her.

His attention, so intent, so unwavering, made her lungs tighten. It made her pulse skitter and race in a panic.

Abruptly, she looked at him, afraid he was going to stare at her impatiently. Show her that he was like everyone else in her life. Remind her that she wasn't worth his time, his conversation, or even his compassion.

But when their eyes met, she saw only acceptance. And patience. He wasn't waiting for her to be a different person. No, he was simply waiting for her to find herself.

That enabled her to find her bearings. She

breathed deeply and forced herself to concentrate on this moment. Not the past, not an uncertain future.

Buoyed by that, she gathered herself and breathed in deeply. Finding success, she inhaled again. And felt hope.

It was as if God had finally spoken to her and blessed her. He'd taken so much, but he'd given her this man.

Oh, she didn't expect Robert to stick around. She didn't expect him to even become her friend. But he was there for her at that moment, and the feeling of happiness that accompanied it was so sweet she almost felt giddy.

Suddenly, Miranda knew she had to tell Robert about her thoughts and her worries. About her hopes too. She had to convince him that she wasn't as bad off as everyone feared.

And, she realized, she had to convince herself that she was worth his time and attention. Somewhere inside of herself she was the same person she'd always been. The girl who had met handsome Phillip Markham at a soldiers' ball and enchanted him. The girl who had bravely hugged her husband with a bright smile before he went off to war, not wanting his last memory of her to be one of tears.

Suddenly, she was living, breathing, feeling.

She was alive.

"I do not want to die," she said at last. "I . . . I,

well, for a time, I wasn't so sure about that, but now I realize I want to live this life that was given to me. Even if it's not perfect." She closed her eyes. Had there ever been a greater understatement? "I mean, even if it is painful, right now I realize I want to feel that pain."

Slowly, he got to his feet. Looked at her steadily. And finally nodded. "Good."

She thought he was going to turn around. She was certain he was ready to leave the room. Be rid of her now that he wasn't afraid she was going to jump or collapse or do whatever else he imagined she was on the verge of.

But he didn't do that at all.

"It's going to be all right, Miranda," he murmured as he approached her. "You are not alone any longer. I will not leave you to face everything by yourself," he said as he carefully wrapped his arms around her.

"I, too, have suffered, but I got stronger. You will get stronger too," he whispered as he brought her into his embrace and held her close.

His warmth, his very being, felt so comforting that she allowed herself to relax. With great deliberation, she placed one hand around his waist, then the other. Leaned her cheek against his clean, starched shirt.

And clung to him.

Robert Truax, former second lieutenant in the C.S.A. and comrade of Phillip's, had become important to her. Not just because he was a handsome man. Not just because he had almost become a friend.

But because he believed in her.

And because right then, right at that moment, she believed in herself too.

She wasn't perfect, but she was alive.

She wasn't strong, but she could be.

She wasn't happy, but she had hope.

Furthermore, she was standing. She was blessed. She was being held.

She had not fallen yet.

15

It was never easy to ask for help. However, Robert had learned the hard way that it was far more difficult to face the consequences of failing by himself.

Because of that, combined with last night's memory of holding Miranda Markham fairly burning in his chest, he'd pulled out his quill and forced himself to compose the letter he hadn't wanted to write. Jess was now an ally, but Robert needed more.

I have learned, sir, that Mrs. Markham's difficulties are even worse than I had surmised. I have told you that her friends have abandoned her, even her best friend. Men who are so far beneath her that they should be doing nothing but begging for a kind smile are treating her as a pariah. Now I've learned that she has been receiving threatening letters for a year and is being blackmailed with the threat of some kind of false proof that Phillip was a traitor. All that on top of insinuations thatshe has dishonored her husband with other men.

In addition, she is still recovering from the loss of her husband.

In summation, she is a woman who has been through too much and has almost given up hope.

As Robert stared at his last sentence, his handwriting barely legible with poor penmanship and hopelessly cramped, he found himself smiling.

Because he'd been able to add one single word that changed everything.

That "almost" meant the difference between a chance of optimism and the knowledge that there was very little anyone was going to be able to do for Miranda Markham.

Last night, she'd realized she had much to live for.

When he'd thrown caution to the wind and enfolded her in his arms, she'd clung to him. That moment, that experience of holding her close, smelling her sweet scent, of knowing that she trusted him when she trusted so few . . . well, it had changed him.

Over the last two weeks, Robert's goals had changed. He'd come to Galveston to honor his friend, to fulfill a promise he'd made to a dying man whom he greatly admired. Then he'd gotten to know Miranda. Little by little, he'd begun to understand Phillip's fascination with his wife.

Then, practically out of the blue, he'd felt a tenderness toward her that had nothing to do with dark promises and everything to do with the woman he couldn't seem to take his eyes off.

He'd become smitten. No, entranced. She was a wonder. No, wonderful. He now wanted to make her happy. Not because he could ease her problems but because he, Robert Truax, was a man she had come to admire too.

He wasn't necessarily proud of his feelings. Part of him felt like he was betraying a close friend's trust. However, the greater part of him, the part that had survived life on the streets and a long war, was far more pragmatic. Life was meant for surviving. And sometimes, if a person was blessed, he might experience love too.

Blinking, he pushed last night's memories from his mind and refocused on his report to Captain Monroe.

Because of the wealth of her problems, and because I did not at first tell Miranda my connection to Phillip and have for the time being lost some of her trust, I feel I must stay here even longer. The sheriff here is Jess Kern. Though I do not remember him, he tells me that he, too, was imprisoned at Johnson's Island the same time we were. He has fostered a tenuous friendship with Miranda. I believe he sincerely wants to uncover the author of the threatening letters, and I have taken him into our confidence. Not about everything, of course, but about our mission to help Miranda. I trust him.

Taking all the above into account, I am humbly asking for assistance, Captain. I fear if I continue to navigate her problems single-handedly in light of all you and I know, there is a chance of failure.

We both know that is not an option. Please advise at your earliest opportunity.

Yours respectfully,
Robert

After marking and sealing the letter, Robert addressed it neatly, blotted the ink, and walked downstairs.

To his surprise, he didn't come across Miranda, any of her servants, or even another guest. In fact, it was unusually quiet for eleven in the morning.

He wondered why. He knew enough about the workings of the house to have a pretty good idea of what everyone usually did at this time of day. Actually, this late-morning hour was one of the busiest. Winnie and Belle cleaned rooms and Emerson was either cleaning fireplaces, washing windows, or tending to the winter garden outside.

Miranda herself spent her time working in her parlor, answering correspondence or greeting new guests. Not that he had seen more than one other guest the entire time he had been there.

But there was no sign of anyone anywhere.

His curiosity was slowly being replaced by worry and a vague sense of trepidation. Stuffing the letter in his vest pocket, Robert headed toward the kitchen. Perhaps Cook had prepared some jam tarts or some other delicacy and they were sampling the items. Miranda had told him that happened from time to time.

Just outside the kitchen, he heard voices. He breathed a sigh of relief and congratulated himself on not jumping to conclusions and making things seem worse than they were.

Opening the door, he grinned. "Cook, what treat have you made today? And please tell me you saved me a sample," he called out.

Then he froze.

Miranda and her four servants were standing together and staring at a pair of thin women dressed in unrelieved black. One was older and looked to be in frail health. She was sitting on one of the hard kitchen chairs, grasping the armrests as if she was using them to keep herself upright.

The other woman had dark hair and hazel eyes. High cheekbones. She looked like the feminine version of Phillip Markham.

But that was where the similarities ended. Whereas Phillip always had a smile on his face and a rather easygoing patience about him, this woman was birdlike and sharp and agitated.

She was also staring at him in the way he'd always looked at two of their Yankee guards. Those men had been sloth-like and unkempt. Unfit and undisciplined. They were men who would have done poorly in Monroe's unit, and presumably weren't even fit for fighting in the Union army since they'd been able-bodied and designated to serving on an island in the middle of the Great Lakes.

Because he was as different from those men as night and day, Robert raised his chin and boldly stared right back at the woman. Phillip had never told him he had living relatives, and why had Miranda not mentioned these two?

"Who are you?" the younger one asked rudely.

Before he could answer, Miranda walked to his side. "This is Robert Truax, Viola," she said in a tremor-filled voice. "He served with Phillip."

Viola scanned him with disdain. "What is he doing here?"

"He is staying as a guest," Miranda said quickly. "I believe he has some business to tend to here in Galveston."

She was attempting to shield him, Robert realized with a bit of shock. Miranda was trying to shield him from these two spiteful women.

He would have been amused if he hadn't been

so sincerely touched. He was six foot one, was well muscled, and had been blessed with a bright mind. He'd grown up unafraid to use his fists to get what he wanted.

In addition, he had been an officer in the Confederate militia. He was used to commanding scores of men. He was used to being the person doing the shielding and guarding.

On top of that, he'd made himself into a gentleman. He prided himself on his ability to shelter the weaker sex.

He accepted that and had enjoyed the feeling of worth that had given him.

He did not enjoy the sight of Miranda fretting about him.

"Yet another man ruining your reputation, I see," the old lady muttered.

When Miranda shook her head and visibly prepared herself to respond, Robert had had enough. "To whom am I speaking?" he asked curtly, in the same tone he'd used to snap at insolent corporals during training exercises.

When the lady did not answer, only inhaled sharply, Miranda once again rushed to the rescue. "Forgive my poor manners. Robert, may I present Viola and Ruth Markham, Phillip's sister and mother. Ladies, as I said, this is Robert Truax. He was one of Phillip's fellow officers in the C.S.A. and one of his best friends. He was also captured and imprisoned at Johnson's Island."

The elder Mrs. Markham sniffed. "But you lived."

It seemed her audacity knew no bounds. Lifting his chin, he stared at her directly. "Indeed, I did."

Noticing that Miranda was wringing her hands, he looked at the servants. All four of them were wearing pinched, uncertain expressions.

That made no sense. He knew enough about the management of a household to realize that a mistress's ill-behaved guest had little effect on the state of the servants. Even as close as their bond was with Miranda, there was no reason, as far as he could see, for why they were standing in the kitchen and looking so awkward and nervous.

"Why is everyone in the kitchen?"

"It is no concern of yours, boy," Viola said.

Before Miranda could run interference again, he spoke. "No one has dared to call me that since I was old enough to make sure they regretted it, Miss Markham. I have no intention to begin accepting it now."

Viola flinched, but otherwise had no response.

"Viola and Mrs. Markham arrived an hour ago, sir. They came to share with me that their lawyer has discovered a way to take the house away from me." After visibly gathering her composure, she added, "After this announcement they insisted on a tour of the home."

"A tour? If this was your son's, I am sure you know it well."

"Mrs. Markham wanted to meet the staff. Her new staff."

"We were interviewing them to see if they have any qualities that would necessitate them staying," Viola said with a note of satisfaction in her voice.

"Is that right?" he drawled.

Miranda's eyes flashed. "I put a stop to it." Her voice turned to ice. "As a matter of fact, I was just attempting to tell them that this was not settled when you came in."

"No, it does not seem settled at all," he agreed as he noticed that both Viola and her mother looked terribly uncomfortable. And Miranda? Well, Miranda looked madder than a wet hen.

Robert was so proud of her. This was the first time, at least in his presence, when she had believed in herself enough to stand up to the naysayers. It proved that she truly had had a transformation the evening before. But again, why hadn't she told him about these two presenting yet another threat to her well-being?

He hated that he couldn't smile at her and tell her how proud of her he was. Instead, he did something that was probably even better, and that was to succinctly inform these two biddies that they were mistaken about the house becoming theirs. Miranda and her staff needed them off the property as soon as possible.

"Miranda was Phillip's beloved wife," he said.

"She was his wife," Mrs. Markham said. "She was also his mistake."

Miranda shook her head. "No, that is not true."

When the old lady inhaled sharply, Robert hardened his voice. "You can say many things, ma'am, but you will never be able to deny your son's complete and utter devotion to Miranda. He adored her. He carried her picture around on his person and gazed at it constantly. He wrote to her daily. And when he wasn't doing those things, he was talking about her. She was his world."

Mrs. Markham looked like she'd just swallowed a particularly sour pickle. "She might have been those things, but she has since become his liability."

"Never that." He made sure to interject enough force in his words to cut off any further discussion, at least there in the kitchen. "Now, I suggest we leave this room and allow Miranda's staff to continue with their duties."

"You are overstepping your bounds, sir," Mrs. Markham said.

"I think not."

Just as the lady was about to speak, Miranda cut in. "Everyone, it is time for this discussion to end. Robert, thank you for joining us, but I feel we all have better uses of our time than continuing this debate. Viola and Ruth, if you would like to stay here for the night, please let Winifred know. She will take you up to your rooms. Otherwise, I fear you have outstayed your welcome. It is time for you both to take your leave."

Ruth got to her feet. When Robert attempted to offer her his hand, she batted it away.

"What about your staff?" Viola asked.

Turning to the four people who were still standing in a small row but now wearing far more relaxed expressions, Miranda said, "Do you need directions for your duties?"

"No, ma'am, we do not," Winnie said with a glare at the two interlopers.

"Very well then," Miranda replied. "Ladies, if you will follow me, please?"

Though Viola looked ready to argue, her mother walked toward the door. Robert stood to one side as Miranda led the ladies out of the kitchen, down the short gap between the kitchen and main house, and finally inside again.

When they heard the last door click shut, Robert turned to the servants. "How bad was it?"

"Not as bad as it could have been," Belle said.

"Do they come here often?"

"They used to come once a month," Emerson replied. "But it's been almost six months since they stopped by. I suppose they were due to make an appearance."

Winnie shook her head. "They're up to something. They must feel that they have something with that lawyer."

Belle shivered dramatically. "I am not going to be able to work for those biddies."

"You won't have to worry about them," Cook said. "They're gonna fire us right away. They're not going to want anyone who was loyal to Mrs. Markham. Mrs. Miranda Markham, I mean."

"I fear you are right," Robert agreed. "However, try not to let their visit worry you too much. Something about their confidence didn't sit well with me. I'll look into it."

"All I can say is that Mr. Phillip would be rolling over in his grave if he knew how his mother and sister were treating his wife. He treated her like gold, he did."

"I wasn't aware that you had worked here when Phillip lived here."

"I've been here for years. Mr. Phillip hired me when he first inherited the mansion. Emerson too. I was here when he brought home his bride, and thank goodness his mother and sister had already moved out."

"Besotted, he was," Emerson said.

Winnie shook her head. "They were in love. He doted on her. And Miss Miranda? Well, she was a sweet little blushing thing. Remember, Audrey?"

Cook fanned her face. "Don't want to shock you, Mr. Truax, but Mr. and Mrs. Markham only had eyes—and hands—for each other. Practically spent their first week of married life in their room."

Robert laughed. "It's going to take more than the amorous affections of a newly married couple to shock me, Winnie!" Sobering, he said, "Your description doesn't sound much like the lady I've met."

"She was hard hit by him going off to war. He came back three times, but each time he returned, he looked more weary and thin. And, I am afraid, more distant. She worried about him fiercely. Then when word came about his imprisonment and then death . . . well, she changed."

"And his family didn't support her?"

"No. The older Mrs. Markham had a different woman in mind for Phillip. When he ignored her wishes, she wasn't happy. Then when he was on leave, he didn't want to give them any time at all and they resented it," Winnie said. "But they were still respectful to her."

"But when the lawyer read the will, everything changed."

"They became mean as snakes, they did," Winnie said. "To our Mrs. Markham and to us."

"I was afraid to be in the same room as them!" Belle said.

Robert didn't even try to hide his smile. "I can imagine why."

"Do you truly think you can help our mistress with them?" Winnie asked.

"Yes," he said after a pause. He almost said he would try his best. Then he realized that such a promise was not only going to mean little, it wasn't true. He'd come here to make Miranda Markham's life better and he was going to do that. If he couldn't handle these women and their lawyer by himself, he would contact as many of his fellow comrades as it took. They'd made each other a promise to see their lives through and he intended to do just that.

No one had ever claimed their journeys would be easy. On the contrary, no one had imagined it would be. Monroe had practically guaranteed that the road to recovering their lives after the war would be anything but simple or quick.

But after the things they'd been through, Robert felt he probably wouldn't even trust something simple or quick. Experience had shown that trial and pain and patience and hard work were what guaranteed success.

That was what he understood and had faith in.

"Now, I had best see how Mrs. Markham is doing with her relatives. Winnie, if you would accompany me, please? If the women are staying, we'll need you to see to that."

"Yes, sir," Winnie said as she bustled to his side. "Though, if I may be so bold, I have to tell ya that I don't think they'll be staying."

"You sound certain," he commented as he opened the back door to the kitchen and ushered the portly housekeeper through.

"I am." With a look of distaste, she added, "They come here to make her miserable, they do. If she's turned the tables on them, then their fun ain't going to be the same. They'll head back to their own home."

Opening the door to the main house, something occurred to Robert. Before they entered the doorway, he said, "Winnie, it just occurred to me that I don't know where they live. Are they on the island?"

She shook her head. "No, they live just on the other side of the bay. They'll have to take the ferry across. But if they can't take it today, they'll stay somewhere else."

"Such as?"

"One of the elder Mrs. Markham's friends. I believe she has at least one or two who haven't turned against her because of the rumors about her son."

Now that they were in the back hallway in the main house, he lowered his voice. "Do you know these friends of hers? Do you know anything about them?"

"I know staff at a couple of their houses, but

we don't speak much to each other. Not anymore."

"Did they not have use for you after the rumors began or did you choose not to associate with them?"

"We chose not to associate with them, of course."

Robert shook his head. "I'm sorry. I was a soldier for years. I have no knowledge of what it is like to be a gossiping woman, or to have a staff to do that."

"It's like this, sir. Mr. Markham being thought of as a traitor is a terrible thing. But no one seems to know how such a rumor started. And Mrs. Markham's disintegrating reputation is difficult to hear but not so hard to believe. But her actions weren't what started the mean talk. And these threatening letters . . . well, they're filled with information that shows the writer knew a lot. A whole lot."

Now Robert wished he and Jess had asked to see all the letters.

Lifting her eyes to his meaningfully, she said, "All that got me to thinking about who has the most to gain from all this talk."

"I see," he said. "Any idea who it is?"

"Well, I've got my ideas, and they begin and end with the two women who were sitting in that kitchen like they have any business even to step foot in it."

"Do you think Mrs. Markham suspects them?"

"No, sir. I don't think any of us has imagined

Lt. Markham's own family would want to hurt his reputation. But they do have resentments about this house."

"Thank you for your honesty, Winnie."

"No, sir. Thank you for caring."

Stunned at how much her words meant to him, he strode into the mansion's foyer. He'd intended to go up the stairs and knock on Miranda's door, but there was no need. She was standing by the front window, her focus completely fixed on the two women's retreating forms.

"Did they leave, Miranda? Or have they simply gone outside to tell their driver and collect their belongings?"

She turned his way. "They are gone," she said with a bit of wonder in her voice. Then, still gazing at him, she smiled.

Truly smiled. It was beautiful.

16

Though she couldn't exactly be sure, Miranda knew there had been a time when she had neither trusted nor loved Phillip Markham whole-heartedly. She was old enough and wise enough now to realize that love was not instantaneous.

It just was sometimes difficult to remember such a time.

She recalled their initial meeting as clearly as if it were yesterday. She'd gone in her family's carriage with her cousin Beatrice to Houston. After hours of primping and prepping, they walked into the assembly hall fairly bursting with exuberance.

An orchestra was playing, flowers were planted in vases, and there were so many men in resplendent gray and gold that Bea had actually gasped at the sight. And in the middle of it all was Phillip.

He had recently graduated from West Point. In addition, his family had purchased him commissions. Therefore, he was a striking, young second lieutenant who was a little in awe of his company when she and her cousin entered.

He and several men his age were talking to a

pair of older-looking officers next to a table laden with lemonade and cookies. His hands were loosely clasped behind his back, and he was nodding at something one of the older men was saying.

Miranda thought he was the most handsome man there.

"Oh! There's James!" Beatrice had squealed.

Miranda giggled when Bea practically dragged her across the room toward the men. "Watch out, Beatrice," she'd cautioned. But in truth, she hadn't minded getting pulled along. The men they were approaching were handsome, debonair, and close to their ages.

They were also standing conveniently far from the long line of seated chaperones. The older women were gossiping and sipping tea. No doubt feeling they had fulfilled their duties by simply showing up.

Walking toward the young officers by her cousin's side, Miranda had felt so grown up and full of herself. At last she was in the big city. She was dressed like a lady and even had her hair styled into an elegant twist. She had on a tight corset that reduced her waist to nineteen inches and enough crinolines and petticoats under her skirt to feel as if she were floating instead of merely walking. She wasn't a particularly vain girl, but she knew she had never looked so fine.

And then Phillip lifted his head and looked

her way. He had curly blond hair, light blue eyes, and dimples. She thought he looked like an angel. And then he smiled at her.

And she? Well, she lost her heart right then and there.

The rest of the night was a blur of emotion. He bowed gallantly when they were introduced. She stammered and pretended she wasn't affected. When he immediately asked for her dance card and filled in his name in three places, she stopped pretending and enjoyed the attention.

Dancing in his arms had surpassed every girlish dream. He held her properly and sure, his right hand curving protectively on her waist. In between dances, he stood on the side and watched her dance with his friends. She'd had no experience in courtship or relationships, but even she knew he'd marked her as his.

And instead of being dismayed or afraid, she'd been glad.

After their three dances and countless glasses of lemonade and one long stroll along the building's back balcony, it was time to go. And then he raised her gloved hand to his lips and pressed his lips to her knuckles. She was so entranced she wished she could feel his touch on her bare skin.

Miranda had no doubt she would have stayed with Phillip until dawn broke if not for Beatrice and her mother's insistence that it was time to leave.

But when she finally turned away from him, trying not to cry, Miranda knew that in that one evening she had forever changed. Phillip Markham might not have been perfect, but he'd been perfect for her. And by the time they settled back into their awaiting carriage Miranda knew she had fallen in love.

In fact, Miranda had known without a shadow of a doubt that if he had proposed to her that evening she would have said yes.

She did say yes not even one month later and they were married the very next day. Her love for Phillip had been wild and overwhelming and all-consuming.

And then, of course, he went to war, and the battles that no one expected to happen did. Phillip fought and marched and commanded men. He'd been imprisoned and finally gone to heaven.

And she learned that just as nothing ever began from nothing, nothing ever lasted forever.

Now, as she looked at Robert Truax standing in the foyer of her boardinghouse so seriously, Miranda didn't know if she was falling in love. Part of her hoped that certainly wasn't the case. If she was falling in love, why, it made no sense.

Robert was nothing like Phillip. He was hard and bull-nosed where Phillip had been caring and amiable. He was rough around the edges where Phillip had always been smooth elegance. He was also direct and blunt and loud and willful.

She'd suspected Phillip was many of those things as well, but he'd always taken care to shield her from his baser emotions and actions.

Robert may have secrets, but he didn't hide anything he was.

For some reason, she found his honesty about himself strangely compelling. Attractive.

He was also going to move on one day soon. Even if he asked, Miranda wasn't sure if she'd leave with him. As hard as her life had been in Galveston, it was also her home.

All she currently understood was that she needed Robert right now. She was grateful for his presence, she liked being in his company, and she was tired of pretending that she didn't care about him.

Noticing that he was still standing still, his expression carefully void of any emotion, she walked to him.

Knowing he was still reeling from her in-laws' visit, she attempted to lighten the mood. "Before they left, my mother-in-law said I was a sinner and an embarrassment to the Markham name." She smiled slightly so he would know that she wasn't too terribly hurt by the hateful statement.

But instead of looking amused, a muscle in his jaw clenched. "And Viola? What did she say?"

"I believe it was something to the effect that she was glad her brother had died so he would not be able to witness the type of woman his wife has become." She did her best to remain looking amused, though Viola's words had been difficult to hear.

Robert sighed. "Miranda, I have heard a lot in my lifetime. But I have to tell you that I've never been forced to listen to any statements more appalling."

"It wasn't that bad. You've been on the battlefield, after all."

"I've also lived on the streets. But try as I might, I can't think of any person who would target a lady such as you with such purposely cruel words." His voice lowered. "I beg your pardon, but I don't believe I had ever had the misfortune to meet such ill-mannered women in my life before today."

Though the women's words did pinch her feelings, Miranda realized they hadn't devastated her. Furthermore, she couldn't help but agree with his assessment.

"They certainly did come here with cruel intentions. I think they would have fired my whole staff and put them on the streets if they had been able to." Thinking of how upset and dismayed they looked, she added, "I'm going to need to visit with them later and assure them that even if the worst happens I'll look after them as best I can."

Robert began pacing. "Have they always treated you as such?"

"No. They were nicer when Phillip was alive.

But they were always rather judgmental, I'm afraid. As I told you, I didn't have a lot of city polish and Phillip was quite a catch. They never thought I was good enough."

"They were wrong. Phillip Markham was a man of many good qualities, and as far as I can tell, you are his equal in every way."

"I don't know if that is quite the case, but it is very kind of you to say. For what it's worth, Phillip was never particularly close to them. They didn't visit all that often."

Robert paused to stare at her. "I can't imagine that he would have wanted them here. What's more, I shudder at how he would have reacted if he'd witnessed such a scene. The man I was honored to know wouldn't have allowed any person to speak to you in such a manner."

"Well, they wouldn't have spoken to me that way if he was here."

Robert resumed his pacing. "I can't believe he comes from that same family! The women were cold hearted and vindictive. Even when we were in prison, I never heard Phillip speak unkindly to anyone." For the first time, humor entered his features. "Not even the guards." He waved a hand. "Why, even when he was bossing us around, he was a gentleman. It used to annoy me to no end."

"I imagine it would have. You don't seem like the kind of man to say please and thank you while being told to march."

He chuckled. "I'm afraid I wasn't that kind of man even on my best days. And that, of course, is why Phillip was about to be made captain and I was advised to shape up and quickly." At last, he stopped pacing and leaned against the banister leading upstairs.

"The problem, I believe, is that Mrs. Markham never wanted Phillip to marry me. She wanted him to marry one of the local girls."

"Instead, he chose you."

"He did. We had a whirlwind courtship. I think she might have come to accept me if Phillip had taken more of a concern for her feelings. I learned after Phillip brought me here that Ruth was hurt that he hadn't brought me to her for approval before he proposed."

"I wonder why he didn't do that."

"There wasn't time." Feeling her cheeks flush, she corrected herself. "Rather, we didn't make time. We fell in love almost on sight and corresponded with each other for barely one month before he proposed. Actually, the moment he was given permission to obtain a week's leave, Phillip came to my house, informed my parents that he couldn't go into battle without making me his wife, and literally whisked me away."

Robert fanned his face dramatically. "My goodness. Who knew Phillip had such impetuousness in him?"

"I suppose I did."

"Your romance sounds like a fairy tale. It's good your parents gave their permission." He paused. "I'm assuming they did give their permission?"

She nodded. "My father said he and my mother worried that I'd simply elope if they didn't give their blessing."

Robert raised both his eyebrows. "I guess you both were rather willful back then."

"Oh, yes. Seriously, I think they would have been shocked if it hadn't been Phillip. But it was." She shrugged. She had never been one to make the deceased into saints or paint them as perfect. But Phillip actually had been very close to perfect. "We got married that evening in Houston and he brought me here the next day. His mother and sister knew what he was going to do, and they left the premises immediately. My mother had all my things delivered here over the next few weeks, and we packed up theirs and sent them to their new home across the bay."

He stared at her for a long moment. "You are blessed to have known such love, Miranda."

"Yes, I am."

"Before all this hullabaloo, I came downstairs to post a letter. Would you care to accompany me?" His voice gentled. "We could take care of your weekly deposit at the bank as well."

"Yes, thank you. I would like to accompany you very much," she admitted. Perhaps it was time to reclaim a little bit of that impetuousness she once had.

Looking down at the gown she was wearing, she knew it wouldn't do. "Robert, would you be able to wait a few minutes? I need to change my gown. I promise I'll hurry."

For the first time since he walked into the foyer, something tender entered his expression. "Mrs. Markham, I may not be the gentleman Phillip Markham was, but even I know never to rush a woman." They had stepped from the foyer into the parlor, and now he walked over to one of the wing chairs situated in front of the for-once roaring fireplace. "I'll cool my heels here as long as you need. So take your time."

The absurdity of his words made her flirt a bit. "Your offer is very gallant, Mr. Truax. However, I'll do my best to make sure your heels don't have too long to cool in front of the flames."

He laughed. "Touché, madam."

His laughter rang in her ears the whole way upstairs.

Even though she'd told him she wouldn't take long, Miranda still tarried. For some reason, she decided her chignon wasn't pinned right. And then she had to try on two different hats.

Finally, she had to collect her latest monies to deposit. She had had even less business than normal, which meant that she had an even smaller amount than usual. If not for Robert's payment, her financial situation would have fallen into even further precarious territory.

Therefore, it was a full forty minutes later when she returned downstairs. "I do beg your pardon. Here I promised I would be quick and I took an even longer time than I usually do."

"I still didn't mind." Walking to the wardrobe, he pulled out her cloak. "Now, let's get you as warm as possible. I do believe there was frost on the ground this morning."

She doubted that, but she allowed him to assist her with her cloak. Moments later, they were walking together toward town. She wasn't clutching his arm, but she might as well have been.

The last time they'd walked together, she had been nervous and tense. Worried about not only everyone around them but also Robert himself. People like Kyle Winter and Mercy had tainted her trust. She'd been afraid of him and couldn't bear to believe anything he said.

Now, however, she felt as if he was her one true ally.

Whether from Robert's appearance or if her time of purgatory had finally ended, several men and women acknowledged her. Oh, they didn't actually greet her and stop to pass the time, but they didn't ignore her completely like they usually did.

The idea that she no longer was going to be despised made her feel like laughing. She settled for a bright smile.

Robert noticed. "What's that smile for? Did I do something to earn it?"

"Maybe." Looking up at him, she said, "Today is the first day in memory that no one on the streets has been treating me like an outcast. I am very happy about that. And I suspect it is because of you standing up for me."

"It's about time that nonsense ended, ma'am. You never were a pariah in the first place."

"Perhaps, but for some reason, people seem nicer. I am glad of that."

His lips curved up. "You, Mrs. Markham, are too easy to please."

"Don't get your hopes up," she teased. "I am only feeling that way this afternoon. Tonight, I feel certain everything and everyone will cause me to complain."

"I'll do my best to stay far away from you this evening then," he said as they stopped at a corner.

She was just about to tell him she wouldn't dare be mean to her social savior when her former best friend walked to her side.

Though it was tempting to say nothing—after all, that was what Mercy had done to her time and again—Miranda didn't want to create an awkward situation. "Hello, Mercy," she said at last. "I trust you are doing well?"

Mercy barely inclined her head. "Mrs. Markham."

When her gaze flickered over to Robert and stilled, he bowed ever so slightly.

"Ma'am."

"Sir, I'm afraid I have not had the pleasure of your acquaintance."

Though she had a feeling she was about to regret it, Miranda performed the introductions. "Mercy, may I present Mr. Robert Truax? He served with my husband in the war. Robert, this is Mrs. Jackson."

"Sir."

He bowed slightly. "Mrs. Jackson."

Mercy tilted her head to one side. "I haven't seen much of you of late, Miranda. Have you become even more a recluse?"

"I suppose I have."

"Perhaps we shall see more of you, now that you have decided to walk the streets with your boarders." She paused. "Or shall I say, too much of you?"

Before Miranda could give that the dignity of a reply, Robert took her elbow. "We should be on our way, Miranda. Let's go while there's a break in the traffic."

"Yes, of course." She allowed him to guide her forward, then started to look back to see if Mercy followed or what expression she was wearing.

"Don't look back."

"I'm only looking to see—"

"Don't. Forget about her."

"I cannot. You see—"

He cut her off again, his voice firm. "You can forget her, Miranda. It's possible. You owe her nothing."

She wondered what kind of man he was. Did he go through life firmly forgetting past friendships? Was that how a man survived without parents to guide him or protect him? "Robert, it isn't quite that easy. You see, she was my best friend for years. We were once quite close."

"If that is truly the case, then that is even more of a reason for you not to be kind to her now. She should have stayed loyal to you." He leaned down closer. "Miranda, she had a choice to make when your troubles started. She could have put you first or put you last. We both know what she did."

It was hard to hear about Mercy's actions in such stark terms. "I wish she had chosen my friendship over the gossip she heard."

"You do?" He looked down at her and smiled softly. Then, to her surprise, he ran two fingers along the slope of her jaw. Right there on the street! "Well, that makes two of us."

Before she could comment on that, he sighed dramatically. "Now that we've taken care of your former best friend, let us tackle the bank and the weasel otherwise known as Mr. Winter before we post my letter at the mercantile."

She dared to smile. Truly, he was being outrageous. "Goodness. He's a weasel now?"

"More or less. Other names are more fitting, but alas, they are not for your ears."

"I've noticed that you are not afraid to put everyone in their place today."

"Yes, it is true. Unlike you, it seems everyone has gotten on my nerves today. I have lost patience with Galveston Island's general population."

"I had better watch myself, then."

"No, my dear." Taking her elbow to carefully guide her up the steps, he said, "Be assured that you have nothing to worry about. There isn't a thing you could do to lower my estimation of you."

His words were so direct, so assured, that they made her a bit wary. He knew her, but he didn't know the things she'd done or contemplated. "Those are sweet words, but we both know they cannot be true. Everyone does something that another finds fault with."

"With you? No, I don't think so," he said without a trace of hesitancy.

Because she knew such words didn't always last and some feelings eventually faded, she didn't protest his effusive praise.

After all, even if he had no regrets, she knew another day things would go dark again.

If time had taught her anything, it was that nothing wonderful lasted.

17

Johnson's Island, Ohio
Confederate States of America
Officers' POW Camp
March 1865

Ever since Phillip had been moved to the bottom floor of their barracks, which was their makeshift infirmary, Thomas Baker had been Robert's new bunkmate. Baker, being only a sergeant, had been originally slated for the POW prison in Columbus, but through the wonders of red tape, and, no doubt, a certain captain's influence, he'd been shipped up to their island prison with the rest of them.

Robert had always liked Thomas well enough. They'd been sent on a few scouting missions together when they were stationed in Tennessee. After only a few hours in each other's company, it was evident they made a good team. Neither of them had much to lose. Because of that, they had little fear. They'd also had a lot of experience using force when necessary. Robert wasn't exactly proud of it, but he could use his fists with the best of them. Thomas was just as scrappy.

Thomas was street-smart, too, and the enlisted

men had held him in high esteem. Robert would fight by his side any day, and consider it an honor to do so.

All that said, Robert wasn't especially thrilled to have him as his bunkmate. The man was bigger than Phillip and, as far as Robert could tell, he'd never slept without shifting positions two dozen times. He was also a talker.

Robert was soon learning that the man required at least an hour's worth of conversation before he closed his eyes for the night. For two men stuck on an island with little to do but write letters to loved ones, pace, and whittle, Robert was amazed that the man had anything to say at all.

But each night Thomas came up with something, usually when Robert's eyes were drifting shut.

"Hey, Rob?"

Not bothering to move from his position on his side, he mumbled, "What?"

"Did you see the new men arrive this afternoon?"

Even though he'd almost been asleep, Robert found himself smiling. "Hard to miss them. They were walking across Lake Erie like their soles were going to slip through at any minute."

"I talked to one. They're from the Tennessee Army."

"Didn't know that. Do you know any of them?" Thomas, like Captain Monroe, had originally joined the Tennessee regiment before getting transferred.

"No. But they seem a well enough sort. Decent."

"Bet they're tired as all get-out." It was a long journey to be taken prisoner, shipped up to Ohio on a train, then eventually forced to march across Lake Erie's frozen bay to their camp.

"Yeah. Maybe." He paused. "One of the officers almost smiled when he saw our barracks. Said it looked like a college dormitory."

"I've heard that too." Phillip had once compared their lodging to his dorm at West Point. Thomas sounded more than a little wistful. Robert wondered where this conversation was going.

"You ever been to college, Lieutenant?"

Robert scoffed. "I never had any schooling."

"Not any?" Thomas sounded incredulous, and Robert couldn't blame him. Most people were lucky enough to have some kind of formal education, he reckoned. He just had never been one of those.

"Nope."

When a couple of men around them grunted, Thomas lowered his voice. "I thought you could read, though. Can't you?"

"I can read. But until I enlisted, only a couple of old men had taught me how to cipher, and a pair of sisters taught me to read a little." He frowned, thinking back to that summer when those girls had befriended him as their charity case. They'd let him use their barn's spigot, given him a cot to sleep on, and had even given him supper every evening.

But when one of them started acting like she liked him, he'd gotten smart and moved on. No amount of learning or stew was worth being some girl's kept boyfriend. Especially when her daddy would've likely shot him for getting close to her.

"What about you?" Robert asked, curious now. "I thought your childhood wasn't much different from mine."

"I was born north of Dallas, in Wichita Falls. I had a house and everything." His voice turned wistful. Almost sweet. "For my first eight years, I had a mom and dad and a big brother too."

Robert was shocked. Thomas was rougher around the edges than he was, and that said a lot. "Were they good people?"

"Yeah. They were real good. My ma liked to sing. She sang most every morning when she hung clothes out on the line. And my brother, Jeremy, was the best. You know how some older brothers act like their reason for living is to beat the tar out of their siblings?"

Of course he didn't; he had no siblings. But he answered anyway. "Yeah."

"Jeremy wasn't like that. He always let me follow him around. And when he was with his friends after church, he made everyone include me. He walked me to school every day too."

Putting off the inevitable question, which was what happened to them all, Robert said, "What about your dad?"

"He was stocky like me. He was a blacksmith. Funny, some blacksmiths are all about the iron, but my dad, he was all about the horses. He loved those horses."

"Now I see why you ride so well."

"Yep, he taught me how to ride. He rode like the wind. He taught me how to trust your horse too. Said a horse won't ever let you down. He was right." His voice drifted off, true sadness lacing every word.

Which prompted Robert to ask the inevitable. "What happened when you were eight?"

"Indian raid."

"What?"

"Shut up, Truax!" a major called out. "It's going on one in the morning!"

"Sorry," Robert mumbled. Flipping over on his back, he whispered, "What happened?"

"Some renegade Indians were out looking for food, I guess. Or maybe they were just sick of being forced from their homes and land and decided to make a point. Anyway, they killed 'em all but me."

"It's good you survived."

"I don't know," Thomas said in his halting way. "My ma made me hide, you see." He lowered his voice. "They all did. Jeremy said he'd beat me good if I showed my face, no matter what I heard. So I stayed hid, 'cause Jeremy didn't lie."

"I'm, uh, real sorry, Baker. That's a real shame about your family." It was more than that, of course. But what else could he say?

"Yeah. But what do you do? Everybody's got something. Now here you and I are, sitting in some Yankee barracks getting yelled at by guards who never saw action."

"This is true."

"And Phillip is downstairs dying inch by inch with that gangrene." Whispering now, he said, "Gangrene's a heck of a way to die."

It was.

The reminder of Phillip downstairs writhing in pain made him get up. "I better go relieve Cap."

"How come it's just you and Cap watching him now?"

"Don't know," he lied. "We might be in prison, but I still do what I'm told."

"Yeah," Thomas said, but it was apparent that he didn't believe Robert.

Not wanting to converse about it further, Robert slipped out of the cot, threw his boots back on, and walked downstairs, then through the middle aisle where most of the men there were sleeping.

No one asked him where he was going. Probably because they'd seen him walk through here dozens of other times.

When he got to Phillip's room, he saw Captain

Monroe sitting next to him. Phillip's blanket was clenched in Cap's hands. The expression on their captain's face could only be described as devastated.

"Robert," he said.

"Captain, you okay?"

"Me? No. Phillip is dead."

The words, though expected, hit him with such force that Robert knew he was swaying on his feet.

Unable to completely grasp it, Robert walked to the side of Phillip's bed and sat on the edge of his cot. Phillip's eyes were closed, but his body didn't look like Robert would have expected it to. He looked tense, almost as if he'd been fighting something.

"What happened?"

"You know what happened, Lieutenant." He hesitated. "The man had gangrene and infection. This was inevitable."

"I know. It's just that when I was with him earlier, he seemed to be breathing easy. He even talked for a while."

Captain Monroe looked up. "Was he making any sense?"

"At first he was talking about Miranda and home, but then about squirrels and rabbits. And weasels, if you can believe that. He must have thought he was a kid out hunting with his pa or something."

Captain Monroe looked like he was about to

nod, then, after looking over his shoulder, he shook his head. "He wasn't talking about hunting with his pa."

"You know what all that meant?"

Monroe nodded. "Yeah. I know."

"Was it . . . was it from one of his missions?" he whispered.

"It was."

"Did he say more while you were with him, sir?"

"Let's not talk anymore about this, Robert." After taking a fortifying breath, Captain Monroe stood. "If it's all the same to you, I think we might as well tell everyone about Phillip's passing in the morning. Let everyone who can sleep do so."

"Yes, sir."

He walked out then, head down. Robert was fairly sure he'd never seen Devin Monroe stand so dejectedly.

The door closed behind him. Leaving Robert alone with Phillip Markham's dead body.

Closing his eyes, he prayed for the man's soul. Prayed he'd find some comfort. And at last prayed for his beloved Miranda, whom he'd seemed to have loved more than anything else in the world.

Then, satisfied that he'd done his best for the man, he moved over to the chair their captain had just vacated and sat vigil by Phillip's side.

He told himself it was because Phillip Markham needed that kind of respect.

But what he really did was look at the door and

think about the last time he'd sat with Phillip.

Phillip had been feverish and vocal. He'd cried. He'd talked about Miranda and Galveston Island. And he did talk about squirrels and rabbits and weasels. He hadn't lied about that.

But then he seemed to be talking to a phantom officer about the success of his latest foray behind enemy lines. Where he'd donned a Union uniform, adopted the East Coast accent he'd learned at West Point, and walked the halls at one of the hospitals.

Through it all, Robert had been stunned and terrified. Terrified to leave him to go get Monroe.

And more terrified to do what Monroe had insisted had to be done.

Soon, however, Phillip had stopped talking and fallen into a deep sleep. Robert dropped the jacket in his hands and sank back against the wall in relief. When Monroe arrived shortly after, Robert never said a word to him, too ashamed that he'd betrayed his captain's orders.

As he left Phillip's room, he noticed the two sick men in cots on the other side of the door staring hard at him. And the guard who was leaning against the wall seeming to stare at nothing.

Those three men had heard. But he walked out without a word.

What had he done?

Certainly not what his captain had been brave enough to do.

18

Belle didn't like fish. She especially didn't like going to the fishmonger early in the morning for Cook. Honestly, she wished Cook would send Emerson every once in a while. That man loved fish and he didn't even mind getting up an hour before dawn.

But of course it didn't really matter what she wanted. Sometimes a woman had to do the job that was asked of her, and this was hers.

After throwing on her cloak and a thick wool scarf to tie around her neck and face, she made the thirty-minute walk to the docks. In the middle of the day, it was a nice journey. Walking in the dim morning light on half-empty streets was another story. To make matters worse, a fog had come in with the tide and blanketed the outside market in cold mist. It was enough to make a girl wonder if she could ever get warm again.

As she got closer to the fishmonger, more people filled the streets. Roughnecks, sailors, and dockworkers were moving slowly through the haze, as were the unfortunate women who had worked the night before. In the middle of it all were domestics like her.

After sidestepping a pair of freedmen standing outside one of the cotton warehouses, she at last got to the pier where her favorite fishmonger set up shop.

"You're here early, Belle," Sam said with a smile.

"I am." She hated sounding so glum when she knew Sam had already been out in the gulf and had returned. "How was your catch this morning?"

"Good." He grinned. "Good enough to sell you a fish or two."

His good nature was infectious. "You always say that," she replied, stifling a giggle.

"You always laugh when I say it too. Makes me proud to get you to smile."

"You're my only reason to smile on this errand. You know I'm not one for getting out early."

He pressed his hand to his chest dramatically. "You wound me every single time you come, Belle." He started to say more, then shuttered his expression.

Surprised by his sudden change in attitude, she turned to see who he was staring at. It was Sheriff Kern. He was talking with some of the men coming off an expensive-looking freighter. She was surprised. The docks usually weren't where the local law enforcement presided. She'd learned they had their own set of rules and regulations. In the distance was another surprise —Mr. Winter. Though she hadn't had much reason to mix with the clerk, Belle certainly recognized him.

But his being down at the docks at sunrise was even more of a surprise than Sheriff Kern.

"You still friends with him, Belle?" Sam asked under his breath.

"Who?"

"Kern."

Belle finally stopped staring and turned back to her friend. "I wouldn't say we're friends, exactly. He's the sheriff." Remembering what she had overheard about Kern's service and imprisonment, she added, "He fought bravely during the war."

"We all fought, one way or another."

"He also has friends in high places."

"What does that even mean?" he scoffed.

"It means we don't run in the same social circles, Sam. He's a good four steps above me."

Sam grunted. "Hardly that. You're better than some of the folks I've seen him keep company with, I'll tell you that."

Wondering if he was referring to Mr. Truax, she asked, "Who have you seen him talking to? Anyone in particular?"

"You know Kyle Winter?"

"I know who he is. And I saw him standing nearby." Curious now, she asked, "Are you saying they spent time together this morning?"

Sam shrugged.

266

She was confused . . . unless the sheriff was doing some detective work. That had to be it. Surely the sheriff couldn't condone Mr. Winter's behavior toward Mrs. Markham. After all, she overheard that he and Mr. Truax were going to work together to solve Mrs. Markham's problems. After glancing around to make sure no one else might be listening, she said, "I doubt they're friends. After all, Mr. Winter treats Mrs. Markham badly and Sheriff Kern is her friend."

"I just assumed anyone who would be friends with Winter would not be a friend of yours."

"No, maybe not. Mrs. Markham doesn't deserve how Mr. Winter has treated her. But why do you think Sheriff Kern—?"

"Sheriff," Sam interrupted, suddenly straightening his shoulders. "Good morning."

Sheriff Kern nodded. "Morning, Sam." Turning to Belle, he smiled slightly. "I was hoping you might be out this morning."

She wouldn't have been more surprised if he'd told her he'd decided to move to New York City. "Oh? I wasn't aware you spent much time in this part of town."

"I do when I have business here. Then someone told me you often come here on this day of the week, so I thought perhaps if we could take a walk together."

"Kind of hard to be walking with your hands full," Sam mumbled.

Kern turned to Sam. "Do you have a problem this morning?"

Across from her, Sam stiffened. "No."

Though Belle wasn't sure what Sam had been getting at, as though Sheriff Kern was not being quite everything he said he was, warning bells were going off in her head. "Thank you, Sheriff, but I had best go right home."

Holding out her hands, she practically grabbed hold of the fish Sam had wrapped in paper and hugged it to her chest. "Fish don't keep for long, you know."

But to her surprise, Kern didn't shy away. "How about I walk you home, then?"

"Well, I, um . . ."

"I insist." He took her elbow and guided her away from Sam's stall and along the narrow passageways of the fish market. Though his hold was strong and unforgiving, she noticed it wasn't painful.

She also noticed that she couldn't help but be aware of his touch. Afraid to meet his gaze, Belle kept looking in front of her. When they got back to Market Street, she pulled her elbow away from his grasp. "There is no need to keep ahold of me, sir. I'm not going to run away."

"I wasn't trying to keep you," he said impatiently. "Only navigate through the crowded market." He waved a hand toward one of the many abandoned buildings on the edge of the warehouse district. "You know it's not safe here. Half the buildings are barely standing after the last storm. You could get hurt."

"By a collapsing building?"

"Vagrants and rats live around here too. I promise, neither are suitable company for you."

He was looking out for her. Trying to shield her. She stiffened as she realized she appreciated his efforts. It was so unexpected. He stopped and looked at her curiously. "Is anything wrong? You seem out of sorts."

"I am fine. I am simply not good company this early in the morning."

"I hope that is all it is." After they walked another half block, he said, "As I said, I was hoping to see you. I want to speak to you."

"About what?"

He glanced her way. "Well, how are things at the boardinghouse?"

"About the same. We got two new boarders last night."

"Any other visitors?"

"No . . . well, no, unless you count the older Mrs. Ruth Markham and Miss Viola Markham."

Sheriff Kern's eyebrows rose. "They were there? Did they spend the night?"

"Oh no. They came in, talking about how they were going to be getting the house soon. We all thought we were going to get fired, for sure. But then Mr. Truax practically ran them off."

"I see."

Belle wasn't sure what he saw. "Has anything happened, sir?"

"I'm not sure," he said slowly. "I plan to ask Mr. Truax about his conversation with those women, though."

They were back in Mrs. Markham's neighborhood. The streets were wider, palm trees and mossy Spanish oaks lined yards, and far fewer people were out than when Belle preferred to be stirring.

Maybe because it felt as if they were the only two people around, their conversation felt more intimate. "Is there a reason you are worried about that?"

To her surprise, Sheriff Kern now looked even more uncomfortable. "I simply want to make sure Mrs. Markham is in no danger."

That, for Belle, was the last and final straw. She was tired of him circling around their conversation, asking things yet not giving her a reason why he was so concerned. "Sir, are you sure it's Mrs. Markham you are worried about?"

He drew to a stop. "Please explain yourself."

"If you had really cared about her, you would have tried harder to figure out who sent her that very first letter. Instead, you made her feel like a fool. And then, when everyone started disparaging her character, you could have put a stop to it."

"And how would I have done that without causing her more undue gossip?"

"I don't know. But it seems to me that you could have tried. Mr. Markham gave his life for the cause. But you—and half the people in this town—act like that wasn't good enough."

"I did not start that talk."

"But you were in a position to finish it, sir. I know that. You could have done something, but you didn't." No longer caring that he was the one in the position of power and she was just a maid, Belle added, "You didn't want to offend the wrong people so you ignored her pain. Just like when someone started sending her awful, hateful letters you didn't want to get involved."

His brow wrinkled. "Belle, I promise, I had no idea who wrote those letters. I still don't know."

"But you didn't even act like you cared to find out. And by your reaction to the news that Mr. Markham's sister and mother came by, you must somehow know how they have been treating her. They act like Mrs. Markham is no better than a harlot. So does half this town. But you have let that talk continue. Only now that Mr. Truax is here do you seem to care."

He was pale now. "Perhaps you have a point."

"I know I do," she bit out as she turned to face him on the street in front of the Markham mansion. "Just as I know I am right about you not wanting to get involved, I know Robert Truax has done more to help her than you ever tried. And that is wrong."

271

"I am trying to make up for it now."

"I see." His tone was earnest, his expression haunted. She wanted to believe him. She wanted to believe he was talking to Kyle Winter to help Mrs. Markham, and she was tempted to ask him if that was the truth.

However, it was more important that she concentrate on Mrs. Markham herself. Actually, what she needed to do was stop trying to figure out if Sheriff Kern was her ally or one of the reasons her employer was so miserable.

"Do you have anything else to tell me?" he asked quietly.

"No. Just that I hope you will help Mrs. Markham solve her problems as soon as possible."

He stilled. "Is there a specific reason you are stating this?" Though she knew her employer deserved her loyalty, something told her the sheriff could indeed be an ally. Heaven knew Mrs. Markham needed more of those. She let her anger go.

At last, she said, "Because maybe I know we don't have much to lose. You see, before Mr. Truax arrived, we were worried that Mrs. Markham wasn't going to survive much longer. However, with Mr. Truax's arrival, I think she now has a reason to live and to be strong." Lifting her chin, she said, "Maybe I want a reason to live and be strong too."

His demeanor changed.

"Do you think I could ever be that reason, Belle?" His voice was plaintive, his gaze hopeful.

Her mouth went dry as she stared at him. He was handsome. He was powerful. When she'd first arrived in Galveston from Louisiana, she would have given anything for a man like him to even give her the time of day.

But now? Well, it seemed she was starting to want more out of life. She was starting to want people in her circle of friends whom she could depend on. People who cared about her even when things weren't going her way. She wanted a man who cared enough to take risks.

She simply wasn't sure if he was that man. She wasn't sure if she could trust him. Apparently, Sam did not.

"I don't know," she finally replied.

Instead of getting mad, he stared at her. "Will you give me a chance?"

Belle swallowed. Here she was, standing with Jess Kern as dawn was breaking overhead. He was asking for her to give him a chance to make amends. To prove that he was good enough for her.

All while she was holding a newspaper full of smelly fish.

It was unbelievable. It was also . . . well, it was also rather flattering.

"I will think about it, Sheriff Kern. If you really want a chance."

"I do." Looking over her, he suddenly smiled. "Will you call me Jess now?"

"Of course not. It isn't proper."

"Will you call me Jess in the early mornings . . . when you are holding fresh fish?"

She couldn't hide a slight smile. "Perhaps." She walked into the house then. Holding the fish to her like a newborn babe.

Maybe he was a man willing to take risks after all.

19

The knock came at half past four.

The moment Miranda opened the door to the man who should have been a complete stranger, she instead found herself smiling as though she'd suddenly met a long-lost friend.

Maybe it was the golden head of hair that looked to be ruthlessly kept short. Maybe it was the man's pale blue eyes that had too many wrinkles at their corners. Or his military bearing.

Or, perhaps, it was the way he looked—as if he was not only the most formidable man on earth but also possessed the kindest heart ever known.

None of that really mattered. It didn't matter how she knew him; she simply did.

As she stood there, fighting a smile, his own eyes scanned her face, seeming to memorize every detail.

And then he bowed from the waist. "Madam," he said, his voice halting and respectful. "You don't know me, but I am—"

"You're Captain Devin Monroe," she finished.

He blinked as if she'd taken him by surprise. Then, after a pause, he smiled. "I am, indeed. And you, I presume, are Mrs. Markham?"

"Yes, Captain, I am. I mean, I was Phillip's wife, Miranda."

His smile grew. "You are everything he said you were, ma'am."

"As are you. Phillip must have been better at describing people than I had ever realized. I feel like I would have known you anywhere."

"I am delighted to make your acquaintance at last."

"I am pleased as well."

After gazing at her face again, he folded his hands behind his back. "May I come in?"

"Oh! Oh, certainly." She stepped back. "I'm so sorry. I can't believe I kept you standing outside my door." She waved a hand. "Please, do come in."

After he'd followed her and she closed the door to shut out the wind, she held out her hands. "May I take your coat, Captain?"

He shrugged it off his shoulders. "Thank you. But please, simply call me Devin."

"I could not," she said as she hung his heavy wool coat in the wardrobe by the door. "You meant so much to my husband. To both of us."

"Then I guess it will have to be Mr. Monroe. I resigned my commissions, you see. I'm no longer in the military."

"I was not aware of that. Robert, I mean Mr. Truax, still refers to you as Captain."

He smiled again. "Old habits die hard with Robert, I'm afraid. He likes things to stay the same if at all possible. Change doesn't come easy. Perhaps you've noticed?"

"I can't say that I have," she said after a moment's reflection. "All I have noticed is that he is more than he seems at first glance."

Appreciation flickered in his eyes. "I dare say we all might fit that description."

She was embarrassed now. Had she just revealed too much of herself?

"Please, won't you come into the parlor and sit down?" she asked in a rush as she led the way. "Or may I serve you some coffee? Tea?" Another thought crossed her mind. "Or are you hungry? Perhaps you'd like a light repast?"

"I have no need of refreshment at the moment. Don't go to any trouble, Mrs. Markham."

His expression looked so serious all of a udden that she sat down too. "All right."

He looked at her again, his eyes showing genuine happiness. Then, catching himself, he shook his head as if to clear it. "I'm sorry for staring. It's just that, well, you are almost all Phillip talked about. It's taken me a moment to put the lady in front of me with the words that so often rang in my ears."

"Phillip and I were a love match. I'm afraid we were both guilty of talking far too much about the other."

"I don't think that is anything to apologize for. Yours was a blessed union."

"Yes. Yes, it was." She folded her hands, then was suddenly embarrassed. "I'm sorry. I should have sent for Robert right away. He said he was asking for your help, and I'm sure he's been expecting you." Moving to get up, she said, "I think he is home. It won't take me but a moment to—"

"Mrs. Markham, I do want to see Robert. But if you can spare the time, I would like to talk to you first."

She felt more awkward than a schoolgirl attempting to please her teacher. "Oh. Yes, of course."

"You see, Robert came here to see how you were faring. I believe you know that."

She nodded.

"He's been mailing me updates about you and his visit. He also told me about the disturbing letters you've been receiving." He raised a brow. "And, I believe, you've also had some trouble with your in-laws?"

Everything he listed had happened. And while she supposed she was grateful to Robert for caring, she wasn't as pleased to hear about her problems on this man's lips. "I am not sure how I feel about Robert giving you updates on me."

"He didn't really have a choice, I'm afraid. You see, one night on Johnson's Island we made a vow to each other, a pact, if you will, to look out

278

for each other. Phillip asked that you be looked after too."

Miranda didn't know whether to laugh or cry. Of course Phillip would have wanted her to be safe and secure. She could honestly see him, dressed in his worn uniform, standing with Robert and Captain Monroe and inserting her needs into their conversation.

It was sweet and so very thoughtful.

But she didn't think they honored that vow all that much. After all, Robert had only arrived to see her a few weeks ago. But she had been suffering for so long before his arrival.

"You don't seem all that impressed with our pact, ma'am."

"I'm sorry, but I am not. The war has been over for some time, and I confess I've been struggling on my own. I never thought your men would seek me out, so I don't want to sound ungrateful or bitter. It's just that, well . . . I hope you have been looking after the other parties in your pact a bit better."

He winced. "We scattered after we got out. I'd like to think the others are doing well now, but I have no idea. I, um, had some issues that I had to take care of directly after the war. I am only just now able to fulfill my promises."

"No, I am sorry. You owe me nothing."

He leaned forward, resting his elbows on his knees. "Mrs. Markham, I disagree. Furthermore, I have heard that you have been experiencing some difficulties of late. Perhaps you could tell me a bit more about what has been happening with you."

She didn't wish to ask one more man for help with her laundry list of hurts. "I will be fine. Sheriff Kern is now helping me. The only problem I've been experiencing that you might find noteworthy is the rumor that has been circulating around Phillip."

It even hurt to say it. "About Phillip's role in the war. Someone is saying he was a traitor. That, I believe, is cause for your concern. I suppose that is why Robert sent for you."

Captain Monroe's whole bearing shifted. He looked angry and hard. At that moment, it was hard to locate the gentleman who had opened the door to her. "Phillip was not a traitor, Mrs. Markham."

"No, he was not," Robert said as he walked into the parlor.

Miranda rose to her feet. "Robert, your captain is here."

"Just arrived," Captain Monroe said as he stood up as well. "I came as soon as I read your last letter."

"So I see." He winked at her before walking directly to Captain Monroe and holding out his hand. "Devin, it is good to see you."

They shook hands, then to Miranda's surprise

Devin pulled Robert to him and clasped him in a manly, rough hug. "We've been through too much to simply shake hands, Lieutenant."

"Yes, sir. I suppose we have." Turning to Miranda, he said, "I hope Devin here hasn't been filling your head with too many stories about our time together?"

She loved how he so easily used that euphemism. Instead of reminding them all that they'd fought side by side in the most terrible of situations.

"Mrs. Markham has just shared how she's been besieged by rumors about Phillip betraying the Confederacy."

"Which is where I came in," Robert said easily. Taking a seat next to Miranda on the sofa, he said, "I have to say that whatever Miranda might have told you about the pressure she's been under is probably at least ten times worse than she has led you to believe. I don't know too many men who could put up with so much, let alone a gently bred woman."

Captain Monroe's expression turned fierce. "I would like to spend a few days here if I may, ma'am."

"Yes, of course," she replied.

Then he eyed her gently. "I would like the opportunity to share some memories of Phillip with you. If that wouldn't upset you too much."

"I would love to hear your stories. Well, if you feel they are suitable for my hearing," she teased.

The captain grinned. "You're looking at a man who has spent the majority of his life in the company of ramshackle men. I doubt any of my tales are suitable for gently bred ladies. But if you think your ears can handle stories with a few rough edges, it would be an honor to share some memories about a man I held in high esteem."

"I might have been gently bred at one time, but now I'd like to think of myself as a survivor, sir. I promise, there is little you could tell me that I haven't heard before."

Robert chuckled. "Just probably not from Phillip."

Feeling her cheeks heat, she averted her eyes. "You are right about that. Phillip was always careful around me."

Monroe exchanged a meaningful glance with Robert.

"What is it?" she asked. "What did Phillip do? Robert, you told me Phillip was not a traitor. Were you telling me the truth?"

Captain Monroe stared hard at her again. Then, seeming to come to a decision, he sat back down.

"Phillip Markham was a smart and capable man, Miranda. He excelled at West Point."

"Yes."

"Did he, by chance, ever speak to you about his relationships there?"

"No. I am assuming they were the usual ones made between men at university?"

"I think one could safely say that is true. But what you might not have realized is that he was popular there. He had many friends. Many close friends from all walks of life."

"Yes?"

"When he attended, the war was not on anyone's mind. No one paid much mind to where men were from. Because of that, he became as close to men from the North as from the South."

"I thought that might be the case," she said slowly. "He never mentioned any man or state by name. But he did say from time to time that a man can't be judged only by the region where he lives or the dialect in his speech." She shrugged. "I think that was his way of reminding me that every soldier in the North wasn't a terrible person, just like every man in the South wasn't perfect either."

"That sounds like something Phillip would have said," Robert said easily. "He was always giving everyone a chance. Even a man like me."

Miranda smiled softly at Robert. "Even you."

Devin linked his fingers together. "Mrs. Markham, what I am about to tell you cannot be shared with anyone. This is for your ears only."

Miranda was sure she paled, but she leaned forward to catch every word.

"When we went to war, I was not with Phillip at first. Did you know that?"

"I did. He was under another captain. I can't recall his name now."

"I would be surprised if he ever told it to you. That captain had been assigned a job directly from Lee himself. He was to find men who could easily slip through enemy lines and gather information."

She felt her cheeks freeze. "What are you saying, sir?"

"That Phillip was one of the men recruited for that job."

She shook her head. "No."

"For two years Phillip Markham went behind enemy lines, donned a blue uniform, and mixed with Union officers."

She shook her head. "No, that is not possible. They would have known he was from the South."

"Some did. Some thought he was from Kentucky, and that state was pretty much split down the middle. But it didn't matter. He changed his name half the time. He changed his posture and his accent. To survive, he became another man."

"But—"

"To fulfill his missions, he never told anyone but his superiors about them. He kept his promises to the generals and such, who asked so much of him. He was loyal to the core."

Hardly able to believe what she was hearing, Miranda nodded.

Captain Monroe looked at her intently. "What I need you to understand, Mrs. Markham, is that there were many jobs and roles in our war. Not everyone who put his life at stake held a bayonet and charged across a field. Some, like Phillip, risked their lives for information. He was a hero, ma'am. He was a hero in every sense of the word."

Miranda knew it would be days before she would fully be able to let that sink in and come to terms with the fact that her husband had led a very different life from what he'd let on.

Perhaps it didn't matter. Maybe she didn't really need to know how much he sacrificed for the cause. But as she looked at both men and saw how unwaveringly proud they were of him, how much they'd believed in him, she couldn't help but feel justified.

She'd wanted Phillip to be everything she'd believed him to be. And, it seemed, he was.

She was just about to thank Captain Monroe for making the long journey to meet her face-to-face and tell Phillip's whole story when she realized the question that had been hounding her had just become more complicated than ever. Perhaps the captain could help after all.

"Robert assured me Phillip was not a traitor, and now I know how false that rumor has been. But if no one knew about his undercover missions except for a very few select group of people . . ." She paused.

Captain Monroe nodded. "Yes, that is correct."

"Then there was no basis at all for the rumor. So who wants me out of this house so much that he would make up lies and threaten me with these letters?"

Captain Monroe exchanged glances with Robert. "That's a very good question, ma'am. Believe me when I say I aim to find the answer to it very soon."

"We'll discover what has been going on, Miranda," Robert said quietly. "I will not leave Galveston without knowing you are safe and secure once again."

Robert's words were reassuring. But they also filled her with a new sense of dread. Robert Truax wasn't planning to stay in Galveston. And what's more, he never had.

He'd come here for a mission. For Phillip. That was all.

20

Lieutenant Robert Truax's house, West Texas
Christmas Day 1866

The captain's arrival was a welcome surprise, but not a completely unexpected one. Once Robert's brain took a moment to register that he was actually seeing the captain and not some apparition from his many dreams and nightmares of the war, he drew himself up to an almost-forgotten military posture and inclined his head.

He had to remind himself that their army days were gone and therefore he shouldn't salute.

"Captain Monroe. Welcome," he said in a crisp, concise voice. "Happy Christmas."

Captain Monroe's clear blue eyes filled with an unfamiliar glint of amusement. "Happy Christmas to you, Lieutenant. Stand at ease now, man. We're not in the army any longer."

Somewhat embarrassed, Robert relaxed his stance. But he still felt awkward. Part of him wanted to hug his captain, the other part of him wanted to present the calm, relaxed stance he'd been so known for back when they directed their men at camp.

He settled for being direct. "What brings you here, sir?"

Devin rested his left hand on the doorjamb. "Well, I was first hoping that you might invite me into your rather grand home."

Feeling worse than foolish, Robert stepped back. "Forgive me. It's bitterly cold out. I shouldn't have kept you standing in the elements so long."

Captain Monroe stepped through the door. "I've stood in worse, soldier," he said as he passed. "I believe we both have."

"Yes, sir."

They'd shared three Christmases together. One in Tennessee, another in the wilds of Pennsylvania, the last in a flimsy wooden barracks in a prisoner-of-war camp.

That Christmas spent on Johnson's Island in the middle of Lake Erie had been bone chilling. Nothing could compare to that.

Robert closed the door with a firm clap and promptly turned the deadbolt. As he did so, he prayed to wrap his head around the fact that it was time to sound smarter than he was acting.

Luckily, his maid, Marisol, strode forward and held out her hands to Devin. "Take your coat?"

Captain Monroe blinked, then unfastened each button with care. After handing his wool coat to

Marisol with a word of thanks, he looked at Robert. "You have servants now?"

Robert couldn't determine if his captain was impressed with his improved financial situation or taken aback that he'd hired people to do things he could easily do himself.

But perhaps the why of it didn't even matter.

"Sir, this is Marisol," he said. "She and her husband, Stan, live in a cabin on my property. They were looking for some work and, well, you know me . . . I need all the help I can get."

"Yes, I reckon you do, Robert." He directed a small smile at the maid, who was a good ten years older than either of them. "I hope you and Stan keep him in line, ma'am."

"We try, but it can be a challenge at times, sir," she admitted with a sparkle in her eyes. "Most days the hardest part of my day is reminding Mr. Robert that I am here to help him . . . and not the other way around."

"I'm not that bad, Marisol."

"Bad enough, Mr. Robert," she teased. "Now, may I serve you both some food?"

"Please do. Gracias."

"It's nothing," she said as she parted. "I'll bring it to you in the library, sirs. Stan's got a good fire going."

Captain Monroe had watched the interplay with thinly veiled surprise on his face. "It seems you are surviving fairly well these days."

"It does seem so. My work for the railway has proved profitable." Robert chuckled as he led the way down dark stained maple hardwood floors into a small room off to the side. His pride and joy, his library. For a man who'd grown up with next to nothing, the very fact that he had enough books to need a place to store them was amazing.

Sure enough, Stan had built a roaring fire in the stone hearth. That, with the pine branches Marisol had found and arranged on the mantel, gave the room a warm and Christmasy air.

Weeks ago, he had admitted to Marisol that he'd never actually celebrated a true Christmas. She'd taken his admittance to heart and had practically begun baking Christmas treats and decorating in the next breath.

"Have a seat, sir. Or, if you'd prefer, please warm yourself in front of the fire."

Captain Monroe walked right up to the fire and held out his hands without a trace of artifice or self-consciousness. "Even after all this time, I still can't pass up the chance to get warm."

"I find myself doing that fairly often too." He shrugged, then said in a rare bit of honesty, "Old habits, I guess. Some blessings are too wonderful to ignore."

Captain blinked. "There you are."

"Pardon me?"

"Between your fine clothes and servants and

fancy house, I was wondering if the man I fought beside at Gettysburg was still under there."

Robert barely refrained from tugging at his collar. "He's still there, sir. Just a little more polished and a whole lot more comfortable."

"That's a good thing, Robert. Don't be embarrassed about the gifts you have received."

"Thank you, sir."

Leaning back, Captain Monroe stretched his arms, then exhaled with a contented expression. After a second's pause, he focused on Robert. "Now, I suppose you are probably wondering to what you owe this honor of a visit."

"I figured you'd be ready to tell me in your own time. Even if you came all this way to simply wish me Happy Christmas, I wouldn't have been surprised." And that would have been the truth too. Robert held the captain in such high regard, he was fairly sure he could do just about anything.

"Though that thought might have crossed my mind, I did come for a reason."

There was a new, unfamiliar wariness in his captain's tone. Robert tensed. "Yes, sir?"

"I have something to ask you, but I'll wait until Marisol and Stan get us settled."

Robert turned with a start, realizing that his commanding officer had done it again. He was able to set him off without any difficulty at all.

"Shall we set everything on the card table, sir?" Stan asked when he entered the room.

"Yes. Yes, that will be fine. Stan, this is Captain Devin Monroe. He was my commanding officer in the war. We served together . . . and were imprisoned together as well."

"Sir," Stan said. "It's an honor."

"It's good to meet you too," Devin drawled.

"Will that be all then, Mr. Robert?" Stan asked.

"Yes, thank you. And, please, close the door when you leave."

Without another word the man did as he asked. Turning toward the table now heaping with food, Robert thought an explanation might be in order. "This is corn tortillas, refried beans, and steak with peppers. Marisol, being originally from Mexico, has a way with food like this."

"It looks good. A real fine Christmas meal."

"Yes, sir. Gives a man a lot to be thankful for." Robert didn't know if he would ever take a full plate for granted. He hoped not.

After he said a quick blessing, they ate. Once again, his captain looked like he enjoyed every morsel, taking in each bite as though it might be his last.

As Robert watched without trying to look like he was watching, a slow, sickening feeling settled into the pit of his stomach. Was his captain sick? Did he guess he was dying or something?

Afraid to know, his appetite left him. He picked at his food and started mentally reminding himself not to embarrass himself or the captain.

After a few moments, Captain Monroe set down his fork, wiped his mouth with the bandanna on the table, and leaned back with a satisfied sigh. "Good food, Robert."

"Thank you. I'll let Marisol know."

"You've got a nice life now. Prosperous. Good fire. Help. Excellent meal." He eyed him carefully. "None of those things are to be taken for granted."

"No, sir, I do not. Since this is the first time I've ever had such things, I don't take them for granted at all."

"Are you happy?"

The blunt question took him off guard. "I am happy being warm and clean," he said. "I'm happy not being a prisoner and not being hungry." Most days, that was enough.

"Ha. So you've developed some simple needs."

Robert couldn't resist smiling. "I've always had rather simple needs. They've just never been met."

"Point taken." Captain Monroe shifted, looking slightly uncomfortable. Then he fastened his clear blue eyes on Robert and spoke again. "I'm here about Miranda Markham."

And just like that, all feeling of contentment vanished. "Yes, sir?"

"Robert, I want you to go check on her."

Even the thought of such a thing made him uncomfortable. "Why?" Remembering Phillip's constant concern for her, he grasped for a reason. "Is she unwell?"

"I fear so."

"What happened?" he asked, growing more concerned. "Did she get that influenza? Did she get hurt? Is she injured?"

"No, nothing like that. I have heard she is having a difficult time. Uh, emotionally."

"She is still mourning."

"Yes. But I fear there is more." He paused, then said quietly, "From my contacts around Houston, I have learned that she has become something of a recluse. Some even fear that she will take her own life."

Robert rose to his feet. "That would have devastated Phillip. She was the reason he fought so hard to live." Maybe knowing there was a love like Phillip and Miranda's had given all of them a reason to live.

Even for Ethan Kelly, who'd received a letter just weeks before their release that his Faye had decided to marry someone else.

"I agree. Hearing that she is on the verge of giving up is difficult. It also doesn't make sense." Instead of standing up again, Monroe simply leaned back and stretched out his legs. Looked at him hard. "I worry that something else might be happening to her. After all, how can a woman who stayed strong throughout a long war suddenly give everything up?"

"I don't know."

Captain Monroe leaned forward. "Will you go see her? Will you go to Galveston Island, call on Miranda Markham, and stay with her for a few days? Maybe even a few weeks?"

"Stay?"

"She has turned her home into a boarding-house. I hear the rooms are rarely filled," he said in his off-hand way. "I imagine you would make her very happy if you were to stay for a week or two."

This request was getting harder and harder to bear. "You want me to stay with her that long?"

"I'd like you to," he said easily, but Robert heard what was blatantly unsaid. It was more of an order than a simple request. "She could use a friend, I think."

"Do you think she'll welcome a friendship with one of her husband's comrades?"

Devin stared at the fire. "Perhaps you don't need to mention that you knew Phillip. It's been my experience that some friendships form best when there is little baggage attached. You might be able to ascertain she will be all right, then quietly leave. I don't think she needs any reminders about the war."

"You don't think she'll recognize my name?"

"She might . . . or she might not," he said slowly. Looking back at Robert, he said, "You have always thought quickly on your feet, Lieutenant.

I'm sure you'll know how to present yourself when the time comes, just as I feel certain you will keep the exact nature of your service to the C.S.A. to yourself."

Before he realized what he was doing, Robert pulled back his shoulders. "I would never discuss my missions."

"Of course not," Devin said lightly. "Beg pardon. After all, it's not like you've decided if you are going to see Miranda."

"I will go," he said. He took care to keep his voice casual and contemplative, though there had never been any question of him visiting Miranda Markham. "I have been thinking about leaving my job with the railroad and finding something new."

"Thank you, Robert."

"But why me?"

Captain Monroe stilled. Stared at him directly. "We both know that answer, Robert."

Robert didn't do him the disservice of pretending he didn't understand what he meant. He'd been mesmerized by Phillip's love for his wife, and everyone at the camp had known it. He'd often gone to sleep wondering what kind of woman Miranda Markham was. Now, it seemed, he was going to find out.

They were still sitting in silence ten minutes later when Marisol stepped into the doorway. "Coffee, gentlemen?"

Devin got to his feet. "Thank you, but no. I should be going."

Robert stood up as well. "But it's Christmas. And it's getting late. It will be dark out soon."

"Indeed."

"I wish you would consider staying, sir. The area around here is not very forgiving at night. Especially not in the winter."

"I'll be fine. I have a feeling the only people who will be brave enough to be out on a night like this are me and any wayward wise men."

"But—"

"I came here for a reason, soldier. Now that is done, I think it's best I go on."

Without another word of warning, Robert led the way back down the hallway. Captain Monroe followed, Marisol on their heels.

All too soon, she produced the captain's coat. She and Robert stood quietly as they watched him fasten the buttons with the same care he had taken as he unfastened them.

When he was buttoned up and had his hat in his hand, he smiled at the woman. "Thank you for a wonderful meal, ma'am. Best I've had in some time."

"It . . . it was my pleasure."

He smiled at that, then turned to Robert. "Thank you for both the hospitality and your loyalty. Both mean a lot to me."

That was the thing. Robert knew his captain

wasn't just giving him lip service. He was completely sincere. And that was why Robert knew that, as soon as the new year came, he would take a train down to Galveston Island and check on Miranda Markham as he was asked to do.

Even though the sight of her was likely going to rip him in two. He owed Phillip that much.

But he owed Captain Monroe even more.

"Merry Christmas, sir. Safe travels and God-speed."

"To you, too, Robert. For all good things, you too."

And with that, he put on his hat and walked outside. Moments later, Robert saw him on his mount riding through the east pasture.

When he closed the door, Marisol was still standing in the foyer, looking at him with concern. "Do you think he'll be all right?"

"I hope and pray so." He shrugged. "I learned something about him years ago. With Captain Monroe, one doesn't argue or question. One simply does as he's bid."

He walked back to the library then. Found all traces of their meal and visit had been magically cleared away.

So he stood in front of the fireplace, raised his hands, and gave thanks for the warmth.

21

Not long after Captain Monroe and Robert made their promises to Miranda, she excused herself, citing a pressing need to answer some correspondence.

Though neither of them had actually believed her excuse, Robert let her go without comment. He knew Miranda likely needed some time to process everything they'd revealed about Phillip.

Soon afterward, Winnie directed Devin to one of the bedrooms down the hall from Robert. Thirty minutes after that, the two men went outside.

Devin was eager to see the Galveston Phillip had described in such detail to them all during their late-night talks. As for himself, well, Robert knew the time had finally come to admit to his captain what had happened the day Phillip died.

To have never told him about his inability to do his duty was pure cowardice.

They'd just stepped off the front porch when Devin looked back at the house curiously. "This house is rather close to the water."

"Yes."

"It would be so easy for one to slip down to the docks without notice."

Robert shrugged. "Perhaps. It has one of the finest locations in Galveston. It's close to the water yet off the main thoroughfare."

Still staring at the canal, Devin said, "Has Miranda told you if there has been much interest in her house because of its location?"

"All I know is that her mother-in-law intends to have the house. She and Phillip's sister resent Miranda's keeping it after Phillip left it to her, and especially for turning it into a boarding-house."

"I bet they do," he mused. "It's Miranda's right to claim her home, though."

"It is. It's her house and her husband's legacy. But since I last wrote to you, I have learned first-hand that they are miserable women who gladly make Miranda miserable as well."

Still staring at the narrow body of water and dock behind the mansion, Devin said, "I don't know a lot about shipping and waterways, but I know a lot about military strategy. Water is desirable."

Robert felt a little slow, and he still wasn't following. "And?"

"And maybe someone decided they would like to have this mansion not for its beauty or sentimental nature, but because of its location. A man could bring all sorts of things into the country this way and no one would ever be wiser."

Remembering just how displeased Phillip's mother and sister had been when he'd told them he would make sure they never got the house, Robert said, "Let's go visit the older Mrs. Markham and her daughter, Viola, tomorrow. They might have some answers to some of our questions."

Captain Monroe's light blue eyes warmed. "If they are as truly unpleasant as you made them seem—"

"They are," he said quickly.

"And if they have truly been as disrespectful and impolite to Miranda—"

"They have."

"Then visiting them first thing tomorrow will be worth waking up for."

Robert smiled to himself. "In the meantime, would you care to see the Strand?"

Devin inclined his head. "I would indeed."

They walked up Market Street, then turned toward the busy city district. When they passed the infamous Recognition Square, Robert walked Devin over to it. "This is the memorial for the dead, sir."

Devin nodded, barely scanning the names. "Where is Phillip's name? Did they list his rank? I still wish I would have been able to get his promotion to go through before his death."

"It is absent, sir."

He turned to Robert. "What is? His ranking?"

"No, sir. His name."

"Why?" His words were fairly barked.

"I was told the memorial was for only the city's heroes. This is what the rumor has done, sir."

Devin jerked off his hat and stood at attention. It was obvious to Robert that he was forcing himself to read every man's name on the off chance he'd recall one of the honored fallen heroes. That, of course, was a vintage Captain Monroe gesture. He'd been exhausted for most of the war and paid attention to correct protocols only when absolutely necessary. Until something untoward happened to one of his men.

Then it was obvious that he would do anything and everything to uphold their honor.

Only when Devin had replaced his hat on his head and was staring at the statue in silence did Robert speak. "Did you recognize any of the names?"

"One. He was in the Texas Rangers with me."

"Good man?"

Devin thought for a moment. "Good enough. Too young to die." At last turning away from the carefully carved list of names, he said, "Thank you for showing this to me, Robert."

"Of course."

Devin looked at him a moment longer, then instead of walking ahead, he took a seat on one of the vacant benches. "You look like you have a lot on your mind."

"I do. When I walked onto Galveston Island, I felt as if I was entering Pandora's box. It's been a challenge figuring out whom to trust. Fortunately, as I told you in my last letter, I have come to trust the sheriff, Jess Kern. But I am glad you are here, sir. Jess, of course, does not know of Phillip's true contributions to the war."

"I am pleased you wrote to me about the urgency of the situation," he said as they left the square. "However, I don't believe that is actually all that is on your mind, is it?"

"No."

"Is it Miranda Markham who has you so tied up in knots?"

That took him by surprise. "Sir, everything we are dealing with has to do with Miranda."

"Don't be dense, Lieutenant. I am not speaking of her problems, I am speaking about her."

"Sir?" Robert wasn't sure if he was offended or embarrassed.

"It has not escaped my notice that she's a beautiful woman. I also have not failed to observe that you've noticed her beauty."

"I would never force my attentions on a woman still grieving."

"Is she, though?"

"I know she misses Phillip. But that said, I don't know how much she misses the man versus what she'd hoped they would be together." Thinking about this further, he said slowly, "Wrapping one's mind around a new reality can be a challenge."

"This is true. However, it is the way of the world. Life and death can interrupt a great many plans."

"Indeed."

"That said, I think you should investigate Miranda's feelings."

Robert stopped and started several times, then at last uttered, "You don't think my . . . I mean, you don't think my admiration for her is wrong?"

"What? To look after her? To admit that you fancy her?" He paused, then grinned. "Or to admit that it is okay to fancy her?"

Robert decided to give up all sense of pride. "Yes to all of those things."

Captain Monroe laughed. "My forte is war, not love. But I will say that, as someone who has just stumbled upon the two of you? It's apparent there's something almost tangible between you. For both of your sakes, I think you should give it a try."

"I might." Staring down at Devin, Robert said formally, "Captain, I need to tell you something, but I'm afraid you're going to be so disappointed and upset, you'll think differently about me."

All traces of humor vanished from his expression. "It's that serious?"

"Yes."

Looking at him closely, his captain sighed. "I'm not going to make you any promises, Robert. I'd like to think I've learned something after all these years in the military."

"So, then . . ."

"So then, spit it out, soldier."

Inwardly, Robert gave a sigh of relief. At last he was going to be able to share his burden. He was ready to face the consequences, even if it meant that the man he admired the most was going to look at him as if he was a failure.

"You remember when Phillip was so sick. When he was slowly dying and started hallucinating."

The muscle in Devin's cheek jumped. "I remember."

"What you may not recall is that earlier that week I made a promise to you."

"No, I remember your promise." Devin stood.

Robert was standing almost at attention and couldn't even meet his captain's gaze. Belatedly, he realized he was staring just above the man's head. It was a classic soldier's pose. Men had done it to him all the time. Whenever they were ashamed or lying or afraid, they would stand tall and look slightly away.

It didn't fool anyone.

He had no doubt that he wasn't fooling Devin at the moment. Not even a little bit.

Feeling even worse because he was still acting like a coward, he continued. "Anyway, sir . . . I promised you I would do whatever was necessary to sustain the integrity of Phillip Markham." And, of course, the integrity of the South.

"Yes. You did."

"When I sat with him that day, he started talking. In an agitated way. At first I truly thought he was lost in a vision of home. Maybe back when he was a boy. He was talking about rabbits and weasels. Foxes and hounds, and you told me later, after he died, that he had been talking in code . . ." His voice drifted off, and at that moment the words Phillip had uttered were so clear in his head he could probably have recited them verbatim. "But I didn't tell you Phillip started talking about his undercover work. Not in code, but plainly."

His captain froze. "Yes."

Feeling as though it had all happened days ago instead of years, Robert felt as if his mouth were full of cotton. "I knew I should quiet him. I knew what my orders were. They were clear, sir."

"What did you do?"

Hating the memory, hating how it made him feel, he forced himself to say each word, even though admitting it all out loud made him feel even worse. "I took off my jacket, intending to . . . to stop him. But I couldn't."

"I see."

Robert glanced at Captain Monroe's expression. It was carefully blank. Feeling miserable, he said, "Sir, there's more. You see, when I left the room, a guard was standing nearby, and two prisoners were there in their cots. The sick men were staring at me with stunned expressions."

"So they heard." His voice was flat.

"They did. And I'm sure the guard heard too." Robert closed his eyes, hating this part of his story the most. Hating how weak it made him sound. How weak it made him feel. "I should have dealt with them there, sir."

"Should have? What did you do?"

"Nothing," he whispered. Then, forcing himself to remember that he was alive while Phillip was dead, he said clearly, "I did nothing, sir. I walked away." Robert swallowed. "And then I chose not to tell you either."

"Why didn't you tell me?"

"I couldn't bear to let you know that I wasn't man enough to kill Phillip. Or brave enough to deal with the three men who heard." Back then, every choice had seemed to have irrefutable consequences. If he'd killed the men, he would have very well been caught and put to death too. If he'd merely threatened them to keep their silence, the uncertainty would have been an insurmountable weight around his neck.

"I see." Devin stared at him for several seconds.

Robert forced himself to stand still. Unwavering. Whatever blame Devin heaped on him was what he deserved.

"Lieutenant?"

He braced himself. "Yes, sir?"

"When I went into Phillip's sick room to relieve you, just minutes after you left, he was dead." Looking hollow, Devin said, "He was already dead."

"What? But you seemed to . . . you never said."

"You're right, I didn't." He swallowed. "You see, I thought you ended Phillip's life."

"You thought I killed him. Yet you never said a word to me."

Monroe shrugged. "How could I? I thought you had done what a soldier—no, what an officer—needed to do. When I said, 'You know what happened,' I thought you knew I was acknowl-edging what you would not want to admit, not Phillip's inevitable death from gangrene. No words could have made you feel any better anyway."

He sighed. "Robert, I thought you had done what was best for our unit, best for the Confederacy, best for Phillip's memory." He laughed darkly. "After a while, I even said it was best for Phillip. He was in terrible pain. For weeks."

"When you said Phillip was dead, I assumed you did what I wasn't brave enough to do."

"I would have. I would have done it without much remorse. However, I did not end Phillip Markham's life."

"So it was one of the three men outside the door. Either one of the Confederate soldiers in the cots or the guard. As I think on what Phillip said, I'm not sure if it would have been clear that Phillip was a spy for us, and not the North."

"So it would seem. He did not look as though he died peacefully."

"All this time I've felt terrible about it. I wished I had been stronger," Robert said, feeling both confused and, for the first time, cautiously optimistic. "After all, I couldn't say how many times I fired bullets with my Remington. I killed dozens of men on the field."

"We all did."

"But I loved him."

"We all loved him too. He was a good man. The best."

"Captain, I think one of those three men must have either ended up back here or told someone here that Phillip was a traitor. That's the only way I can figure out how that rumor started. Someone either truly thinks Phillip betrayed the South or wants everyone to think that. Either way, he is bent on destroying Phillip's name and Miranda's life."

"I don't know if we'll ever find who killed Phillip. I'm not even sure if it matters. What's done is done." Looking grim, Devin said, "But whoever did kill him saved you and me from doing it. It might not be right, but I'm grateful for that. Ending Phillip's life would have been a heavy burden to bear."

"How is it that even after all this time, we're still uncovering the pain and secrets of war?

"How can we not? We are men with hearts and souls, after all. We're scarred by our experiences. We also promised each other that we'd never forget."

As Robert stared at his former captain, he realized that was one promise that had been almost too easy to keep.

22

"Any idea what you intend to say or ask these ladies?" Captain Monroe said under his breath as they rode their rented horses up a windy dirt road on the outskirts of Houston.

From the livery's directions, Robert deducted that the Markham women lived in the modest ranch at the end of the lane.

"Not a one," Robert replied. From the time they'd left that morning for their trip on the ferry to the quiet ride to Viola and Ruth's home, he'd been playing over different scenarios. Sometimes he imagined appealing to their love for Phillip.

Other times, he thought it was a better idea to go in strong and assured, using Captain Monroe's rank to an advantage. They'd seemed like women who valued Phillip's military career. Therefore, it stood to reason that they'd value his captain's reputation as well.

Robert even imagined using a bit of force. Flatly refusing to leave or doing his best to keep the women from their scheduled activities until he got some answers.

But that didn't seem like the right method either.

"I've considered a lot of avenues," he replied at last. "Unfortunately, none of my ideas feel like the right course of action."

Instead of looking aggravated, Captain Monroe grinned. "Guess we'll figure it out when we get inside."

"If you have any bright ideas, feel free to take the lead. I'll be happy to follow your directives again. Sir," he added belatedly.

"Will do, but I don't imagine I'll know what to do any more than you will." He paused to move his horse around a parked buggy and a patch of debris on the ground. "To be honest, a part of me would like to simply yell at the women until they've told us what we need to know."

Robert was shocked. "I thought I was the only man who thought that way."

"I don't think you are," Monroe said as he dismounted and tied up the leads. Eyeing him in a bemused way, he continued. "Moreover, I spent far too much of my life on the battlefield. All men lose control at times, I believe."

"You think so?"

Monroe shrugged. "There's only so much one man can take before he gives in to emotions he usually tries to keep in better control." He paused. "That's when prayer comes in handy, I think."

After Robert tethered his mount, he steeled his

shoulders and walked to the front door. Winifred had been extremely agitated when she discovered he and Devin planned to visit Mrs. Markham's in-laws that morning.

Though the housekeeper didn't say it, he had a sneaking suspicion that she feared those women would hurt his feelings. He didn't know whether he should be touched that she thought he possessed delicate feelings or simply be amused that she was hoping to protect him.

Now, though, it was time to get some answers and get back to her. He rapped his knuckles on the door twice.

"It will be fine, Truax," Captain said as they heard a quiet rustling on the other side of the door.

"I know. I just want to help her."

"You will. Once more, don't forget—no matter what happens, the future is already in God's hands. He knows what was meant to be."

Robert replayed that sentiment over and over again as Viola herself opened the door and stared at him and the captain as if they were thieving carpetbaggers intending to fleece them out of their life savings.

"You," she bit out. "What are you doing here?"

Ironically, her foul greeting made his mission easier. "Good morning to you, too, ma'am. I came to speak to you about Miranda."

"I have nothing to say to you."

"I beg to differ," Captain Monroe blurted as he walked right in, ignoring the small push on the door as he strode forward. "I have traveled a fair distance to speak to you and your mother. I intend to do just that."

Viola blanched. "Excuse me, but you may not barge into my home like you own it."

Her words rankled Robert to no end. "Tell me now what you said when Miranda told you that same thing."

"She never dared to say anything of the sort," Ruth Markham announced as she appeared from one of the back rooms. "She knew better than to speak to me with such disrespect."

Captain Monroe looked at her coolly. "Where may we sit?"

"We will not be leaving until we've gotten the answers we've come for," Robert advised. "How long we stay is up to you."

While her mother looked as if she was actually tempted to argue, Viola sighed. "Come into the drawing room. We'll conduct our business there." Then she turned and started down the short and narrow hallway.

After a brief second, her mother followed, her uneven gait looking painful even to Robert's untrained eye.

When they were alone in the entryway, Devin looked his way and smiled. "It seems the manner to deal with these women has been solved. We simply need to be direct, blunt, and if all else fails, rude."

"Agreed." He realized there had been a grain of hope that the women would be cordial enough to speak to him in an easy and open manner. It was obvious now that he hadn't been more wrong.

It made him sick to think that Miranda had been dealing with them all by herself for years now. They were thoroughly unpleasant.

Once all four of them took their seats in the small room that was filled with doilies, knick-knacks, area rugs, heavy drapes, and an excessive amount of cat hair, Devin looked directly at the women.

"Even though you have not asked, I would like to introduce myself. I am Devin Monroe. I was Phillip's captain during his last two years of service in the army."

Ruth's expression softened. "He spoke of you often, Captain. He idolized you."

"I hope not. I was only his commanding officer," he said modestly. "However, I will tell you I thought very highly of your son. He was a good man, a good lieutenant, and above all, a true gentleman of the South. It was an honor to have known him."

"But he still died while in your care," Viola blurted.

"Phillip was not a child, ma'am," Robert replied.

"Furthermore, he was suffering the effects of a gunshot wound. It festered while in captivity. There was nothing we could do."

"Perhaps."

"There was nothing anyone could have done. Like too many others to count, the Lord had decided it was his time to die."

Ruth's face pinched. "Sir—"

"We did not come all this way to discuss old injuries or Phillip's death," Devin smoothly intervened. "We want to know who is behind the letters to Miranda."

"What letters?" Ruth said.

"The threatening ones," Robert said. "The letters that disparage her marriage, her character, and her very self. The letters that come frequently. The letters that tell her to move."

Ruth frowned. "I have no knowledge of such things."

Captain Monroe eyed Viola carefully. "And you, ma'am? Do you have any knowledge of them?"

"I am not sure."

"I did not ask a difficult question," Robert said, leaning forward so his elbows rested on his knees.

Viola shook her head. "Perhaps, but still . . ."

"I saw the last one," Robert pushed. "It was not only vicious in content, but poorly written. Were you not able to have access to a good education, Miss Markham?"

Viola's face flushed. "I had a proper education. Just as Phillip did. I did not write letters such as the ones Miranda received."

Captain grinned. "So you actually do know about them, yes?"

Viola looked from her mother to Robert to Captain Monroe. Then, finally, she nodded. "I know about them," she whispered.

"You know more than that," Captain Monroe pressed. "If you did not write the letters, did you feed the information to the person who did?"

"I fail to see why any of this matters to you."

"A good woman has been tormented by them."

"You are painting a picture of Miranda that simply isn't true. She is far from being helpless, sir."

"Then let us make no mistake about this. I am not a helpless woman." He hardened his voice. "I expect you to answer me. Immediately."

"Mother, are you going to let him make such accusations against me?"

Ruth took a moment, then said, "I, too, would like to hear the truth about these letters, Viola. Speak."

A hand flew up to her chest. After several shaky breaths, Viola whispered, "I . . . I may have told him some things."

Robert leapt on that pronoun. "Him?"

Viola closed her eyes. From the position of her body, it was obvious that she was hoping the men would feel sorry for her circumstances and desist.

But Robert had no intention of backing down. "Who is he?"

"I shouldn't say."

Captain Monroe eyed her with a dark expression. "Oh, you should, ma'am."

Viola looked toward her mother. "Mother, say something."

Ruth, in contrast to her daughter, looked deflated. It was as if she was coming to terms with how their efforts to drive Miranda away sounded in the light of day and she wasn't proud of it. At all. "Viola, what have you done?"

"Nothing!" She leapt to her feet. "I only did what had to be done." She waved a hand. "Look at *where* we are living, Mother. At *how* we are living. We shouldn't be here. We should be in our home. In the home I was born in. In the house you raised me in!"

"I know that. But I didn't think you would have resorted to such tactics. It is most unbecoming."

"I need the name of the man," Devin said, his voice as hard and as unflinching as steel. "Now."

"Tell him, Viola," Ruth said. "You will not get any sympathy from me. Writing threatening letters is beneath us."

"Mamma—"

"Now, if you please," Captain Monroe said.

Viola glared at him, then exhaled, looking like her mother's twin. "Kyle Winter."

Robert surged to his feet. "So that worm of a bank clerk wrote these letters? The sheriff and I have suspected him. But why? Why do this?"

"Because his brother was killed at the Battle of the Wilderness."

Captain Monroe shrugged. "So were thousands of brave men. How was that Miranda Markham's fault?"

"Mr. Winter said Phillip told secrets about the South, maybe about the North too. Someone who was at Johnson's Island with Phillip told him so. He caused the fight to go so badly against the Confederacy."

Captain Monroe shook his head. "Winter was either misinformed or made that up. Phillip was . . . no traitor. He did not betray the C.S.A. You have my word on that."

Viola shook her head. "No, that isn't right. Kyle said the Union troops were too over-whelming in that battle. He was sure they knew too much about our soldiers' plans and strategies." Her voice rose. "He said there was no way they would have so soundly trounced our boys if not for Phillip's betrayal."

Robert shook his head. "Phillip did not betray us. We were out-funded, out-manned, and out-gunned. The Union army had almost twice as many men." He sighed, hating what he was about to say but unwilling to lie. "By the time that battle was fought, the South's loss was all but a certainty. The fact is that we were losing the war even then."

Mrs. Markham raised her voice. "The South had not fallen."

"No, ma'am, but many factors were against us. And even if not, please believe me when I tell you that Phillip did not cause the rout."

Viola stared at him mulishly. "His brother still died."

"So did my brother!" Captain Monroe snapped. "So did half of America's brothers. It was war. It was terrible. It was bloody. But it was not Phillip Markham's fault."

Viola's eyes widened. She looked to be completely at a loss for words. "You sound so sure."

"I am sure," Monroe retorted. "But what I don't understand is your reasoning."

"Mine?"

"Yes, Miss Markham. What I want to know is why you didn't stand up for him."

She froze. "I tried."

"I don't think so." Staring at her intently, he asked, "Why didn't you stand up for your brother's memory? Even if you weren't close, he was your own flesh and blood."

Instead of answering, Viola colored and put her head down.

And it was Ruth who replied. "I believe I have the answer, gentlemen," she said, her voice flat. All trace of fire had disappeared.

"I did not know about the letters, nor that the hurtful rumors about my son"—she turned to stare at Viola—"came from Mr. Winter with Viola's knowledge. And while I do not care about that woman still living in the home my late husband built for me, I am dismayed that my own daughter betrayed Phillip's memory by helping Mr. Winter with these tactics."

Ruth straightened her shoulders before going on. "I am, however, certain I know the reason for her actions. Kyle Winter promised Viola if and when Miranda returned the house to us, she would be living there as his wife."

Incredulous, Robert turned to Viola.

"You agreed to Winter's plans in order to get married?"

"He said he loved me." She shook her head. "No, he does love me."

"He doesn't love you," Devin said. "Love isn't full of conditions or threaded with threats and pain. He was using you. I would be surprised if he even ever intended to marry you at all."

"You are wrong," Viola whispered. "You are all wrong."

"Believe that if you must," Captain Monroe said, his voice flat. "However, we both know if you believe that, you are lying to yourself."

"There's more," Ruth said. "I have also suspected that, rather than truly interested in marriage to Viola, Winter has desired the mansion itself. It's quite valuable, you know. And now that I know what he has done, I can see no better way for him to avenge his brother's supposed betrayal than to take over all Phillip's family has left. But I fear I have been turning a blind eye in my desire to return to my home and be rid of my son's wife."

Robert looked to his captain. "We have what we came for. I suggest we leave."

"I agree."

"Wait!" Ruth called out as she struggled to her feet. "What is going to happen to us now?"

"I have no earthly idea."

"Are you going to tell the sheriff?"

"Of course," Robert answered.

"But we are her family."

"I don't see how it matters," Devin replied. "You have already made your choices, you have been party to blackmail, and you will be answering for your actions for years to come and for eternity."

"You don't understand," Viola cried out. "We deserve . . . we need—"

"You need compassion and forgiveness and trust," Robert bit out as he slapped his hat back on his lap. "I suggest you begin searching for those things again. In the meantime, if you so much as glance in Miranda's direction, I will make sure you will be brought to Sheriff Kern."

Ruth had the audacity to roll her eyes. "Kern. He is no one. He has no power at all."

"That, Mrs. Markham, is about to change," Captain Monroe said before bowing slightly, leading the way out the door of the drawing room, and heading outside.

Robert followed, glad they had several hours before they were going to have the opportunity to face Kyle Winter. Robert knew without a doubt if the man walked in front of him at that moment . . . well, those would be the last pain-free steps he'd walk in months.

As far as he was concerned, it was past time for the man to get a taste of what it had been like to walk in Miranda Markham's shoes.

23

The men had left early that morning. Hours later, Miranda learned they'd asked her staff for directions to Viola and Ruth's home.

Miranda was mystified why the men hadn't asked her about the women or for directions. After all, she had been to their home several times, though only when Phillip had been home on leave. Had they worried about upsetting her? Were they planning to visit other locales besides that house? Or was it simply a matter of them not wanting Miranda to be present when they spoke to Viola and Ruth?

Especially because she had no idea what they thought the two women could tell them about her troubles, other than their own desire for her to leave this house, Miranda hoped Robert and Captain Monroe hadn't wanted her present when they talked to the ladies. Because, quite frankly, she had no desire to be around the women ever again. They were callous and selfish, and she'd had enough of their difficult dispositions for a lifetime.

Now that she had support and the dark depression that had hovered around her psyche for months had at last lifted, Miranda felt renewed. Instead of sitting and worrying, she was eager to do things again. To make plans for her future. To live. For the first time since she'd moved in, she was thinking about doing some redecorating. The idea of pulling down some of the old velvet drapes that hung over almost every window and sew some new, lighter curtains was appealing. Actually, the idea of working on any project for the house was as tempting to her as candy had to be to a small child.

With that in mind, Miranda slipped on an easy-fitting calico day dress and concentrated on work. A new guest had arrived just a few hours ago. She was an elderly lady, the mother of a ship's first mate or some such. She wanted to spend some time with her boy while he was in port.

The idea of the woman coming so far to spend a few precious hours with her son made Miranda smile. Perhaps that was the silver lining after spending so many years under war's thumb. No one took family or time spent with them for granted.

At that moment she remembered what she had told Robert after the two women's last visit. That she would let them know she would always look out for them. And she would, because that was what Phillip would have wanted.

After knocking on the guest's door and making

sure she had everything she needed, she decided to sort through some of Phillip's favorite books. She had only begun when she heard a knock at the door.

Hoping it was Robert and Captain Monroe—perhaps they left their keys?—she rushed to the door. But instead of spying the two men she was coming to trust implicitly, she came face-to-face with a tall, extremely handsome man with a military bearing.

The moment he gazed at her, he smiled.

His smile was a beautiful thing. Straight, white teeth, framed by high cheekbones and a solid jaw. "You are Miranda."

She nodded. "I am Miranda Markham. However, I'm afraid you have me at a disadvantage. May I help you?"

He removed his hat. "My name is Ethan Kelly. I served with your husband, Phillip. I am actually looking for two gentlemen I believe are staying here. Robert Truax and Captain Monroe. Are they here, by any chance?"

There was something unique in the way he spoke. Maybe it was his cadence? He spoke in starts and stops. Maybe it was the way he was staring intently at her, as if a cannon could go off behind him and he wouldn't pay it any mind.

Suddenly, she knew who he was. Just as he did with Captain Monroe, Phillip had described him well. "You're Major Kelly, aren't you?"

"I was. However, I'm plain old Mr. Kelly now."

His smile was so warm, she felt as if she were greeting an old friend. "Please, do come in, Major Kelly." The moment she ushered him inside and closed the door, she held out her hand. "I'm honored to make your acquaintance. I feel like I am greeting another old friend. Phillip spoke so highly of all of you."

His brown eyes softened. "He was an excellent man. And he certainly thought the world of you."

"I'm beginning to realize that. Robert and Captain Monroe said much the same thing. He . . . well, he was a very good husband."

After taking his coat, she offered him a seat in the parlor. She was about to ask if she could call for tea or coffee or a light repast when Belle rushed forward.

"I'm sorry I wasn't here to get the door, ma'am," she said. "I went out to run some errands for Cook and lost track of time."

"You have nothing to worry about. I don't mind answering the door from time to time." Smiling in Major Kelly's direction, she said, "Especially to friends."

Belle's apologetic stance turned curious as she turned to look at Major Kelly.

He was already on his feet. "Miss," he said. "Good morning."

"Good morning. Sir." She opened her mouth.

Closed it, then shook her head. "I'm sorry. I meant, thank you."

Miranda hid a smile. Her sweet maid looked entranced. Miranda didn't blame her one bit. Major Kelly was truly handsome. So handsome, he looked like he belonged on the stage.

But what Miranda also noted was that he seemed to be looking at Belle in appreciation.

Feeling a bit like a third wheel, Miranda cleared her throat. Instantly, both turned to face her. Belle's cheeks were lightly flushed.

"Major Kelly, this is Belle Harden. She works for me as kind of a maid of all work. Belle, this is Major Ethan Kelly. He served with Phillip."

Belle's eyes widened. "You're a major?"

"Yes. Well, I was."

"Goodness."

Major Kelly laughed. "I promise you, those days are in the past, thank goodness. And, well, I have to say that plenty of people were not terribly intrigued or impressed by my rank. My sergeant, for example, could have easily run our unit without my interference."

"I am sure I don't know about that," Belle breathed.

"Belle, I was just about to offer Major Kelly some refreshment. Would you prepare some coffee and a tray for us?"

"Of course. I'll get right on it." But to Miranda's

amusement, her maid didn't move a muscle.

"Thank you. That will be all."

At last, the maid blinked. "Yes, ma'am." She turned away with a snap of her skirts and exited the room again. The minute they were alone Miranda couldn't help herself. She burst out laughing.

"I must admit that was a first for her and me, sir. She usually looks far less, well . . . far less spellbound by visitors."

"I'll take your word for it," he said with a hearty chuckle of his own. "At the risk of sounding too full of myself, her appreciation did my vanity good."

"I imagine it did, though at the risk of embarrassing you, sir, I would venture that her reaction is not as outlandish as you are making it out to be."

"In my current job, I promise you, I rarely get stared at like I'm someone of worth."

She noticed there was more than a trace of bitterness underlying his words. She wondered why. Was he thinking of the war or everything that had happened since? "You know, the first time Phillip left, when I knew he was going to be marching into battle, I barely slept. I was worried about him. Worried about him getting hurt, being without help, and dying. The stories that came back from the front . . . well, they were very bad."

"They were accurate. Our battles were difficult. Many, many men didn't survive."

"What I'm trying to say is that I didn't think I would ever have a longer evening than those nights. Long evenings spent with worry and doubts . . . but I discovered that life after is sometimes harder to handle."

"Yes. I would agree." He frowned. "And then one hates to complain because we're alive."

"Why are you here, sir? Are you on business with the men?"

"Devin Monroe contacted me. He relayed to me what Robert had relayed to him in a recent letter. I dropped everything and got on a train here from San Antonio."

She shook her head in wonder. "I find it amazing that you would come so far for me."

"You shouldn't find it surprising at all. We all wanted to be here for you. Thomas Baker would be here as well, if he could."

"Your loyalty seems to know no bounds."

"For the men I served with, it does not."

"I appreciate it more than I can say." Good manners might have expected her to say his visit wasn't needed, but she was too happy to not be alone to say that.

"Please don't mention it. Like I said, I am glad to be of use. It's good to have a worthy cause to fight for again."

"What do you do now? If I may ask?"

"I do several things in San Antonio. But by trade, I suppose you could say I'm mainly a gambler, ma'am."

A gambler! Staring at him, Miranda reflected that he certainly didn't look like any gambler she'd ever met. The gamblers she had crossed paths with in Galveston had come off the boats. Most were rather fidgety, pale, and thin men. This gentleman, on the other hand, looked tan and fit. Realizing she was staring, she said, "I must admit I haven't met many gamblers."

His lips twitched. "That is a very good thing, madam." He shrugged. "I am good at it, which some might say is not to my benefit. I, however, like to think it is a useful skill."

"Indeed." Smiling softly, she said, "I am not one to judge, sir. I have found that we'll all do what we must to survive."

"Indeed, Mrs. Markham. I have found that to be continually true."

It felt good to be back in the saddle. It felt even better to be riding alongside his captain. They'd spent countless hours on horseback together during the war, throughout most of Tennessee, Pennsylvania, and everywhere in between. Ironically, they'd never ridden together in their home state of Texas.

"These horses are in surprisingly good condition," Robert said as he patted his gelding's flank.

"I inspected several stables when I arrived in Houston two days ago. I wanted to have a good idea where the best horseflesh was in case we needed some mounts."

"What?" Robert had no idea that he'd been in Houston for any length of time before heading to Galveston.

Monroe shrugged. "It never hurts to be prepared."

"Obviously not." As Robert clenched his legs, prompting his mount into a canter, he said, "You never fail to surprise me, sir. I'm glad you're here."

"I am too. What's happened to Miranda isn't right."

Thinking of how Viola and Ruth betrayed both Miranda and Phillip, Robert thought that was something of an understatement. "At least we now know who has been behind the letters and the rumors."

Devin's expression hardened. "What do you know about this Kyle Winter?"

"Enough to know that it will be a pleasure to pay him a visit and escort him to Sheriff Kern. Jess will be glad his suspicions about Winter have been justified. He even followed the man early one morning to see what he was up to. He ended up down by the water, but when he engaged Winter in conversation, his excuse for being there didn't hold up. Now I wonder if Ruth is right about Winter's interest in the canal. You were right to suspect its worth had something to do with this."

"Too bad we can't dispense our own justice and string him up from a tree."

Thinking of how Winter had talked down to Miranda in front of the other customers of the bank and even in front of him the first time he accompanied Miranda, Robert didn't disagree. "I agree with you one hundred percent, Captain. This man deserves to be treated the way he treated Miranda. Harshly and without remorse."

"Where to next? The Iron Rail or the bank?"

"The bank," Robert said after a moment's reflection. "The next time I see Miranda, I want to be able to tell her that her troubles are over. At least with Kyle Winter."

24

Miranda had hoped Robert might be back in time to accompany her to her weekly visit to the bank. Unfortunately, he was nowhere to be found. After watching the clock tick past early afternoon and creep toward four o'clock, she knew she could wait no longer.

As she slipped the week's worth of receipts and notes into her reticule, Miranda resigned herself to the next hour's difficulty. Lord knew, she'd survived the encounter with Mr. Winter on her own plenty of times before. She would simply have to suffer through his rudeness again.

Unless . . .

Gazing up the stairs, she thought about Major Kelly. He was as close to Phillip as Robert and Captain Monroe were. He'd also already told her he took his vow to Phillip seriously. She hated to be so weak as to need him to accompany her on this errand, but in the scheme of things, it surely wasn't much to ask, was it?

And he did seem to be simply waiting for the men to return too. Running this errand with her would help make the time go faster.

Making a decision, she walked up the stairs

and knocked on his door before she lost her nerve.

He answered immediately. "Yes, Mrs. Markham?"

He'd taken off his suit jacket, vest, and tie. He'd also rolled up his sleeves. He looked so much like how Phillip had after church on the few Sunday afternoons they'd had together. She soaked in his appearance, savoring the memory that she'd pushed away for far too long.

Then she recalled herself. "Major Kelly, I don't wish to inconvenience you, but I have a favor to ask."

He smiled, as if she'd truly made his day by needing him. "All you have to do is ask and I'll help in any way I can."

She smiled back before concentrating on her words. She wanted to beg his help in just the right way, so he would understand why she was asking. At the same time she wanted to be sure he knew this favor wasn't going to take up hours of his time. "You see, every Friday I must make a deposit to the bank. The teller there . . . well, he is rather rude. He . . . well, he says disparaging things to me."

He blinked slowly, as if he was trying to come to terms with what he was hearing. "He is rude to you. To Lieutenant Markham's widow."

"He . . . well, he is one of the people who has been saying Phillip was a traitor. And . . . well, he has suggested that my character has much to be desired."

"Your character?" he asked slowly.

"Yes. On account of the fact that I have turned Phillip's house into a boardinghouse."

"This is your house too, Mrs. Markham."

"Yes. And, well, I have had no choice but to take in boarders. The bills must be paid."

"Of course." His eyes narrowed. "Therefore, you would rather not go to the bank alone."

She swallowed. "Yes. Um, well, I did go by myself for several years. But since Robert has been here, he's accompanied me and the task has been much easier to bear. That is why I decided to ask you to come with me. If you wouldn't mind, that is."

"It would be my honor to go in Robert's place, ma'am. When would you like to depart?"

"As soon as it is possible. I am supposed to be there before five. I usually am there before four."

The muscle in his jaw jumped. "Let's not make him wait, then. I'll be downstairs presently."

Afraid she was making too much out of what was usually a routine errand, she said, "Please, take your time. I need to put on a bonnet."

"I'll await at your pleasure, ma'am."

"Thank you."

"There is no need for thanks. You have given me a way to help you. I am grateful for that."

Breathing a sigh of relief, Miranda walked to her room, only to find her door open and Belle dusting the furniture.

She started when she saw Miranda walk in. "I'm sorry, ma'am. I didn't realize you were coming back in here right now."

"No need to apologize. I came in to put on a bonnet and gloves. I've asked Major Kelly to accompany me to the bank."

"I'm glad of that. With you standing next to him, I have a feeling Mr. Winter will think long and hard about his manners today."

"I would be very happy if that was the case." She took a simple black bonnet out of the box, then sat down at her dressing table to fashion it on her head.

Belle came to stand behind her. "If I may, Mrs. Markham?"

"Of course."

Carefully, Belle took down her hair, brushed it, then pinned up her tresses again. As she looked in the mirror, Miranda saw that her hair was in essentially the same style as it always was. However, Belle had pulled her hair back less severely. The looser arrangement was more becoming. She looked more feminine, even younger.

Miranda was amazed. "I wasn't aware you knew how to fashion hair." And surprised Belle would want her to be more attractive in the presence of the man she had so recently admired. Actually, she suspected it was Sheriff Kern who had caught Belle's eye, but whoever Belle cared for, that was her business.

"I learned a long time ago." Blushing, she said, "Sometimes my mother would ask me to dress her hair." She picked up the hat, eyed two of the pale pink roses in the vase on her table, and threaded them into the brim. Then she pulled out one of Miranda's more ornate hat pins and secured it.

Looking in the mirror, Miranda tilted her head this way and that. The effect was very pretty. "I don't believe I've ever been so thankful to have received such pretty roses in the winter."

"They do you proud, ma'am."

"Major Kelly is waiting for me downstairs," she said as she pulled on her gloves. "Wish us luck."

"You won't need any luck. Mr. Markham's friends are at last making everything better."

"They are." She glanced at Belle and realized they were both most likely thinking the same thing. It was going to be so very hard when Phillip's comrades left.

When she appeared on the stairs, Major Kelly glanced up at her and smiled. "You look as pretty as a picture. All the men in Galveston Island will undoubtedly be green with envy."

After she double-checked her reticule for her deposit, she closed the top of it with a firm snap. "The women we pass will no doubt feel the same way."

Major Kelly's laughter rang through the house. "I am beginning to understand why Phillip was so smitten, ma'am. Now, let's go take care of this odious errand."

Thinking that was the best descriptor yet, she allowed him to help her put on her cloak and then led the way outside.

Thirty minutes later, Miranda was trying her best not to clutch Major Kelly's arm as a lifeline. Because the atmosphere at the bank had not changed a bit. Not in the slightest. Not without Robert there.

Once again the various officers of the bank looked down their noses at her, the other customers barely acknowledged her, and Mr. Winter seemed to be as determined as he ever was to make sure she felt like a second-class citizen.

She could feel Major Kelly's ire rise as he took in every slight. From the hard expression that had appeared in his eyes, she was starting to even think that he was practically cataloguing each person so he could get retribution at a later date.

After Mr. Winter finished with the wife of one of the city's well-known cotton suppliers, he shuffled some papers on his counter, obviously taking his time to force Miranda to stand even longer for his bidding.

Major Kelly tensed up. She laid a hand on his arm. "I know it is hard, but please, don't make a fuss."

He leaned down. "Someone needs to make a fuss. This is inexcusable."

"I agree. But when you and Robert and the captain leave, I'll have to be here in Galveston by myself. And unless something changes, I'm going to have to continue to make my weekly deposit. This errand is hard enough. I don't want things to get worse."

"We will not leave you like this. Things will get better, I promise," he said before stepping forward to Mr. Winter. "Mrs. Markham has business to take care of," he said in a loud, authoritative voice. "She has waited long enough. You will see her now."

Mr. Winter lifted his chin. "I'll see her when I am ready."

Major Kelly's expression turned to ice. "I suggest that moment be now."

Unperturbed, the clerk wrinkled his brow. "I don't know who you are, and I don't care. As far as I'm concerned, you are simply another man warming the bed of a traitor's widow."

Major Kelly slammed his hand on the counter. "Bring me whoever is in charge here. Now."

"I don't answer to the likes of you."

Kelly glared at him, then turned and spoke to the room at large. "Who is in charge in this institution?"

The whole room—easily at least twenty-five people—went quiet. After a moment, Mr. Carrington stood up and approached. "I am. Is there a problem?"

"From the moment we arrived, Mrs. Markham has been both ignored and derided."

"Sir, I'm sure you have misunderstood the situation."

"Do not tell me what I witnessed. Furthermore, I don't care to learn why you have permitted such behavior in your establishment. But I will tell you that it will stop now."

Mr. Carrington blanched. "You should watch yourself, sir. If you are the latest guest in Mrs. Markham's boardinghouse, your concern is of no interest to me."

The cold, harsh stare Major Kelly sent to the bank president should have stopped him in his tracks. "I beg your pardon, but I am certain you should rethink your decision. As far as I'm concerned, there is everything for you to worry about."

"I beg your pardon," Mr. Winter said. Still standing behind the counter, he leaned his elbows on the top. "But you have obviously no idea to whom you are speaking. This is Mr. *Marcus Carrington*."

Miranda had had enough. "This gentleman is Mr. Ethan Kelly. He served as a major for the C.S.A. and was held prisoner on Johnson's Island. He is a decorated war hero. Do you truly dare to pawn off your prejudices of me onto him?"

The bank president paled. "You are Major Ethan Kelly? Of the Kelly family in Houston? Who rode with the Texas Rangers?"

"I am," Major Kelly replied, his voice like ice. "Are you going to tell me now that we have a problem?"

As low murmurings flew through the occupants of the room, the bank president paled further. "Of course not. I am sorry, Major Kelly." He snapped his fingers. "Winter, please see to Major Kelly and, uh, Mrs. Markham right now."

With a sigh, Miranda stepped forward, only to be pulled back by her escort. "I'm afraid, Mr. Carrington, that your apology is not sufficient."

After freezing for a second, the bank president stepped forward, his rotund appearance looking as if it was shrinking before their eyes. "Pardon me, sir? What else do you need?"

"I need you to apologize to Mrs. Markham. Immediately. Next, I will hear you order this . . . this clerk of yours to speak to her in a more respectful way."

Mr. Carrington looked at Major Kelly, then his clerk, then glanced around the room.

Miranda was surprised to find that most everyone present was glaring at the bank president. It seemed there were few people in Galveston who would disrespect such a war hero so publicly.

After swallowing hard, Mr. Carrington turned to her. "I do beg your pardon for my clerk's mistreatment of you, Mrs. Markham. I hope you will not hold it against us."

She was so surprised, she merely nodded.

"And?" Kelly prodded.

Sweat formed on the gentleman's brow. "And . . . and I will give you my word that you will be treated better in the future. I assure you."

Miranda wasn't sure if she believed such a pretty speech. She actually doubted the promise would last after Phillip's friends left. "Thank you."

"Very good," Major Kelly said with a nod of his head. "Now you will help Mrs. Markham with her deposit."

"What? No, that is Mr. Winter's job."

"Not today."

Mr. Carrington visibly debated whether to argue. Then, with a halfhearted shrug, he said, "Very well. Kyle, stand aside."

Mr. Winter paled. "But, sir—"

"Don't say another word," Mr. Carrington said.

But instead of listening, Mr. Winter puffed up, his whole body filled with indignation. "But you know who she is. You know who her husband was."

Major Kelly stepped forward, obviously intent on boxing the man's ears.

But before Kelly could do a thing, Mr. Carrington pointed to the back door. "Out, Winter. Now."

At last Mr. Winter stepped away. Looking increasingly upset with every step, he left the room and slapped the door shut behind him.

"Idiot," Kelly muttered under his breath.

Miranda stayed completely quiet.

By the time Mr. Carrington finished noting her deposit, which he did with shaking hands due to Major Kelly's fierce glare, Mr. Winter still had not returned.

Since several men and women were still waiting to be helped, the bank president himself beckoned the next person in line forward.

As Major Kelly took her arm, one of the women who had been standing in line eyed her in a confused way. "You certainly have some friends in high places, Mrs. Markham."

"No," Kelly interrupted. "I am the one who has that honor. Miranda is one of the finest women I've met. She was the wife of one of the best men I had the good fortune to serve with."

"Yes, well. There are some who say—"

"I would watch who you listen to from now on, ma'am. You may begin to regret your choice of causes."

Two men and one woman nodded. "It's about time someone put that clerk in his place," one of the men said. "It's been difficult to watch how they've been treating you in here, week after week."

Though Miranda ached to ask why he had never stood up for her, she merely nodded as they exited, her hand clinging to Major Kelly's arm like it was her lifeline.

The moment they walked down the stairs, Miranda blew out a breath of air she hadn't even realized she'd been holding. "Major Kelly, you are a force to be reckoned with."

"No, ma'am. I am simply old enough to be tired of having to put up with such foolishness."

"Thank you," she said. "Robert scared them, but you somehow made the threat stick."

Major Kelly looked pleased. "To tell you the truth, it felt really good to throw my weight around. I hadn't done that in a while."

"You don't do such antics in San Antonio?" she asked as they walked toward the edge of the Strand, next to the rows of cluttered warehouses, some damaged in storms or during the Galveston battle.

"No," he said quietly. "My—" Stopping abruptly, he reached for her elbow. "Get behind me, Miranda."

Startled, she did as he asked. But when she peeked around him, she saw what he was guarding her against. None other than Kyle Winter was facing them with a pistol. He was holding it in both of his shaking hands. Miranda wondered if he'd ever held a gun before. She hoped it was not loaded, but she had to assume it was.

"Come with me," he ordered her.

"Yes, yes, of course."

"You will not go anywhere with him," Major Kelly said. "I would have to be incapacitated for that to happen."

"That can be arranged," Mr. Winter said. Just before he shot Major Kelly in the thigh.

25

"Hallelujah!" Devin Monroe exclaimed the moment they walked off the ferry and stepped foot onto Galveston Island. "I thought we were never going to get back on this island in one piece."

Robert chuckled. "I've been with you through battles and marches and prisoner-of-war camps. Through it all, you've never done more than press forward, hardly flinching. But today was a new experience."

Still looking a bit green, his captain attempted to draw himself up. "I don't usually get seasick. The sea was unusually rough."

"It was choppy, I'll give you that. But you were also unusually squeamish." He started laughing again. There was no hope of even trying to keep a straight face.

Devin looked away. "All I'm saying is that one would think our day's trip would have been easier. We were only going to Houston and back. Not Timbuktu."

"One would think," Robert quipped. Then as he remembered how callous the women were and how much they didn't seem to have a single moment's regret for their treatment of Miranda, he said, far more soberly, "Unfortunately, it was even worse than I remember."

"I swear, I think it was easier to direct two hundred men than those two women."

"Of course it was. The men listened. Those females did not."

"Neither did the ferryman." Devin rolled his eyes. "If he told me once, he told me a hundred times that he wasn't allowed to operate the ferry unless he was filled to capacity."

"He did stay true to his word."

"His sense of urgency has much to be desired," Devin said under his breath. "If there was ever a day that I wished I was still a captain and had some say in this world, today was it."

"Indeed, sir." Because he had experience with his captain's extremely rare loss of patience, Robert took care to look impassive. But inside, he was grinning like a loon. It had been quite a sight to see his captain, who held the respect of even generals, get beaten down by a pudgy ferryboat captain with a chip on his shoulder.

As they started down Water Street, Robert tipped his hat at an awaiting lady, then spoke. "Sir, it's late. I suggest we relax the rest of the evening. We can compare notes in the morning and visit with the bank clerk then."

"I like the way you're talking, soldier," Devin said with a grin. "I'm freezing cold and in need of a hot beverage, a bath, and a roaring fire." He paused. "Not necessarily in that order."

Robert was about to agree when he noticed Miranda's servant Emerson standing just beyond the ferry platform with a panicked expression on his face. "Something's happened," he said as he strode ahead.

The moment Emerson spied him he breathed a sigh of relief. "Oh, thank the good Lord. I didn't think you'd ever show up, sir."

That comment only made his heart beat faster. "What has happened?"

"Everything, it seems," he sputtered.

"Explain yourself," Devin ordered.

"Oh, yes, sir. You see, well, I have some news to tell you about Major Kelly. You see, he arrived earlier and . . ."

Emerson's words were almost too much to take in at once. Mind spinning, Robert turned to his captain to try to make sense of things. "Did you know Ethan was coming here?"

"I wasn't sure he would join us, but I hoped he would. After I received your letter, I wrote Kelly and told him what's been happening with Phillip's wife. I told him you've additionally been uncovering information right and left. I can only assume he took it upon himself to lend a hand."

"Well, he may be regretting that decision," Emerson said. "On account that he got shot, you see."

Time seemed to freeze. "Shot, you say?" Devin asked, his voice hoarse.

"Yessir." Emerson pointed down the street behind them. "Right outside the bank it was."

"Is he alive?"

Emerson brightened a bit. "Oh, yessir, he is. Matter of fact, he's with the surgeon now. He's a good one too."

"How good?" Devin asked.

"I promise, Captain, that he's a real particular doctor. Not a sawbones in the slightest. Keeps his offices spick and span, he does. Major Kelly is in good hands."

After mumbling something under his breath, the captain said, "Take me to him, Emerson. I need to see this for myself. I've yet to meet a surgeon I would trust not to make things worse."

"I'll go too," Robert said, wondering who would shoot Ethan and why. "If he needs anything, I can go fetch it. Emerson, please tell Mrs. Markham where we are, and that we'll talk to Sheriff Kern as soon as we can."

But Emerson shook his head. "No, sir. You see, that ain't all. From what I understand, Major Kelly accompanied Mrs. Markham to the bank—"

"Miranda was with him?" Robert nearly shouted.

"Yessir. And he got mad when people there were being rude to her. Then he called out Mr. Carrington."

"Who is that?"

"The bank president himself!" Emerson declared proudly. "After Major Kelly told him who he was, and Mr. Carrington put two and two together and all, he apologized to Mrs. Markham."

Robert was interested in the story but was more interested in seeing to his old friend and making sure Miranda was safe and well. "Tell us about it later, Emerson. After you tell me how Mrs. Markham is. Did she accompany the major to the physician?"

The little man gulped. "No, sir."

"Pardon me?"

"You see, I ain't done."

"Finish up, if you please," Captain Monroe said.

"Well, Major Kelly wanted Mr. Carrington to help Mrs. Markham instead of Mr. Winter."

"That man is a worm," explained Robert. "If I could prevent him from even looking Miranda's way again, I would."

"Oh, yes, sir, he is," Emerson said. "See, you see . . . Mr. Carrington agreed, but Mr. Winter got mad."

"And then?" Monroe said impatiently. "Get to the point."

"And then Mr. Carrington told him to leave. And when Miss Miranda and Major Kelly left the building, Mr. Winter shot Major Kelly and took Mrs. Markham!"

He could sense Monroe's unease, but for Robert,

time seemed to stand still. "Took her where?"

"I'm not sure, exactly. But by all accounts, everyone believes they darted into the warehouse district."

Robert's pulse started to race, not from fear but adrenaline. It was the same reaction his body had when they were mere minutes from going into battle. "Where is Mrs. Markham now, Emerson?"

"That's what I've been trying to tell ya," Emerson said with a pull on his collar. "Mrs. Markham is with Mr. Winter in the warehouses and no one has seen hide nor hair of her for hours." Looking both appalled and dejected, he said, "I'm sorry to tell you, sir, but she's been kidnapped."

Robert looked at the captain. His lips were pressed together in a thin line. "Did you say 'hours'?" After Emerson nodded, he barked, "When, exactly, did this happen?"

"At least three hours ago, I reckon. Maybe toward four?" Emerson scratched his chin. "You two have been gone a long time."

Though every muscle in his body ached to head directly to the warehouse district, Robert knew it would be far more prudent to ascertain as much information as possible before going off half-cocked. "Who has been searching for her?" he asked, hoping and praying the servant would give him a name and not a shrug.

Emerson's expression cleared. "Oh. Sheriff

Kern is, Mr. Truax. The moment he heard about what happened, I heard he grabbed his pistol and went after them."

Some relief filled him, but not enough. With a start, he realized he didn't trust anyone to protect Miranda other than himself. "Who else?"

"I don't know." Emerson looked up at the sky as if he was attempting to pull the information out of thin air. "Maybe one of his deputies?" He frowned. "I have to tell ya, though, I'd almost rather Mrs. Markham be lost with Mr. Winter than 'rescued' by one of Kern's men. They're a sorry lot, to be sure."

Captain Monroe exchanged a glance with Robert. "What do you think? Do we have time to get our weapons?"

Though Robert was reluctant to spend one more minute simply standing and pondering, years of fighting made him cautious and able to see the benefits of thinking through the situation. "I don't think we have a choice, sir. If Winter shot Kelly, he's liable to shoot again."

"Good point. Lead us to the quickest way back to the house, Emerson," Captain Monroe ordered. "And be quick about it. We have no time to spare."

"Yes, sir," Emerson replied, then turned sharply to his right and picked up his pace, fairly running down a back alley, Robert and his captain on his heels.

As they ran, Robert left the rest of his thoughts unspoken. Mainly that if Winter shot Kelly, he might have also already injured Miranda. And that as soon as Winter met either him or Monroe face-to-face, he would be receiving his retribution. There was no way Ethan Kelly had survived Gettysburg and several months in a Yankee prisoner-of-war camp only to be bested by a disgruntled bank clerk with an ax to grind.

There was no way that was ever going to happen. Not if he could help it.

The moment they tore open the front door, Belle, Winnie, and Cook ran to meet them.

"Do you have her?" When the answer became obvious, Winnie sniffed. "Oh, where is she?"

"I don't know, but we're going to find her," Robert said. "We came in only for our weapons."

As he and Monroe rushed up the stairs, Belle followed. "Sirs, beg your pardon, but is it true about Major Kelly? Has he really been shot?"

Captain Monroe spared her only the briefest of glances. "That's what Emerson says. We haven't seen him."

"I know you both are going to find Mrs. Markham, and I'm real glad of that. But . . . would you mind terribly if I went and sat with the major?"

"I think that is a fine idea," Robert said as he reached into his knapsack, pulled out his Colt and a box of bullets, then began loading the revolver.

"Oh, I'm so glad. I would hate for him to be alone."

"I would too," he said as he raced back to the hall. Monroe was already trotting down the stairs. "Thank you, Belle."

"Of course. Please, please go find Mrs. Markham."

"I will find her tonight," Robert promised. He didn't dare add that he was hoping and praying he would find her alive.

"You need me to do anything besides look after your major?"

"Pray," Monroe called out as he swung open the door. "And, Belle?"

"Yes . . . yes, sir?"

"You tell that sawbones that Kelly keeps his leg," he said fiercely. "You hear me?"

"Oh, yes, sir!" she called. "I'll make sure that happens. You can count on me."

Robert hoped that really was the case, because it was now apparent that he was going to need to place his complete trust in her and Kern. And the Lord, of course.

He sincerely prayed that would be enough.

26

Galveston's warehouse district was a run-down hodgepodge of derelict buildings, thriving cotton warehouses, and empty storefronts. With every storm that had passed through the area, water and wind had caused a good bit of damage to some of it.

Never all.

For that reason, it was an area in constant change. It lay in between the port and the red-light district, and the businessmen who oversaw the area were generally thought to be unscrupulous. They were men just coming out of years of war with nothing to lose. Because of all that—as well as the well-known rat population—Miranda had stayed far away from this section of the city.

Until now.

She was currently sitting alone on the second floor of what surely was once a fishery. The building smelled abominable and creaked and groaned painfully with every burst of wind. Her hands were tied behind her back with rope, she was bruised, and she had a cut on her cheek that she feared would always leave a scar.

If she survived.

After shooting poor Major Kelly, Mr. Winter

had jerked her forward, pulling her into the crowded alleys and passageways of the warehouse district. She'd screamed and cried, but no one they passed had given her any mind.

Any attempts of rescue wouldn't have been fruitful anyway. Mr. Winter had been dragging her along like a man possessed, calling her foul names and accusing her of awful things. She doubted he would have been any kinder to any poor soul who would have attempted to rescue her.

After he dragged her into the fishery, he forced her to climb the rickety stairs into an abandoned loft. Then he talked and talked, hardly taking a breath.

As much as Miranda could ascertain from the madman's ramblings, Mr. Carrington's bowing to Ethan Kelly's wishes had pushed Kyle Winter over the edge, and he'd finally had enough of waiting for his schemes to work. He told her how he blamed Phillip for his brother's death, and how he had been courting Viola to claim the house and its prime location as his ultimate means of revenge. Then how while Viola imagined they were going to live happily as husband and wife, he planned to sell the house to one of the many ship captains who often came in, to one of the Yankee profiteers, or to one of the men making fortunes in cotton as both the North and South struggled to pull themselves together.

He was going to destroy everything Phillip Markham had ever known, and, he said, the only real obstacle was her. She was made of far stronger stuff than he'd ever imagined.

Then he pushed her into a small space about the size of a storage room. The action had caused her to trip and fall. She'd landed clumsily. Because of that, she'd cut both her arm and cheek as well as bruised most of her limbs.

The moment she struggled to stand upright, Mr. Winter yanked her to her feet, then proceeded to pull her to the back of the musty space.

While she was still disoriented, he tied her hands, secured her to a rusty pipe, and left.

That had been at least two hours ago. Maybe three. She had no idea where he had gone or if and when he would return.

Now it was dark, though some shadows played along the walls, making the already-scary situation worse. She kept imagining someone was attempting to break into the room to join her. Whether it was a rat or a vagrant, she would have no way to fight back.

Miranda had known her situation would get even more horrific when darkness fell. She wouldn't be able to see anything and the temperature would drop even more. She'd been right.

Already bitterly cold, she rested her head against the wall of the room and closed her eyes. Tried to calm her nerves.

It was ironic that she'd fought her depression for months, contemplating suicide in much the same way a cook considered a new recipe. She'd spent hours in a fog, wondering whether it would be better to die by slicing her wrists or jumping through a window.

Only her respect and love for her staff had prevented her from doing either.

Or so she'd thought.

Now she wondered if she actually ever had wanted to die at all. Maybe it hadn't been fear that had stopped her but a deep-seated need to survive.

It was certainly how she felt now. She was willing to do anything to fight that dreadful Kyle Winter and his schemes to destroy her husband's memory, his very home. She did not want to spend her last hours on earth in an abandoned fishery. She certainly didn't want his to be the last face she ever saw.

There was no way she could ever simply lie down and give in to a man like him. If she died in his captivity, it would make his life so much easier. It would be like he won. And she would be doing the exact opposite of what Phillip had done.

She couldn't let that happen. She was not going to make anything easy for Mr. Winter, and she was not going to die without putting up at least half as much of a fight as Robert and Devin had told her Phillip did.

She didn't know how she was going to survive, but she would. To perish this way was unthinkable.

It took Belle asking for directions several times before she located Dr. Kronke's offices. Of German descent, the doctor hadn't been in Galveston long, but it seemed he had already developed a formidable reputation.

Injured soldiers and ailing sailors alike seemed to praise his efforts. By the time Belle located the man's door and knocked twice, she had decided that Major Kelly was receiving the best treatment possible.

To her surprise, the doctor opened the door himself. Peering at her closely, he tilted his head. "Yes?"

"Hello. I'm, uh, Belle. I'm looking for Major Kelly. He received a gunshot wound to his leg, I believe?"

The doctor beamed. Beamed! "He did, indeed."

She thought his smile was strange, but it did give her a curious sense of hope. "Is he still here? May I see him?"

"Of course. Come in!" He stepped back.

She walked into a tiny receiving area, the whole space barely big enough for two rather uncomfortable wooden chairs and a small, very fine wooden table in between them.

The walls were covered in light blue wallpaper and framed prints of what she could only assume were scenes from Germany hung on his walls. It was a pretty, cozy little room, and a surprise when she'd expected to see a rather bare doctor's examining room.

He peeked at her a little more closely through his wire-rimmed glasses. "Are you the major's sweetheart?"

"Me? Oh, goodness, no. I'm, uh, well, I work for Mrs. Markham," she sputtered, feeling her neck flush. As he continued to stare at her with interest, Belle continued, attempting to make some kind of coherent sense. "She runs a boardinghouse. She's currently, um, hosting three men who served in the army with her husband."

He tilted his gray head. "So you are here for her?"

"No . . ." Why was she there, exactly? How could she explain her need to see Major Kelly? "Sir? I mean, Dr. Kronke, is he all right? We're all very worried."

"Yes, I imagine you are. As for your Major Kelly, he is doing well so far. I was able to remove the bullet without any consequence. He lost some blood, of course, but overall he doesn't seem too worse for wear." He shrugged. "We'll see what happens over the next twenty-four hours. Infection is any wound's worst enemy."

Belle was fairly proud of herself for not turning weak or light-headed at the mention of the officer's loss of blood. "May I sit with him?"

"He might not wake up for some time," he warned. "It might even be hours."

"That's okay. I don't want him to be alone."

Dr. Kronke grinned. "Of course you don't. Well, my dear, if you are willing to keep this major company, I'll even give you a job. When he wakes up, you may give him sips of water."

"Yes, I can do that."

After beaming at her again, he tottered to another door and quietly opened it. She followed right behind and was immediately struck by the scent of antiseptic, clean cotton, and lavender, of all things. When she fingered the bowl of dried herbs, the doctor chuckled.

"You have seen my weakness, I see. I have found that I grew weary of the smell of blood and sickness. The lavender soothes me."

"It soothes me too," she said, meeting his gaze with a half-smile. Then all thoughts of dried herbs were forgotten as she spied Major Kelly lying motionless in a small, neatly made cot.

The doctor bustled over to the lone utilitarian chair resting against the wall and carried it to the major's bedside. "Here you are, dear. I'll have someone bring in a pitcher of water and two glasses to you shortly."

"Two glasses?"

He bowed slightly. "Sitting bedside is hard work. You might need to take a sip every now and then too."

He turned and walked out the door before Belle could thank him for his kindness. When the door shut, and she was completely alone with Major Kelly, Belle allowed herself to look her fill of him.

He was still in his shirt, but his trousers had been removed. A white sheet covered him up to his waist, with only his left bandaged leg exposed. A small moss-colored blanket was neatly folded at the foot of the bed. Fearing he might be cold, she shook it out and placed it on his body and around his wound. He shifted and groaned from her administrations.

She started from the noise, then sat back and smiled. "Groan all you want, Mr. Kelly. All that means to me is that you're sleeping hard."

Minutes later, a serious-looking young man a few years younger than her entered with the promised pitcher and glasses on a small tray. He set them down without a word, ignoring her thanks.

Belle poured herself a half glass, sipped carefully, then kicked her legs out a bit.

Then, because she had never been completely comfortable in silence, she began to talk. In choppy, halting sentences, she told him about growing up in northern Louisiana and then finding her way to New Orleans and eventually ending up in Galveston.

It was the first time she'd ever dared to speak out loud about her whole past.

But even though no one's ears heard but her own, the confession felt cleansing.

27

"So I hate to ask the obvious," Captain Monroe ventured as they made their way down two side streets that lined the warehouse district. "But do you have any idea where in this maze of alleys she might be?"

"Nope," Robert said.

"I see. Do you happen to have a plan that consists of something more than wandering around and peeking in doorways?"

"There's no reason to be sarcastic, Devin. We're not leading hundreds of troops into battle; we're searching for Miranda and a crazy bank clerk in a run-down warehouse district. Officer Candidate School didn't cover this scenario."

"Point taken. So . . . what do you suggest we do?"

"I thought we'd first patrol the area and interview anyone we see. Someone here had to have seen Winter and Miranda."

"And if no one did? What next?" Monroe didn't seem to be even trying to hide his skepticism.

Robert shrugged. "If no one did, then your guess is as good as mine. I guess we'll have to start searching through every structure until we find her."

After a pause, Devin smiled. "Sounds good."

Robert didn't respond. He could feel the same anticipation he was sure was running through his former captain. Though he was afraid for Miranda and hated that she was scared, possibly hurt and alone, he couldn't deny the satisfaction that ran through him.

Frankly, it felt good to be of use. Ever since they were captured and sent to Johnson's Island, he'd felt at a loss for what to do with the rest of his life. From the time he was a child he'd been used to frequent activity combined with the quiet sense of desperation that told him he needed to do everything possible to survive.

Their long period of captivity, though it had been filled with pain and more than a little suffering, had also been filled with guilt, knowing they were likely to survive while so many of their friends and allies would not.

After his release, when he'd spent two long years working seventy and eighty hours a week for the train lines, making money hand over fist, it hadn't brought him all that much satisfaction.

But this? Walking by his captain's side, revolver in hand, with a noble purpose in his heart? He hadn't experienced this feeling in years.

When they saw a pair of men and one woman loitering outside a warehouse, they stopped. The trio looked at them curiously.

"We're looking for a woman," Devin said.

"Brown hair. Attractive blue eyes. She was taken into the area against her will earlier this afternoon."

The woman rolled her eyes. "If it didn't just happen, we ain't seen her. We've been working inside all day."

Robert had no doubt she spoke the truth. When he worked for the trains, he had the opportunity to step inside several warehouses and factories just like this. Workers were hardly given breaks, and they were supervised closely.

"I need to find her," he pleaded, not caring in the slightest that he sounded suspiciously like he was begging. "Who in the area might have seen her? It's imperative I find her as quickly as possible."

"I don't know, and I don't care."

Devin shot Robert a look that conveyed he'd told him so. "Let's go, Lieutenant. We'll ask someone over on the next block."

"No. Wait a sec," one of the men called out. "Who are you gents, anyway?"

Before Robert snapped that it didn't matter who they were, Devin spoke. "I'm Devin Monroe," he said easily, his voice as smooth and calm as if they were being introduced at an officer's ball. "This is Robert Truax. We're staying at Miranda Markham's house. She is the one we seek."

"Mrs. Markham has gone missing?" the woman asked.

"Yes. Kidnapped, in fact. Why, do you know her?" Robert asked.

The three exchanged glances. "Were you friends with her man?" the man asked suspiciously.

"We were. Her husband, Phillip Markham, served under me during the war." Devin paused and looked at him more closely. "Why? What do you know?"

"I know him," he replied. "I mean, I used to. We grew up near each other."

"You lived on Market Street?"

The man shook his head. "Nah. He was on Market. I was with my ma at one of the cottages nearby. But we still saw each other a lot."

"I'm sure you did," Devin said laconically, just as if they were discussing the latest weather report. "Did you stay in touch?"

The man looked surprised to be asked, then a bit embarrassed. "Nah. He went off to some fancy boarding school in Virginia and then on to a high and mighty military academy of some sort."

"He attended West Point. What did you do?"

"Me? I went to the shipyard. Good, honest work, it is. I worked there before the war. Then ended up here after." His chin lifted. "But I saw him later too."

"When?" Robert asked.

"After Gettysburg. I was getting sewn up from some shrapnel and he was walking through the hospital wards. When he saw me, he stopped and talked awhile." His expression softened. "He acted like we were friends. He acted like he was happy to see me."

"I'm sure he was glad to see you, as well as relieved you were surviving," Devin said. "Friends from home were always a bonus to us."

The man shrugged. "I don't know about that. All I do know is that we both served." Looking adamant, he blurted, "I don't care what no one says. He didn't betray nobody."

"No, he did not," Captain Monroe said.

The man stared at him in wonder. "You're sure, aren't you?"

"I wouldn't be here if I weren't."

The man seemed to weigh his words. He looked at his friends. Then, after an interminable amount of time, he pointed to a run-down, boarded-up warehouse. "Winter took Mrs. Markham over there."

Robert stepped forward, his expression intent. "You sure about that?"

The man didn't back down. "Sure as I can be without stepping foot in that place. It's an old fishery and smells to high heaven."

Monroe ignored the description and glared at the three of them. "How can you be sure it was them? We didn't tell you it was Winter who had her."

"Well, I know who Winter is and the woman

was fighting him like her life depended on it."

"She was crying, sir," the woman whispered. "Then she stilled and looked our way."

"Yes?" Devin asked impatiently.

"That's when I saw her eyes. You see, I know who Mrs. Markham is too. She's got bright blue eyes, she does. Plus, she is a high-class lady. She stuck out like a sore thumb in these parts."

"She does have blue eyes," Robert said. "Beautiful eyes."

"Almost violet, they are," the woman said.

"Why didn't you go after them?" Devin asked.

For the first time, the man looked embarrassed. "Winter had a gun. And, well, you learn, living and working around here, to keep out of other people's business. Sticking your neck out don't count for much."

Robert felt as if he was about to expire on the spot. Looking at the building across the way, he gave a quick prayer of thanks. He'd needed the Lord to give him a hand, and it seemed that he had in the form of this loquacious fellow.

Devin put his hand out and steadied him. "Chin up, Lieutenant. She was alive then. That is something."

"Let's just hope she's still alive now. If she isn't, I don't know if I'll be able to bear it."

"Let's hope you don't have to find out."

"Do you need some help?" the vagrant asked. "If you want, I could go in and lend a hand."

Though Robert was more than ready to dismiss the man's offer, he knew how important it was for everyone to feel valued. "Thank you," he said finally. "If you and your friends could stand at the doorways and stop anyone who tries to escape, that would be a tremendous help."

The man seemed to stand a full six inches taller. "Thank you, sir. I can do that."

"Let's go," Devin said. "We can't wait another moment."

Robert couldn't have agreed more as he strode to his former captain's side and entered the building, his Colt cocked and ready.

Miranda heard the footsteps on the stairwell before her captor did.

Thirty minutes ago, Mr. Winter had returned and then had started pacing in the loft, stopping often to look out the dirty windows. For what, Miranda wasn't sure. She'd anticipated Mr. Winter yelling at her, or manhandling her, or doing much worse.

Instead, he seemed to be thoroughly confused about what to do with her next. Wherever he had gone before didn't seem to have helped him.

When Miranda heard the footsteps get closer and saw Winter turn toward them, she braced herself. She had no idea what was going to happen next, but she was prepared for it. She knew now that she was going to fight as much as she could. She was not going to give up. Not going to give in without a fight.

The footsteps were hard claps against the wooden floor. Only men in heavy boots made such a noise.

Trembling, Miranda kept her eyes focused on the door. Mentally preparing herself to call out for help. To scream. To do whatever it took to help herself and get free.

"Miranda!" A voice called out. "Miranda!"

"Don't say a word," Mr. Winter said.

Heart pounding, she drew in her breath. Ignored the cocking of his Colt.

And did the one thing she knew she had to do. No matter the consequences. "I'm here!" she called. "In here."

28

The clerk had a pistol trained on Miranda. Her eyes were wide with fright and glued on Robert.

Obviously waiting for him to do something. To save her.

That moment, all training, experience, and common sense flew out the window. "Don't do it, Winter!" Robert called as he raced into the room.

His exclamation seemed to be all anyone needed to push them forward. Devin cursed behind him, then cocked his own pistol and trained it on Winter.

Miranda shifted and pulled at her hands, which Robert now realized were tied to an old pipe.

And Winter pivoted and turned his gun on them. His hand was trembling. Right then and there, Robert figured there was only a fifty-percent chance that the clerk could hit either him or Devin.

That clerk's insecurity and nervousness was all Robert needed to calm down and focus. "Put the gun down, Kyle. You do not want to hurt anyone."

"We've all hurt people. This isn't any different than what happened to my brother in Virginia."

"It's everything different," Devin called out, his voice perfectly composed and his dark eyes looking completely cool and unemotional. "Your brother died in war. On the battlefield. You are harming an innocent woman."

Winter shook his head, his gun waving with the motion. "I wasn't allowed to fight," he declared with a pained expression. "My brother, my parents, even the doctors said I was too unfit. Too unhealthy." His voice cracked. "Can you even believe that? The South needed everyone. Every able man. Boys volunteered! Everyone but me. And then he died."

"Don't dishonor him by behaving in this manner, then," Devin said. "If you want to serve the South, don't start shooting innocent women and soldiers who already gave so much for our cause."

"I have no choice." Turning back to Miranda, he said, "Her husband betrayed my brother. Her husband shared secrets and spied." Lowering his voice, he said, "Somebody needs to pay. But still, here she is, living in his grand house, smiling at the Yankees who give her money to stay there. Flirting with men. She deserves nothing. And since my brother is dead, I have to be the one to take care of her."

"Killing her won't change the outcome of the war, son," Captain Monroe said as he edged forward. "The hard truth is that our side lost. All of us on both sides of the Mason-Dixon are grieving for people we buried. There probably isn't a person in this country who hadn't wished and prayed for more men to have survived the war. However, that wasn't what the Lord intended to happen."

"What does God want? Do we even know?" As if his right arm was paining him, Winter lowered it. The Colt now hung limply in his hand. Still cocked and ready to go off at any second.

"He wants us to value what we still have," Robert answered, realizing as he spoke that he was sure about his answer. "God wants us to find solace in each other. To remember to give thanks for what we have. To love the people we care about and show kindness to people we don't. He wants us to live and breathe and learn from our past." Taking a fortifying breath, he added, "He does not want us to find retribution. That is for him to do, not us."

Kyle's eyes filled with tears. For a brief second, Robert felt hope, hoped that he'd said something that would have struck a chord with him and defused the situation.

But then Kyle inhaled sharply and shook his head. "No!" he shouted as he raised his gun again.

And pointed it directly at Robert.

"No!" Miranda called out just as a shot rang out.

It came from Devin.

When Kyle Winter collapsed, Robert knew he'd died instantly.

Out of habit, Robert put the safety back on his revolver and slid it back into the waistband of his jeans, nestled in the small of his back. Then he ran to Miranda.

Thick tears were racing down her cheeks. "Oh, Robert. I was so scared. I was afraid he was going to kill you."

"Thanks to Devin, he did not." Kneeling by her side, Robert brushed some of her tears away, then gave in to temptation and kissed her cheek. "I was afraid for the same thing. I was afraid he was going to take you from me. I have never been more scared."

As her tears continued to flow, he reached for his knife. "Let's get you free."

Two sharp swipes with his knife freed her. The moment the rope fell to the ground, he inspected her wrists. Her tender skin had been rubbed raw and was bleeding. Her wrists were bruised and swollen. When she cried out in pain, Robert suddenly wished he had been the one to pull the trigger. "I'm so sorry," he whispered as he gently enfolded her in his arms.

"How is she? Will she be all right?" Devin asked. While Robert had been freeing Miranda from her bindings, his captain had knelt at Winter's side.

Still holding her protectively, Robert said, "I think so." Leaning back a little so he could see her face, he asked, "Miranda, did he hurt you anywhere else?"

"No. I'm a little bruised, but beyond my wrists, I'm unharmed." Releasing a ragged sigh she said, "I honestly think he was trying to get up the nerve to kill me."

"Thank the Lord he couldn't summon the will to do that," Devin replied.

"No, thank the good Lord that you both found me in time." Treating them both to a watery smile, she said, "I was willing to do whatever it took to survive, but I was frightened half to death."

When she shuddered again, Robert enfolded her back in his arms and held her close. "You okay?" he asked Devin.

"Me? Yeah." Looking toward Winter, he added grimly, "It gave me no pleasure to end his life, but I am grateful he didn't harm either of you."

"Not as grateful as I am," Robert replied. "I owe you."

Looking grim, he shook his head. "You owe me nothing, Robert. I've lost enough people I care about. I'm in no hurry to lose one more. Keeping you and Miranda alive was a selfish move on my part."

Robert was about to say he understood when they heard the pounding of footsteps on the stairs.

Turning, his body went on alert again as he loosened his hold on Miranda.

But instead of moving away from him, Miranda clung. "Who do you think that could be?" she asked.

He didn't bother to reply as he continued to stare at the doorway. There was no telling who was coming to join them, but the chance that it was yet another person out for trouble was high.

"Get down," he ordered as he freed his gun. To his relief, she didn't question him, but simply did as he asked.

Devin had already pulled out his Colt again. His face impassive, he slowly lifted his arm and watched the empty doorway.

The pounding on the wood floor grew louder.

When it was obvious the intruders were men and they were heading their way, Robert exhaled and cocked his gun.

The moment two men appeared with guns drawn, Robert uttered, "Right," just as he placed his finger on the trigger.

"Don't shoot!" Kern called out.

Robert had already pulled the trigger. He only had time to raise his arm so the bullet pierced the wall above them. Behind him, Miranda gasped.

"Easy, now," Kern said. He, as well as his deputy, looked visibly shaken.

Robert dropped his arm with a wince. He'd

almost killed a lawman. Unable to help himself, he swore under his breath. When he felt Miranda's reassuring hand, he glanced her way. "You okay?"

Her blue eyes were tinged with worry, but she gifted him with a tremulous smile. "Yes."

Now that he was reassured, he laced his fingers with hers, then turned his attention back to the other men.

Beside him, Devin was complaining. "You almost got yourself killed, Sheriff."

"I kind of noticed that."

"I kind of noticed that you were nowhere to be found when we got here. Where have you been?"

"Trying to track down the four of you," Kern said. "I think we went to every single run-down and abandoned building except for this one."

"I've seen more rats today than I care to admit," his deputy complained.

"We saw our fair share of rats ourselves," Devin said.

Kern's eyes narrowed. "Is that right?" Looking from Miranda, who was clinging to Robert's arm, to Robert himself, to Devin, he started to speak, then stilled as it became obvious that he had finally located Kyle Winter.

He was lying facedown on the floor behind them in a pool of blood.

Kern walked over to the body, crouched down,

and pulled on Winter's shoulder, rolling him over. Winter's gun was lying next to his hand. "Looks like he was armed."

"He was seconds away from shooting Miranda," Devin said. "Then when he pointed his gun at Robert . . . I had no choice. I shot to kill."

The deputy whistled low.

Robert curved an arm around Miranda, who was now trembling again. Holding her closer, he whispered in her ear. "Don't look."

While Miranda kept her face hidden, Robert eyed both Winter's body and Kern's reaction.

After a moment, Kern lumbered to his feet. "Looks like you two men took care of things for me." He raised his eyebrows. "Can't wait to hear what happened."

"I'll be glad to fill you in, Kern," Robert said. "But after I get Miranda home safely and tend to her hands and wrists."

"That works with me. I'll walk back with y'all. I'm going to need to ask Mrs. Markham some questions. I'd prefer to get those out of the way so I don't have to bother her again."

The last thing she needed at the moment was to be pestered. "Sheriff, I think tomorrow will be soon enough."

"No, tonight will be fine," Miranda interrupted. "I'm not made of spun glass, Robert," she said into his ear. "And besides, I have a feeling our sheriff is going to want to check on someone else at my home."

"Point taken." Looking at Kern, Robert nodded. "Yeah, come on with us."

Kern turned to his deputy and pointed to Winter's body. "Take care of this," he said before gesturing for Miranda, Robert, and Devin to lead the way out of the loft.

Just before they started down the stairs, Kern said, "The more I learned about Kyle Winter, the more I started to worry about y'all. That man was a loose cannon. Though I would have liked to have put him on trial, I'm not disappointed to be spared that undertaking." Looking their way again, he said, "I really am glad you all survived this ordeal relatively unscathed."

Devin Monroe smiled. "Truax and I made a promise to each other long ago. We take care of our own."

Kern smiled in return. "It seems your loyalty knows no bounds."

29

Almost two hours later, Miranda was sitting on the sofa in her parlor beside Robert. The moment they'd returned home, all four servants had rushed to her side.

Upon seeing her condition, Belle—who had just returned from Major Kelly's bedside—ushered Miranda to her room. Once there, Belle had helped her change into a fresh gown.

Cook arrived mere moments after that with a pitcher of warm water and some rags. While sitting at her dressing table, the two women had gently bathed Miranda's wrists and wrapped them in the clean cotton.

"I don't think you will scar, ma'am," Cook said with a frown at her wrapped wrists. "Though your left looks pretty bad, I'm afraid."

Miranda had to agree. Both of her wrists were swollen, bruised, and cut. However, her left one looked the worst. "It's a small price to pay for surviving that experience," she said with a shudder. "I was so afraid. I felt certain Mr. Winter was going to kill me today."

"Those men are true heroes, they are," Cook said.

"I owe them my life," Miranda agreed. She'd given Cook and Belle a brief account of her ordeal while they'd cleaned her wounds.

"They did save you, but I think you saved yourself, too, Mrs. Markham," Belle said. "You didn't give up."

Another time, Miranda probably would have pushed aside any praise. But at this moment, she was feeling glad that she had been as brave as she possibly could. "I'm so glad I didn't give up. And now I just need to give my statement to Sheriff Kern."

"Would you like me to stay with you, ma'am?" Belle asked.

"I would appreciate that very much. Thank you," Miranda replied, exchanging a knowing look with Cook. It was beginning to become pretty apparent that she wasn't the only person to have been recently granted a chance for love.

When she got back downstairs, Robert immediately walked to her side. "How are you feeling? Do you want me to tell Kern to go away? It's near midnight. I'm sure you can tell him your story tomorrow."

"I'd rather get it over with. When I finally go to sleep tonight, I want to know I can put this all behind me, not dread going over it yet again."

"I can understand that." He looked at Belle.

"I'm going to stay with her, too, sir. Just in case she needs anything. I can help serve refreshments as well. Cook went to go prepare something."

Robert nodded as he escorted Miranda to the sofa. "Let's get this over with, then."

He sounded so weary, so disgruntled, she couldn't help but smile. "I promise, I don't mind speaking to Sheriff Kern now. I'm grateful to be alive."

His expression softened. "Well said, Miranda. Indeed, we have much to be grateful for. More than I ever imagined."

An hour later, Belle walked Sheriff Kern to the door. Though it was apparent Mrs. Markham, Mr. Truax, and Captain Monroe were surprised—and perhaps amused?—at her bold offer to see Sheriff Kern out, Belle didn't care.

The day had been so stressful, so incredibly nerve-racking, it had made her want to finally take some chances. She would always regret it if she didn't at least make a bit of an effort.

When they reached the impressive carved oak door, Sheriff Kern bowed gallantly. "Thank you for seeing me out, Belle. Given the time of night, it is very kind."

The right thing to do would be to say it was no trouble, open the door, and wave him on.

But if she did that, she might never have another chance like this.

"Do you have to go right this minute?" Belle blurted.

"No." He looked at her curiously. "Is there something you need?"

"Only a moment of your time. If you aren't in too big a hurry, can we stand outside for a moment?"

His dark eyes flickered. "I'm never in too big of a hurry for you, Belle. But it's chilly. Do you have a cloak or something to put on?"

She grabbed a blanket that she'd folded on one of the chairs by the door. "This will do."

After the front door closed and they were alone under the dim gas lantern by the door, Sheriff Kern looked at her with concern. "Now, what is on your mind? Is anything wrong?"

Because she was so nervous, her voice was sharper than she intended. "Do you mean beyond my employer getting kidnapped and almost killed?"

He looked down at his feet. Sighed. Then raised his chin to meet her gaze. "I'm sorry. Of course you are right. There has been more than enough 'wrong' today." Still eyeing her carefully, he added, "It's just that, well, you seem . . . well, you seem distraught. I was afraid something else happened tonight that you didn't feel you could share in front of everyone else."

"Something did."

"What happened?"

"I was worried about you."

"Me?"

"I was so worried that you would come to harm. The moment I heard you were out looking for Mrs. Markham, I worried."

"You did?" Then he looked embarrassed. "I didn't hardly do anything."

"Of course you did! Why, you were out searching in the warehouse district all evening for Mrs. Markham!"

"This is true, but Truax and Monroe were the ones who found her. Not me."

"That hardly matters."

"Winter pulled a pistol on Mrs. Markham. Monroe's quick reflexes prevented a terrible tragedy from taking place. So I would say what he did does matter. It matters a lot."

Now she was the one who was feeling foolish. Backing up, she said, "I'm sorry. It's just that I didn't want you to go home without me saying anything. I am very glad you are all right . . . sir."

"To be honest, even though you said that day at the docks that you would give me a chance, I didn't think you cared about me," Sheriff Kern admitted.

She was stunned. "Why would you say that?"

Looking increasingly uncomfortable, he looked down at his linked hands. "Well, I heard you spent much of the evening with Major Kelly." Raising his chin, he shrugged. "I don't blame you, though."

"What?"

"After all, I'm just a man, Belle. I fought in the war and have settled here in Galveston. I now try to keep the peace in this melting pot of Northerners, Southerners, refugees, and foreigners from all parts of the world. Never have I gained a reputation like Ethan Kelly's."

She realized then that, even though she thought of him as powerful, he was just as confused about his self-worth as the rest of them. And for some reason, that made her feel more at ease around him than ever before.

Choosing her words with care, she said, "To be honest, yes, I was glad to sit with Major Kelly. He's helped Mrs. Markham and Mr. Truax, and because of that I would sit with him as long as anyone needed me to."

His expression was still guarded. "He is wealthy and handsome."

"Indeed. And yes, I think he is dashing."

"I am far from that."

She couldn't help but smile. Did he really not know how handsome he was?

"Well, he is not the kind of man for me." Based on some of his mostly unintelligible ramblings at Dr. Kronke's, she also was pretty sure Ethan Kelly was hiding some secrets of his own. She had no desire to discover them.

"He's not?"

She shook her head. "First of all, I don't think

someone like him would ever care for me. We are too different."

"Ah." He stared at her for a long moment. What was he thinking? Had she been too bold?

She turned to leave. "Sheriff Kern, I do beg your pardon. I shouldn't have run out here."

"Wait. I'm glad you did."

"Truly?"

He nodded. "There's something about you that I can't get over, Belle. Maybe it's the way you look so fragile, but you never give in. Or maybe it's the way you always put other people's needs before your own." His voice lowered. "Whatever the reason, I can't always seem to think coherently when I'm around you."

"How do you think we might solve this problem?" She smiled as she felt his gaze float over her.

"I think we need to see each other more often," he said, his voice strong and sure.

"I've heard that practice does make certain tasks easier," she teased.

He nodded. "When is your next afternoon off?"

"In two days."

"May I take you out then? We could go to that new tavern in the Tremont and have some supper."

He was asking her out. Just like a real lady. "Yes, Sheriff Kern, I would like that."

"I only eat meals with people who call me Jess. Will you finally call me by my given name?"

"I'll let you know . . . in two days' time," she said with a smile.

"I'll look forward to discovering your answer then, miss." He tipped his hat and nodded, then started down the stairs.

And when Belle opened the door, the lantern by the door illuminating her way, she was delighted to hear his chuckle float toward her.

Sweetening her dreams.

30

Two weeks later

They had done it.

Miranda would no longer be receiving threatening letters. Phillip's honor and reputation were restored—some folks were even saying his name should be added to the monument on Recognition Square.

People were talking to her again, though she suspected it would take some time for Mercy to be willing to face her. She even had more reservations for guests than she had room for.

Mr. Winter was dead and Major Kelly was recovering well from his wound. Captain Monroe had left that morning.

She was going to be just fine now. Better than fine, actually. She felt like smiling all the time. At last, all the darkness that had permeated her life had lifted and she felt optimistic and grateful again. She was feeling blessed.

So yes, Miranda knew she had every reason to celebrate each day's new dawn. And she would . . . even though she was going to miss Robert terribly.

Last night after supper, he'd told her he felt it was time for him to go. Though everything inside her had wanted to beg him to stay, she couldn't think of a single reason that would convince him. After all, he'd certainly accomplished everything he'd set out to do.

Therefore, instead of crying or attempting to cajole him to stay even one day longer, Miranda had simply nodded her head and attempted to look happy for him. This act had been important. After all, she was stronger now. She didn't want his last memory of her to be of her crying yet again.

When he came down the stairs, duffle in his hand and a determined expression on his face, Miranda prepared herself to see him off with as much grace as possible.

She needed to do this. She wanted to do it. Robert Truax had fulfilled his mission and she was grateful for his service. To expect anything more from him was selfish. And while she had a great many faults, selfishness had never been one of them.

As he set his bag on the floor near the door, she walked to his side. She was wearing a crimson dress today. It was slightly daring, but the bold color had felt right. She was ready to conquer the world—or at least Galveston, Texas—thanks to him.

"I guess you are all set?" she asked.

"I believe so." His voice was quiet, his gaze reflective as it skimmed over her face and body. "You look beautiful today, Miranda. Fetching."

"Thank you." Like always, she felt every word he said all the way down to her toes. "Would you care for something to eat before you go? I know Cook would be delighted to make you something. Or even a small repast to take with you on your journey."

"I . . . I think not."

"Are you sure? I promise, it's no trouble. Cook, Winnie, Belle, and Emerson are almost as grateful to you as I am."

"I'm sure, Miranda." Shifting from one foot to the other, he looked down at his spotlessly shined boots before staring at her again. "To be honest, taking my leave of you is going to be extremely hard. I don't know if I'm strong enough to drag it out."

Extremely hard? Strong enough? "What . . . what do you mean?" When something lit his eyes, she hurried to explain. "I mean . . . I thought you were eager to leave."

"I am eager to remove myself from temptation," he blurted. The moment the words were out, he inhaled sharply, just as a fierce blush lit his skin.

Miranda couldn't recall another time she'd seen him either blush or act so ill at ease.

"I beg your pardon, ma'am," he said, now standing tall and straight, and seeming to stare at a point directly above her head. "I didn't mean to place that burden on you."

Unable to help herself, she reached out and pressed her hand on his arm. "I'm confused, Robert, not burdened. What, exactly, are you saying? What are you tempted by?" She was beginning to have a very good idea, but she needed to hear the words.

He pressed his lips together, as if he had been waging a private war with himself, then blurted, "You, of course."

Her. He was tempted by her.

His words warmed her insides and caused her cheeks to flush. Happiness and hope sprang forth, and she yearned to clutch those two long-lost emotions tight to her chest.

But that didn't mean she understood what his temptation meant to him. "I'm sorry, but you said you wanted to leave." Though it was tempting to simply let him be the one to bare his heart, she realized she was stronger now. It turned out that she, too, could be completely honest. "I wish you wouldn't, though."

"Miranda, as much as I would hope other-wise, I fear you and I could never suit."

And right then and there, hope and happiness vanished. "Because you feel I am too fragile," she said, forcing herself to state the obvious. "Too weak."

He shook his head. "Never that." Stepping closer,

he reached for the hand that was still on his arm and placed it in his own. "Miranda, I knew Phillip well. I know what kind of man he was. I know the kind of man you deserve. I am nothing like him."

He caught her off guard. "What are you talking about?"

He looked down at his feet. "I have no formal education. I have no pedigree." He rolled his eyes. "Sometimes I'm surprised I even have a name. I'm as far from a West Point graduate as one might get."

She was so taken aback, she almost laughed. "Robert, I never cared about where Phillip went to school. I only cared about him."

"Yes, well . . ." He swallowed. "There was much in Phillip Markham to care about."

"Just as there is in you, Robert." She squeezed his hand gently. "I know this, because I've grown to care about you too."

Longing filled his expression before he firmly tamped it down. "Miranda, when the relief you are feeling about being free from Winter's tyranny subsides, you will realize that you are a wonderful woman with a bright future. You are beautiful. Any man would want you. And you, my dear, will get to have your choice of whom to pick. You won't have to settle for someone like me."

"Settle for you?" she asked, incredulous. "Robert, you saved me. In more ways than one. Before you arrived, I wasn't only scared and afraid . . . I had run out of hope." Didn't he understand what a gift he'd given her? Didn't he understand what a difference he had made in her life?

Robert closed his eyes as if even the idea of her giving up hope was painful. "I helped you, but you saved yourself."

"Yes, but—"

"You didn't give up," he interrupted. "You learned to trust. You fought Winter and were determined to stay alive in that wretched warehouse."

"Actually—"

"Just as importantly, you helped me."

"How?"

"You gave me a reason to continue living. You let a man like me believe that goodness was still present on this earth. Even after a war. Even after so many very good men died." He lowered his voice. "Miranda, you let a man like me believe there really are people like you in this world. And for that, I will always be grateful."

It seemed there was only one thing left to say.

"Don't leave me, Robert."

He stepped closer, slipped one of his hands around her waist. "Miranda, I don't think you understand. The reason I'm leaving is that I cannot simply be your friend. You see, I've fallen in love with you."

"I've fallen for you too," she said through a

smile. Hardly able to believe that she was the one who was taking the lead, she strengthened her voice. "Please, don't leave. Stay here with me. Help me."

He smiled then. "Do you want me to remain here as your husband or your boarder?"

She laughed then. "Robert Truax, are you proposing marriage or are you waiting for me to do so?"

He flushed, then before she quite knew what was happening, he pulled her into his arms and kissed her soundly. "I told you I don't have the words I need."

"I think you are finding them."

"I want you to be mine. Say you'll marry me."

"I will, Robert."

He smiled, then kissed her again and again, holding her close, being everything she ever needed.

It seemed that Robert Truax did a great many things well. He had been a fine soldier, an influential officer, and a brave protector. He was personable and confident. Chatty and romantic.

But a man of words he was not.

That was why, when he leaned down to kiss her again, Miranda realized that she was tired of talking.

Though words were always well and good, there were times—like the present—when they weren't even needed at all.

DISCUSSION QUESTIONS

1. The five men at the Confederate Officer Prisoner of War camp are central characters for the entire book. What is your first impression of them?

2. Miranda Markham is without hope at the beginning of the novel. Is there any part of her character that you can relate to?

3. How do you feel about Robert Truax not telling Miranda the complete reason he is visiting? For that matter, what would you have done if you were Robert and were asked to check on Miranda? Would you have gone?

4. As the book progresses, it is evident that there are many people in Galveston who betrayed both Miranda and Phillip. Do you think Miranda should have left?

5. What is your impression of the inn's staff? What do you foresee happening with Belle?

6. The men at the camp have sworn their loyalty to Captain Monroe. Do you think he is

worthy of their trust? Who in your life would you follow without question?

7. The novel focuses on the toll the war took on a handful of people in a southern Texas town. Do you think it was realistic? How do you think some of these same themes might be played out in the world today?

8. In what ways was Miranda strengthened throughout the book? Do you think she is a worthy match for Robert?

9. The verse from Psalm 51, "Create in me a clean heart, O God. Renew a loyal spirit within me," is a favorite of mine. I thought it fit both Robert's and Miranda's faith journeys well. What does this scripture mean to you?

10. What former soldier are you most interested in reading about next?

ACKNOWLEDGMENTS

Dear Readers,

Thank you for reading this book! I hope you enjoyed this first book in the *Lone Star Heroes* series and getting to know Captain Devin Monroe and his friends and comrades as much I did.

I have to share that the inspiration for this series came from my kitchen table! One evening, my husband and I were cooking together, and I told him about a discovery I had made regarding Johnson's Island. Soon, we were talking about a series based on former POWs who made promises to look after each other for the rest of their lives. I scribbled notes on old pieces of notebook paper, stuck them in a folder, then pulled them out when my editor expressed an interest years later. That is how this book began.

With that in mind, I owe many thanks to the people who helped make this novel come together so well. First, I am grateful to my husband Tom, who not only helped me plot a whole series but also traveled with me to the C.S.A. Officer Cemetery on Johnson's Island and ventured down to Galveston one hot July weekend to do research. Tom is the best. Really.

I also owe many thanks to my friend Tiffany Crona and her mother Mary Wharton, who helped me discover more research materials about Galveston Island in the 1870s. I did take a few liberties with some of the information I discovered. Those inaccuracies are purely my own!

I'm also grateful to my agent Nicole Resciniti of The Seymour Agency. She helped make the dream of publishing this trilogy a reality. Thank you, Nicole!

I'm so appreciative of my editor for this project, Becky Philpott. Becky, thank you for chatting with me about Texas and soldiers and prisoner-of-war camps one sunny day in San Antonio. Thank you, also, for your belief in me and my writing. Every author dreams of having a champion like you.

Thank you, also, to incredible editor Jean Bloom for making this story actually follow a timeline that makes sense. You are amazing, Jean!

Finally, no note would be complete without praising God for His words, and my family, especially my brother and sister. We, like so many others, know how devastating both suicide and depression can be for loved ones. I'm so thankful for them!

With blessings and my thanks,
Shelley Shepard Gray

ABOUT THE AUTHOR

Shelley Shepard Gray is a *New York Times* and *USA Today* bestselling author, a finalist for the American Christian Fiction Writers' prestigious Carol Award, and a two-time HOLT Medallion winner. She lives in southern Ohio, where she writes full-time, bakes too much, and can often be found walking her dachshunds on her town's bike trail.

She also spends a lot of time online. Please visit her website: www.shelleyshepardgray.com.

Find her on Facebook at Facebook.com/ShelleyShepardGray.

Center Point Large Print
600 Brooks Road / PO Box 1
Thorndike, ME 04986-0001 USA

(207) 568-3717

US & Canada:
1 800 929-9108
www.centerpointlargeprint.com